THE BODY IN THE FRIDGE

I felt around for my red wool robe and slipped my feet into my lamb's-wool-lined moccasins. "Coming!"

Gus stood at the bottom of the stairs. He'd flipped on the overhead lights in the restaurant, providing a warm, homey glow in contrast to the dark that crept in through the windows.

"What did you say?" I asked.

"There's a dead guy in my walk-in refrigerator. You leave him there?"

I didn't answer. It was a ridiculous question. I marched to the big refrigerator and swung open the heavy stainless steel door.

There was a dead guy in there.

He was seated on the floor, his back resting against the lower two shelves, his chin on his chest . . .

Books by Barbara Ross

CLAMMED UP

BOILED OVER

MUSSELED OUT

FOGGED INN

Published by Kensington Publishing Corporation

Fogged Inn

Barbara
Ross

KENSINGTON BOOKS
http://www.kensingtonbooks.com

KENSINGTON BOOKS are published by

Kensington Publishing Corp.
119 West 40th Street
New York, NY 10018

All Kensington titles, imprints and distributed lines are available at special quantity discounts for bulk purchases for sales promotion, premiums, fund-raising, educational or institutional use. Special book excerpts or customized printings can also be created to fit specific needs. For details, write or phone the office of the Kensington Special Sales Manager: Kensington Publishing Corp., 119 West 40th Street, New York, NY, 10018. Attn. Special Sales Department. Phone: 1-800-221-2647.

Kensington and the K logo Reg. U.S. Pat. & TM Off.

ISBN-13: 978-1-4967-0037-7
ISBN-10: 1-4967-0037-6
First Kensington Mass Market Edition: March 2016

eISBN-13: 978-1-4967-0038-4
eISBN-10: 1-4967-0038-4
First Kensington Electronic Edition: March 2016

10 9 8 7 6 5 4 3 2 1

Printed in the United States of America

*This book is dedicated to my mother-in-law, Olga Carito,
the incredible proprietor of the Seafarer Inn
and the person who introduced me to beautiful
Boothbay Harbor, Maine.*

Chapter 1

"Jule-YA! There's a dead guy in the walk-in."

My brain swam slowly out of a deep slumber. My boyfriend, Chris Durand, rolled over in my bed. "What was that?"

"Dunno. Gus. Something about the walk-in." I knew, from unfortunately frequent experience, that my landlord, Gus Farnham, had opened the door that connected his restaurant downstairs to my studio apartment above and bellowed up the stairs.

"What is it now?" Chris mumbled. We'd been sharing the restaurant space for a little over a month. Gus served breakfast and lunch as he had for more than fifty years. Chris and I ran the restaurant for dinner. Gus was very particular about how he wanted things left, and as careful as Chris and I had been, we'd managed to annoy the old curmudgeon practically every day. Chris pulled the duvet around his shoulders. "Time is it?"

I grabbed my phone off the bedside table. "Five after five."

Chris groaned. We'd finally gotten to bed after one in the morning—four scant hours before. "Can you handle it?" he asked. "He called you."

"Jule-YA!" Gus bellowed again. "There's a stiff in the refrigerator."

I heard it that time. He definitely had my attention. I felt around for my red wool robe and slipped my feet into my lamb's-wool-lined moccasins. "Coming!"

Gus stood at the bottom of the stairs, hands on hips. He'd flipped on the overhead lights in the restaurant, providing a warm, homey glow in contrast to the dark that crept in through the windows.

I blinked the sleep from my eyes. "What did you say?"

"There's a dead guy in my walk-in refrigerator. You leave him there?"

I didn't answer. It was a ridiculous question. I marched to the big refrigerator and swung open the heavy stainless steel door.

There was a dead guy in there. He was seated on the floor, his back resting against the lower two shelves, face upturned. His eyes were wide open, as if in surprise. He looked as if he were alive, but I could tell he wasn't. I'd seen dead bodies before. Just to make sure, I took a big gulp of air to steady myself and felt the base of his throat for a pulse.

His skin was cold. Dead cold and refrigerator cold. I snatched my hand back, took another deep breath to tamp down the emotions swirling in my chest—repulsion, sadness, fear of an unknown future—and sprinted out of the walk-in Indiana Jones style, as if the floor were crumbling behind me.

"Think I didn't check him already?" Gus groused from behind me. "You know how he got here?"

Deep breaths. "Nope."

"So you never seen him before?"

"I didn't say that." I walked back to the bottom of the stairs and opened the door. "Chris! You need to get down here. Now!" Chris mumbled something I didn't understand, but I heard his feet hit the floor. "You call the cops?" I asked Gus.

"Nine-one-one. As soon as I spotted him." As if in response, I heard the sound of sirens approaching.

Gus, who had better ears than anyone his age had a right to, heard them too. "Don't need to make all that racket. He's dead."

Chris came down the stairs, light brown hair tousled from sleep, still buttoning his flannel shirt over his bare, well-muscled chest. We'd been together for five rocky months, yet the sight of him still made my heart beat faster.

"You were in bed?" Gus asked him. Gus and his wife, Mrs. Gus, had risen at 4 AM every morning for decades. She, so she could bake the delicious pies Gus served at the restaurant, and he, so he could open early to feed the lobstermen and fishermen of Busman's Harbor, Maine. As a result, Gus had trouble believing anyone was still sleeping at five o'clock. Chris and I had explained to him time and again that we were often up late closing the restaurant and then cleaning up to his exacting specifications, but he treated the information as if it were irrelevant. Last night, due to circumstances well beyond our control, we'd been up even later.

There was a loud banging on the restaurant's front door. "Guess I forgot to unlock it," Gus said, and went to answer.

"Take a look in the walk-in," I whispered to Chris.

He did, backing out in a hurry, eyebrows raised, green eyes wide. Gus came clattering down the stairs that led from the restaurant's street-side public entrance into its front room. My childhood friend Officer Jamie Dawes and his partner, Officer Pete Howland, were behind him. Two EMTs and half a dozen firemen brought up the rear.

"I told 'em they didn't need all these people." Gus crossed his arms, a portrait of Yankee disgust at excess of any kind. "The man is deceased."

Jamie and Officer Howland entered the walk-in. They were back out in less than a minute. "He's dead," Jamie told the EMTs and firefighters. "Double-check me for your logs and then you can go along." A young EMT strode into the walk-in and returned moments later shaking his head.

"Can I cook them breakfast?" Gus asked.

"No." Jamie didn't hesitate to answer. "You're closed down. At a minimum, having a dead guy in your refrigerator constitutes a health code violation. Everybody out," he said to the assembled crowd. Then he looked over at Gus, Chris, and me. "Not you three."

"Can I change?" I was suddenly aware of my robe and slippers.

"In a minute." Jamie and Howland stood in

front of the three of us. "You know who this guy is?" Howland asked.

"Not his name," I said. "But he was in the restaurant last night, sitting at the bar. He was here when you came in." I looked at Jamie. He nodded. Even though it had been a crazy, stressful night for him, there had been only nine people in the restaurant in addition to Chris and me when Jamie had arrived. He would remember the stranger.

"Either of you got anything to add?" Howland looked from Chris to Gus.

Chris shook his head.

"I was home in bed last night," Gus protested.

"You can go get dressed," Jamie told me.

"Thanks. What happens now?"

"Unattended death. We call the medical examiner."

I arrived back downstairs dressed in the same basic clothes I'd worn almost every workday since I'd returned to Busman's Harbor the previous March—work boots, jeans, and a T-shirt. The number of layers varied with the season, though little else did. Since it was the first day of December, my ensemble featured a turtleneck underneath the T-shirt, a flannel shirt over the top, and thick socks between my bare feet and the work boots. I'd run a brush through my shoulder-length blond hair, the beginning and ending activity of my Maine daytime beauty routine.

Jamie and Chris were seated at the restaurant's

counter, while Gus stood behind it. I smelled coffee and was grateful the police had at least allowed Gus to brew it. I took a seat on the stool next to Chris.

"Where's Officer Howland?" I asked.

Jamie answered. "Outside, waiting for the ME. We were just talking about"—he gestured toward Chris—"when you last saw the gentleman."

"Do you remember?" I asked Chris.

"No. Not really." Chris looked at me.

"I'm certain he wasn't here that second time I came in," Jamie said. "That was around a quarter to one."

"One in the morning?" Gus wasn't happy. "The police coming around twice? What kind of place you runnin' in my building?"

"Long story," I said.

"I'm all ears."

"Not now," Jamie cautioned. "First, which one of you was the last one in the walk-in?"

"I was." Chris sat, elbows crossed on the counter. "We were open late, as you know." He threw a warning glance at Gus, who looked ready, once again, to demand an explanation. "Julia did the dishes and then minded the bar while I cleaned up. I put the last of the food away a little before ten."

He looked at me for confirmation. I nodded, adding, "When everyone finally left, I put the lemons, orange slices, and cherries from the bar into the little fridge underneath it. I didn't go back in the walk-in."

Jamie leaned back on his stool. "Interesting you

say, 'When everyone finally left,' since everyone apparently did not."

"Sorry, I meant . . ." I floundered. What did I mean?

"And what time did you think the gentleman left?" Jamie looked at me.

I squinted to help myself remember. "A little after ten. Chris closed the kitchen and came to help me. The guy threw some cash on the bar and drifted out right after that."

"Drifted?"

"Drifted," I repeated. "Ambled. Sauntered. Strolled. Moved casually toward the door."

"Was he drunk?"

This time I looked at Chris for confirmation. We both had experience judging people's levels of inebriation, Chris from his work as a bouncer, me from managing the Snowden Family Clambakes in the summer. "I would say he was relaxed, maybe had a little buzz on," I said, while Chris nodded his agreement. "I wasn't worried about him, if that's what you're asking. I certainly didn't think he was going off to die in our refrigerator."

"Did he tell you his name?" Jamie asked it slowly, as if to emphasize the importance of the question.

"No," I answered. "And, as I said, he paid in cash."

"And to confirm, neither of you had ever seen him before last evening."

Chris and I shook our heads.

"He doesn't appear to have a wallet on him," Jamie said. "Or a phone. I don't want to move him until the ME gets here. Maybe they're in his back pants pocket."

"He told me he was staying at the Snuggles," I offered. The Snuggles Inn, a gingerbread-covered Victorian bed-and-breakfast, was across the street from my mother's house and was run by Fiona and Viola Snugg, dear family friends and honorary great-aunts.

"Thanks. That's helpful."

"ME's here," Officer Howland called from the front door. "She's parking."

Jamie stood up. "Bring her down."

Chapter 2

Gus moved from behind the counter to clear the way for the tidy figure of Dr. Joellen Simpson to enter the walk-in. Dr. Simpson was a family practitioner with a good reputation in Busman's Harbor, and was also, apparently, our part-time medical examiner.

As soon as Howland and Jamie followed her into the walk-in, Gus stalked to a table on the far side of the dining room and motioned for Chris and me to join him.

"Now you're going to tell me what the heck is going on." He gave us the full Gus treatment—a squint that emphasized his great white eyebrows—to show he meant business. "How in heck did you leave a dead guy in my refrigerator?"

"I'm not sure," I said.

"We didn't." Chris was more emphatic.

Chris and I had been running our restaurant, which we cleverly called Gus's Too, for five weeks. The idea had been all Gus's. He'd proposed that he

serve breakfast and lunch and that Chris and I
share the space and serve dinner, or as Gus called
it, "suppah."

The offer had seemed like a lifeline at the time,
and I'd grabbed it like the flailing survivor I was. I'd
returned to Busman's Harbor in the spring after fif-
teen years away for school and then work, the last
eight in a venture capital job in Manhattan. My goal
had been to rescue my family's clambake business
from bankruptcy. With a lot of help from friends
and family, and a few major calamities along the
way, that mission had been accomplished. At least
for this year.

But by the middle of October, the clambake was
closed down for the season and I was at a cross-
roads. Return to my life and career in New York, or
stay in Busman's Harbor with the man I loved?

Then Gus had offered the restaurant as well as
the studio apartment above it. Chris, I had discovered, was a brilliant home chef. I had experience
running my family's food business. The town, Gus
felt strongly, needed a place to gather during the
winter months. So win-win-win. Or so I'd thought.

The night before in the restaurant hadn't been
typical, that was for sure. For one thing, we'd had
only four reservations, but for the Monday night
after Thanksgiving that seemed reasonable. Lots of
people were still out of town and others were presumably home gorging on leftovers. Most of our
business was walk-in trade anyway. I wasn't worried.

But then, as the sun went down, the fog rolled in.
Fog in coastal Maine is like rain in Seattle. If we all

stayed home because of it, we'd be home half the year. But this fog morphed into something more serious that our local weather people liked to call "frizzle." As the temperature hit thirty-two degrees, the fog froze, leaving everything it touched—roads, cars, windows—coated in a thin, slippery veil of ice.

At 7:00 PM, Chris and I had stood looking at each other across the empty dining room. Perhaps no one would come at all.

"I'm going to put more sand on the walkway." Chris wasn't skilled at doing nothing. He'd done his kitchen prep. The pea soup was made, the stuffed chicken breasts prepared. The sweet and smoky aroma of slow-cooked braised short ribs wafted across the restaurant. It was the perfect do-ahead entree for our short-staffed kitchen.

"You just got back inside from the last time you sanded," I had pointed out.

At that moment, we heard a car come to a stop. One car door slammed, followed by a second. Caroline and Henry Caswell descended the stairs into the restaurant.

"We're so happy to see you!" I'd meant every word of it. I took their heavy wool coats and hung them up on the hooks that lined the wall outside the restrooms.

"You look lovely," Caroline had said.

At night, I traded in my work boots and jeans for black slacks and a nice top. I pulled my hair back and put on a little makeup. The restaurant was supposed to be a casual gathering place but nice enough for a couple to have a "date night." We had spruced it up with candles and checkered cloths over the linoleum tabletops. After New Year's Eve, we'd be the only eat-in restaurant open in town, so we were trying to meet a lot of needs.

The Caswells lived just up the peninsula in Baywater, a "Community for Active Adults over Fifty-Five." On a previous visit to the restaurant, Caroline had told me they both had connections to Maine going back to their childhoods, but like so many Maine retirees, they'd gone elsewhere to make their money. They had been early and loyal supporters of Gus's Too, coming in at least once a week, the closest thing to regulars at our fledgling operation.

I had led them through the archway into the dining room. "Table or booth?" I asked, gesturing around the empty space. They selected a booth in one of the far corners.

The word that came to mind whenever I saw the Caswells was "pixieish." They were both small and lean with white hair and twinkling eyes—his blue, hers brown. Caroline even wore her hair in a pixie cut.

"How is it out?" I asked. "Tough traveling?"

"The fog!" Caroline had answered as they took their seats. "You could barely see five feet in front of the car."

"And the ice. Terrible," Henry affirmed. "But it's Maine, right?"

"We're just glad you could make it."

"We wouldn't have missed it," Henry said.

"We spent the holiday at our eldest daughter's

house in Massachusetts. All three of our girls and their families were there. We are so lucky." Caroline had said it like she truly felt it. "But there's not a thing to eat in our house."

"Plus, we had the gift certificate that had to be used by today," Henry added.

I had handed them their menu books with the paper inserts that Chris and I changed daily.

"Oh, pea soup," Caroline said when she looked at her menu. "How appropriate. For the fog."

"We couldn't resist. It's hearty—full of pea flavor and ham. I tasted it this afternoon."

"Your beau is a great cook," Henry said.

I took their wine order. Merlot for him, chardonnay for her. I'd been selling the gift certificates only since the week before we'd opened, and none of them had an expiration date. But who was I to contradict a good customer, particularly one who had just driven in terrible weather? I'd kept mum on the whole gift-certificate-deadline topic.

I just finished telling this part of the story to Gus and Chris when a thunk and a bump echoed from inside the walk-in, and we all turned our heads to stare. "Now you know why I don't allow strangers in my restaurant," Gus said.

It was true. Against all laws—of the United States, capitalism, and common sense—you didn't get food at Gus's unless he knew you or you arrived with someone he did know. When I first moved back to Busman's Harbor, I'd viewed Gus's rule as a characteristic, if extreme, example of the native Mainers' feelings about people From Away. But during the high season last summer, with day-trippers clogging the streets, I'd come to treasure the refuge of Gus's, where not only did everybody know your name, everybody knew *everybody's* name.

Chris and I had ignored Gus's policy. If you wandered into our restaurant for dinner, you got served. And though I knew Gus hadn't created his rule to prevent strangers from dying in his refrigerator, I was having a bit of a rethink about our position vis-à-vis the whole strangers thing when Dr. Simpson walked back into the room, trailed by Jamie and Howland.

"You call the state police. I'll call the State Medical Examiner's Office in Augusta," Dr. Simpson said to the officers. It sounded like she was repeating instructions to a reluctant student.

"But you said you don't know how he died," Howland protested.

"Exactly," Dr. Simpson confirmed. "I don't know how he died. I'm a part-time ME. I can sign off on unattended deaths with obvious causes, and accidents. But you've got a guy who looks like he's in his middle forties, who's not where he's supposed to be, with no obvious cause of death. I need an autopsy and tox screens, and until we know what's going on here, you need to treat this like a crime scene."

"Can we at least roll him over and see if he's got

a wallet or a phone in his back pocket?" Howland asked.

Simpson shook her head. "Absolutely not."

"Wait a minute. How long am I going to be closed?" Gus demanded.

"As long as it takes." Jamie's mouth was a grim line. He'd had, if anything, less sleep than I had, and he appeared to be fraying a bit around the edges.

There was a banging on the restaurant door. I scooted to answer it.

"Hello, darlin'." It was my brother-in-law's father, Bard Ramsey, and three of his lobstermen cronies. The local lobstermen gathered at Gus's most days for breakfast, especially now that winter was closing in and most of them had their boats out of the water. "What's goin' on?"

Bard looked pointedly at Jamie and Howland's cruiser parked on the street and Dr. Simpson's navy blue compact SUV next to it.

"Gus is closed," I explained, reluctant to say more.

"No, he isn't. Everyone knows Gus only closes for February when he and Mrs. Gus go to visit their kids out west." Bard craned his thick neck, attempting to look down the stairs into the restaurant. "Something happened to Gus?"

"Gus is fine." I wasn't sure what else I should say, but Bard and his friends didn't budge, so I added, "There's a bit of a situation."

Which was like opening Pandora's Box Full of Questions. The lobstermen bombarded me with plenty, until I finally announced I had to go. I shut the door, wondering what kind of rumors I'd just started.

As I reentered the dining room, Jamie clicked off his cell phone. Dr. Simpson finished her call too. "They're on the way," she said to Jamie. He turned toward Chris and me. "You'd best cancel any reservations you have booked for tonight."

"Gus is open every day, but Julia and I don't serve dinner on Tuesday and Wednesday evenings," Chris informed him.

He nodded. "That's a break. Did you lock both outside doors last night?"

"Yes," Chris and I said at once.

"Which one of you did it?"

"I locked the kitchen door." Chris raised his hand.

"What time was that?"

"About eleven."

"I locked the street door," I said. "At around twelve forty-five."

The layout of Gus's restaurant was quirky. The old former warehouse sat on pilings on a boulder that thrust out into the harbor. The harbor walls were steep at that point, so Gus's public entrance, which was at street level, led to a staircase that customers took down to the restaurant level. The front room housed a lunch counter and a few small tables. An archway opened to a second, much larger dining room, which had faux-leather red booths along the walls and tables at its center. The dining room offered one of the town's best views of the back harbor, the working part of the waterfront.

The second exit, the kitchen door, was at the back

of the first room, behind the lunch counter and the open kitchen area where Gus cooked. The passageway to the walk-in refrigerator and the little hallway that led to the door to my apartment stairs were also back there. The kitchen exit opened onto a flat area of asphalt that offered a few parking spaces and a Dumpster. From there, a steep driveway climbed back to street level.

"Did you lock the refrigerator?" Jamie asked.

Gus glanced at the old walk-in with something that looked like affection. "Wouldn't even know how. Bought it used in '84. Never had a key."

"Right." Jamie addressed Chris, Gus, and me. "You all can go. We know where to find you."

"The hell I will," Gus said.

"Can I stay upstairs in my apartment?" I asked.

"Better not," Jamie answered. "And we'll need your permission to search it. I'll get you the form."

"You don't think the dead man was up there?" I couldn't keep the alarm out of my voice.

"I don't think anything yet."

"Who was at the door?" Gus asked.

"Bard Ramsey and some of the other lobstermen," I answered. "I told him you were closed."

Gus sighed. "I'd best phone Mrs. Gus before someone calls to ask her if I'm dead."

"Officer Howland will stay to secure the scene," Jamie said. "I'm heading over to the Snuggles Inn to see if we can find out who this guy is."

"You should bring me with you," I said.

"Why?"

"So the sisters aren't alarmed when they see you."

"They've known me all my life, Julia, just like you."

That was true. I'd grown up across the street from the Snuggles Inn. Jamie, who was my age—thirty—had always lived, still lived, in the house next door to my mother's.

"You're in your uniform, on their front porch at, what?" I looked at my phone. "Seven in the morning." *My, how time flies when you're not having fun.* "You know it will go better if I'm standing next to you."

Jamie hesitated. He was well acquainted with Vee Snugg's love of the dramatic. "Okay," he finally said. "Get your coat. Hurry."

I ran upstairs; put food and water in bowls for Le Roi, my Maine coon cat; grabbed my coat; and called good-bye. Le Roi lifted a lazy head out of the folds in the duvet, blinked, and went to sleep again.

Chris was waiting at the bottom of the stairs when I came back down.

"It's definitely the same guy," he whispered.

"Yup. I saw the, uh, scar," I responded.

"Me too. How the heck . . . ?"

"I don't know." I inclined my head in the direction of the cops and the ME. "Let's talk soon. Where are you headed?"

"At eight thirty I've got to take Mrs. Deakins to the supermarket. I'm going back to my cabin to trade my truck for my cab."

During the busy season, Chris had three jobs. He worked at his landscaping business, drove a cab he owned, and was a bouncer at Crowley's, Busman's Harbor's most touristy bar. Now that the summer was over, short cab hops were as good as it got. He and I were still working out the logistics of having two places to live. It seemed like his truck, or his cab, or my car was always in the wrong place.

"Okay," I said. "Call me soon. We need to talk."

His lips brushed my cheek and he was out the door.

Chapter 3

Jamie left the squad car at Gus's, and we walked out of the back harbor and up the hill toward Snuggles Inn. The day was overcast, and a fierce wind cut through my coat. Jamie was a good deal taller than my paltry five-foot-two, and I had to push to keep up. Nothing was very far from anything else in Busman's Harbor proper, and soon we were on the Snuggles' front porch. Jamie rang the bell, and a deep bong echoed inside.

"Coming!" Viola Snugg, called Vee, opened the front door. At seventy-five years of age and slightly after 7 AM, Vee cut an elegant figure. Her luxurious snow-white hair was swept up in a perfect coif, and she was wearing, as always, a tailored dress, hose, and high heels. As I'd predicted, her eyes took in Jamie in his uniform and she immediately stepped backward, clutching her hand to her ample bosom. "Oh my. How can I help you?"

"May we come in?" Jamie asked.

"Of course, Jamie, er, Officer Dawes. And Julia."
She threw me a quizzical look.

The Snuggles was, as always, tidy and inviting.
Vee directed us to the front parlor. "You're here
about our guest," she said to Jamie before we sat
down.

"Why do you say that?" Jamie asked.

"He didn't come back last night." We all settled
into our seats—Jamie and I on the Victorian settee
the Snugg sisters had inherited from their grandparents, Vee in the straight-backed, upholstered
chair opposite. I had the feeling Jamie sat down
only because he didn't want Vee to think she had to
remain standing.

"How did you discover he didn't return to his
room?" Jamie asked.

"He arrived a little after five last evening. He had
a reservation for two nights. Fee and I greeted him
and suggested he might like to have his evening
meal at Gus's Too." Not a hard recommendation to
make, considering we were the only place open on
weeknights during the off season, except for Hole
in the Wall Pizza, about which the less said, the
better.

"He went off about six o'clock. Fee and I watched
a little TV. At ten, I went up to bed. Fee stayed up to
let him in."

Like most B&Bs in town, the Snuggles gave their
guests keys to their rooms but not to the outside
door. Since Vee got up early to make the guests
the full English breakfasts for which the inn was

renowned, it was her sister, Fiona, called Fee, who stayed up late to let in any stray guests.

"I found Fee sound asleep in her easy chair at six o'clock this morning," Vee said. "I woke her up and sent her to bed. She said our guest never came home."

"Which room is his?" Jamie asked.

"Four," Vee said. "I'll get you the key." She disappeared through a swinging door and reappeared before it had stopped moving. I knew she'd grabbed the key off a board in the kitchen that held spares for all the rooms.

Jamie stood. "I'm going to look at his room. Alone." He threw me a look that told me to stay put. "Miss Snugg, can you come upstairs with me and wake your sister? Tell her I need to speak with her as soon as I'm done."

They bustled out of the room. Vee raised an eyebrow in my direction, forming a silent question, as she followed Jamie up the winding stairway.

I stayed in my seat and looked around the room. It was high Victorian and should have been heavy, dark, and uncomfortable, but it was one of my happiest places. I was suffering from a lack of sleep and normally the warm room would have made me woozy, but my nerves were wound up tight from the events of the morning.

Jamie must have finished searching at the same time Vee got the roused Fee out of her room. All three trooped down the stairs. Fee was covered from head to toe in a high-necked, plaid flannel gown, a matching flannel robe, and slipper socks. Behind her thick glasses, she blinked at the interruption to her sleep.

"Now, Jamie Dawes, you tell us what this is about," she demanded. I rose and met the three of them in the foyer.

Jamie glanced at me and inhaled deeply. "Your guest passed away last night. At Gus's restaurant."

Both sisters' mouths dropped open. "How terrible," Fee said. "Julia, were you there when it happened?"

I didn't answer. I undoubtedly had been, if being behind the restaurant bar or upstairs in ignorant slumber counted. I noticed Jamie hadn't given any of the details. Like that the body hadn't been found until this morning. Or its location.

"We heard the sirens last night," Fee added.

Again, Jamie didn't contradict or clarify, so I stayed mum. The sirens had been about something else entirely.

"Right now, what we really need is your guest's identity," Jamie said. "I didn't see anything in his room to help me. Just a clean shirt and underwear on the bed. No wallet or phone. Not even a suitcase."

"He had a backpack when he arrived," Vee said. "I'm sure of it. I noticed it particularly because it seemed too large for a couple of nights. I thought he might be on an extended visit along the coast."

Jamie looked at me. "Did he have a backpack at the restaurant?"

"No. I'm certain."

Jamie turned back to the Snugg sisters. "Do you remember if he had the backpack when he left for dinner?"

"We didn't see him go out. We were back in our den watching the news on TV. I heard the door slam. That was it," Fee answered.

"And it definitely was him leaving?"

Fee looked mystified. "Who else could it have been?"

"He'd have his wallet and probably his phone with him, wouldn't he?" The remarkably smooth skin over Vee's nose pinched in suspicion. "He'd have to pay for his dinner."

"Do you know his name?" Jamie asked.

The sisters looked at one another. "I'll fetch the guest register." Vee took a few steps to the table in the center of the room.

"I'll get the reservation book," Fee said, shuffling toward the kitchen in her slipper socks.

Vee held out the guest register to Jamie and me. "Here we go."

Jamie squinted at the opened page, taking the register from Vee and holding it closer. "What do you think that says?" he asked me, tipping the book one way and then another, hoping to read the scrawl of a signature.

"I think it begins with a Q," I said. "Or maybe that's a J?"

"Can you make out the last name?"

To me, the last name looked like *nnnnnnnnn*.

"I got nothing," I told him. We stood together, turning the register from side to side as if it were a kaleidoscope that would suddenly reveal a discernible pattern. It was hopeless. The man's signature was a cipher.

Fee bustled back with the reservation book—a simple calendar on which they wrote guest names with arrows going through the days they were staying. "What does this say?" she asked. Her handwriting was no better. The four of us stared at the calendar.

"Justin?" I suggested.

"Or Jason," Vee said. "Maybe Jackson?"

"Or Jacob?" Fee said. "What did he say his name was?"

Jamie sighed. "I take it he didn't pay with a credit card."

"No," Fee answered. "He paid in cash, up front for two nights."

"In the high season we require a deposit in full on a credit card to hold the room," Vee explained. "But in the off season . . ." She trailed off, gesturing around the silent house. Justin or Jason or Jackson had been their only guest.

"Did he have a vehicle?" Jamie asked.

"No," Vee answered. "He told me he came on the bus. And there's no car parked anywhere around."

Jamie sighed again. "Maybe he paid for the bus with a credit card." He straightened up. "I've got to go. Someone else will be around with more questions," he told the ladies. "Julia, where will you be?"

"Mom's, I guess."

"Stay and have tea with us," Vee urged.

I could tell they wanted to ask a lot of questions I either couldn't or didn't want to answer. "I'd love to, but maybe later."

I kissed Vee's powdery cheek and Fee's unmade-up one, and I slipped out the door behind Jamie.

We stood on the Snuggles' wide front porch, empty of furniture for the coming winter.

"Maybe the ME will roll him over and his wallet will be in his back pocket," Jamie said.

"Maybe they'll do an autopsy and find he had a heart attack," I responded.

"Maybe," Jamie said.

"Maybe."

Neither of us spoke with any conviction.

Jamie walked off in the direction of the back harbor and Gus's. I crossed the street to my mother's house and let myself in the unlocked back door.

The kitchen of my childhood home was oddly comforting, even though the overcast day let in a gloomy glow and the room was chilly. My mom had recently taken a job at Linens and Pantries about a half an hour away in Topsham. On days when she was out of the house, she turned the heat down low. The job was a new thing for her, and in the beginning it had been a rough transition, but she'd stuck with it. She'd survived Black Friday and the rest of Thanksgiving weekend and was back at work today.

I sat at the kitchen table with my coat still on, pulled my phone out of my bag, and called Chris. "Where are you?"

"Parked outside Hannafords, waiting for Mrs. Deakins." Instead of driving off and returning, he was saving gas by waiting for his fare in the supermarket parking lot. Also, that way he would be there to help her as soon as she came out of the building.

"So that was crazy this morning," I said.

"I have a feeling it's going to get a lot crazier when the medical examiner and the state police get here."

I grunted, acknowledging that was probably true.

"So what did happen?" Chris asked. "What time did he arrive last night, do you remember?"

"A little after seven thirty, I think." That was what I remembered, but it didn't jibe with what Fee had said about the stranger leaving the Snuggles at six. Gus's was a five-minute walk from the inn. What had the man done from six to seven thirty? In nicer weather, he might have taken a stroll around the village, but last night had been dark, cold, foggy, and icy.

"Who was in the dining room by then?" Chris did the cooking, and even though the food preparation area was open to the front room, his focus would be on the meals. Mine was supposed to be on the guests. So I wasn't surprised he was relying on me to remember which customers had arrived when.

"The Caswells were already there," I answered.

"They were the first ones. And the Bennetts were definitely there."

"The Bennetts. Which ones are they?"

"You know, the Bennetts, Phil and Deborah."

"Sure." He didn't sound sure.

I clarified. "He's tall, full head of white hair, skinny arms and legs, but he has a gut. Acts kind of full of himself."

"You mean like he was something in the real world." Living in a resort town, Chris had plenty of experience with entitled retirees.

"Yes, like that," I confirmed. "She's the blonde with the . . ." Here I floundered a bit.

Chris chuckled. "You're making that face, aren't you?"

"What face?" I asked innocently.

"The one where you pull the skin on your face back to your ears and breathe like a fish." He was laughing now, and so was I.

"You got me," I admitted. "She's the one with all the plastic surgery." I cleared my throat. "It's not nice to laugh at our guests."

"I'm not laughing at our guests. I'm laughing at you."

"It does feel a little mean," I said. "Why do women do that to themselves?"

"Whoops, here comes Mrs. Deakins. I gotta help her with her grocery bags. Love you."

"Love you too."

And he was gone.

The Bennetts had arrived after the Caswells, and

before the man who was now dead in Gus's walk-in. I was certain of it. I'd just brought the Caswells their wine when the Bennetts entered the restaurant.

"Quiet tonight," Phil Bennett remarked when I had taken his coat.

"It's the weather," Deborah had said. "Terrible out."

"Your walkway could use more sand. I nearly lost my footing." Phil's clipped tone made it sound as if he were speaking to an incompetent staff member.

"Of course. I'll get right on it."

As I had moved away to hang up their coats, the Bennetts noticed the Caswells. I wasn't surprised the two couples knew each other, or at least had a nodding acquaintance. All four of them appeared to be around the same age and had probably met at some town meeting, volunteer opportunity, or social event. But that wouldn't make them best buddies necessarily, so when I returned with the menus to find the Bennetts sitting in the opposite corner of the dining room, I wasn't surprised by that either. If you're having dinner with your spouse in a practically empty restaurant, there's no point in listening to the conversation of the only other guests, or in having them overhear you.

"Can I get you something to drink? Wine, beer, or a cocktail?" I asked the Bennetts.

"Alcohol. That's something new," Phil had responded.

It was. We'd just gotten our liquor license on the Tuesday before Thanksgiving. Gus had never had one for his breakfast and lunch place, and it had seemed to take forever for ours to come through, though I was assured by the town employees I dealt with it had been at record speed. Before that, working on a temporary license, the restaurant had been strictly BYOB, which had further shaved our razor-thin profit margins. We'd had just enough time and cash before the Thanksgiving holiday to stock the bar.

"I'd like a perfect Rob Roy," Phil said.

"And you?" I had trouble, as always, looking Deborah in the eye. She'd had so much work done, her face was like a mask. Her cheekbones were prominent, her nose perfect, her eyes wide open, but the total effect was somehow frightening.

"Ginger ale."

We didn't have a real bartender, but Chris had worked as a bouncer for years and stepped behind the bar at Crowley's in emergencies. My experience level was about the same, filling in for sick or otherwise absent bartenders at the Snowden Family Clambake. We figured we could fake our way through, but just in case, I'd stowed a little book of cocktail recipes behind the bar.

The bar itself had been a bit of a controversy. Gus had never had one, but Chris and I felt strongly that we needed one. Gus's vision was for a neighborly gathering place, and that wasn't going to happen without a bar. And it wasn't going to happen on nights the New England Patriots played if we didn't have a TV.

Gus had a long unused candlepin-bowling lane

on the opposite side of the front room from the
lunch counter. I'd convinced him that Chris could
use his carpentry skills to cover the lane over without harming it and put the bar in that part of the
room. Chris had also built a back bar to house a
sink, small fridge, and TV. It stood behind the bar
a few feet out from the wall where it wouldn't harm
either the candlepin lane or Gus's "décor," which
consisted entirely of white-washed wallboard. Gus
was insisting we uncover the lane in the spring
when we closed the dinner restaurant and Chris
and I moved back to our tourist season pursuits.
We'd agreed, even though I had never, ever seen
anyone bowl there.

I returned to the Bennetts with their drinks.

"Thank you, Julia," Phil had said, tasting his.
"Excellent," he pronounced.

Whew.

The Bennetts had owned a summer home out on
Eastclaw Point since I was a kid, and every year they
brought houseguests out to our clambake. We
offered a harbor tour on the way to Morrow Island,
our private island. Twice a day, during the high
season, we served two hundred guests a real Maine
clambake meal—chowder, steamed clams, twin
lobsters, corn on the cob, a potato, an onion, and
an egg—cooked over rocks heated by a roaring
wood fire.

I looked from Phil to Deborah and was struck
again by her face. I tried to remember from my
teen years working at the clambake if Deborah had

always looked like that. The smooth mask created by the surgeon's scalpel was the only image I could conjure.

Phil looked at his menu. "What is this fish?"

I cleared my throat. "Hake. It's a light, white fish. Tonight, we're serving the loin, which is the thicker cut, nearer the head."

He knit his brows together. "Never had it." The implication was clear. If Phil Bennett hadn't eaten it, it wasn't worth eating.

Chris, it had turned out, not completely to my surprise, was a genius at creating meals that were both elegant and affordable. If we wanted to be popular with the locals, we had to keep our prices down. Chris had chosen hake because it was fresh, tasty, and inexpensive in the early winter.

"I'm sure you'll love it," I urged.

Phil had thrown me a skeptical look. "What's this pineapple-avocado salsa the hake is served on? Is it spicy?"

"Not spicy," I answered. "But sunny and happy. The perfect antidote to a foggy, icy evening." I'd grinned like an idiot, hoping for a smile back. No dice.

"What else does it come with?"

"Rice and broccoli." *Which is printed clearly on the menu you're staring at.* Out of the corner of my eye, I saw Henry Caswell wave to get my attention.

"Hrrumpf," Phil responded

"I'll leave you to make your decision."

As I left the Bennetts and crossed the dining room toward the Caswells, ready to take their order, a man had entered the front room. He was alone and without a reservation, which hardly mattered given the empty state of the restaurant. When I'd offered him a table he said, "I'll sit at the bar, if you don't mind."

Chapter 4

The buzzing of my cell phone woke me up. Four short hours of sleep had taken its toll, and I'd dozed off sitting upright in my mother's chilly kitchen.

"Julia? Jerry Binder. I understand you found our body."

Lieutenant Jerry Binder of the state police Major Crimes Unit in Augusta. Suddenly, I was wide awake. "Not exactly."

"We're over at Gus's," he said. "I need you to come by and walk me through this."

"On my way."

When I got back to the restaurant Gus's pickup was still in the parking area, and Dr. Simpson's little SUV, a crime scene tech van, and the State Medical Examiner's official car were parked on the street. Chris pulled up in his cab before I reached the front door.

Officer Howland waved us inside.

"Julia, Mr. Durand, come on in." Binder met us

at the bottom of the stairs. He had warm brown eyes, a ski-slope nose, and a fringe of brown hair surrounding his otherwise bald head. Tom Flynn, his second-in-command, was behind Gus's counter, talking to someone who was inside the walk-in. No doubt its door had been open all morning as the ME and crime scene techs wandered in and out. We'd have to throw away everything that was in there. But I supposed we'd have had to anyway. As Jamie had said, the health department no doubt took a dim view of food that was stored with a corpse.

"Is he still . . . ?" I asked.

"No," Binder answered. "Loaded in the medical examiner's van and on his way to Augusta."

Dr. Simpson and the state ME talked in low voices in a corner. When Binder mentioned her title, the ME looked up, nodding a greeting to Chris and me. Gus sat slumped on the last stool at the counter. Jamie stood behind the counter, looking as exhausted as I felt.

"You're here," I said to Binder. "That must mean you suspect something." The only cities in Maine big enough to employ homicide detectives were Bangor and Portland. Murders, child abuse, and other serious crimes were investigated by two state police Major Crimes Units, one for the southern part of state, one for the northern. If Binder and Flynn were in town, it meant they suspected this was more than an unattended death.

Binder gestured toward Dr. Simpson. "Your sharp-eyed local ME spotted an injection site between the

ring and index fingers on the deceased's left hand."
Binder looked at Jamie. "Any sign of drug use,
prescription or otherwise, in the victim's room at
the B&B?"

"No, sir," Jamie answered without hesitation.
"But then, there wasn't much of anything there."

Dr. Simpson and the ME pulled on their coats
and prepared to leave. Binder indicated one of the
larger tables in the center of the room. "Let's go
back to the beginning, shall we?" he said to the
rest of us. "Why doesn't everybody sit down." We
gathered around the table. I sat across from Binder
and Flynn. Chris sat next to me, a comforting presence. Gus and Jamie were at the ends.

"Mr. Farnham," Binder said as Flynn pulled out
his pen and notebook, "You weren't here last
evening."

"That's right."

"And your role in all this is that you found the
body this morning."

"Well, that, and the body's in my damn refrigerator."

Binder allowed a small smile. "Yes, and that. But
what I'm getting at is, you weren't here last night,
which is what I want to talk to Ms. Snowden, Mr.
Durand, and Officer Dawes about. So, if you'd like
to go home, we'll contact you later when we're ready
to take your statement."

"The heck I will."

Binder hesitated a moment, then seemed to
accept Gus wasn't leaving. "Okay." He turned to face

Chris and me. "I understand the deceased ate here in the restaurant last evening. What time did he arrive?"

"Around seven thirty," I said.

Binder looked at Chris, who nodded his agreement. "I was cooking," Chris explained. "Julia would be more aware than me. But that's what I remember too." We'd already been over this ground with Jamie.

"Who was in the restaurant when he got here?"

"Chris, me, Caroline and Henry Caswell, Deborah and Phillip Bennett."

Flynn wrote the names down and read the spellings back to me. "That's it?" he asked.

I felt a little defensive. "It was a Monday night and right after the Thanksgiving holiday."

Flynn glanced at his notes. "So the Caswells and the Bennetts were here, and then the victim arrived. Tell us about that."

"There's not that much to tell. He came in by himself. I offered him a table. He said he wanted to sit at the bar." Binder and Flynn looked at me expectantly, so I went on. "I turned on the football pregame show with the sound off for him, gave him a menu, and offered him a drink."

"Please describe him," Binder said.

"You saw him in the walk-in."

"I'd like your impression from when he was alive."

"He looked like he was in his middle to late forties." I'm not great at judging ages. I was going by the wrinkles around his eyes, a certain heaviness to his body. "He had long, dark, wavy hair that fell to below his collar, and large features—big blue eyes, big nose, big mouth. Big eyelashes," I added. "Thick, both top and bottom." Unusually thick, which was why I'd noticed.

I paused, trying to sort out my first impressions from what I'd seen this morning. My memory of the empty eyes staring up at me blotted out everything else. I took a deep breath and looked at Binder.

"Did you notice any distinctive—"

"You mean the scar."

Binder nodded, and I continued. "I didn't see it at first. He had long hair, and the scar kind of crept up from his neck to his ear. It was pretty well hidden. If anything, I might have vaguely thought he'd had acne when he was younger." I stopped, looking across at Chris. Binder and Flynn waited silently. "Later, I noticed his ear."

"Tell me about that," Binder coaxed.

"We just set up the bar. We only have the basics. He asked me for a lot of specialized labels, fancy ryes and such. Finally, I put every bottle I had on the bar, and he chose."

"What did he go with?" Flynn asked.

"Wild Turkey." I shrugged. "That's as exotic as brands get at Gus's Too. Anyway, all this required a fair amount of conversation. I was distracted because two more couples came in and needed to be seated, but I did notice his ear. It's some kind of prosthesis, isn't it?"

"Yes," Binder confirmed. "The ear is not his."

"Will that help you identify him?"

"Only in the sense that we know we're looking for a man who was missing an ear. According to the ME, ears aren't like prosthetic limbs with unique serial numbers. Their only function is cosmetic." Binder paused. "Who were the other couples?"

"The Smiths and the Walkers. Michael and Sheila Smith, and Barry and Fran Walker."

Flynn wrote that down, obviously for follow up later.

"And then what?" Binder prompted.

"Just regular restaurant stuff." Suddenly, we were busy. Not that the restaurant was crowded, but everyone had come in at once. I juggled taking orders, getting drinks, and bringing the Caswells their starters—pea soup for her, salad for him. Chris was a skilled home cook but not yet used to the pace of restaurant cooking. For us, this constituted a rush.

"Until?" Binder prompted.

"Until a little more than an hour later, when Officer Dawes came in and told us no one could leave." The Caswells had been settling up. They hadn't ordered dessert, and their gift certificate was going to cover just about the whole meal. Everyone else was eating his or her entree. Jamie had come to the door, in his heavy policeman's raincoat, and told us there'd been an accident.

Binder looked at Jamie. "Officer Dawes has already told us about the accident."

There was a single road in and out of Busman's

Harbor. Main Street started at the two-lane highway at the end of town and traveled through the downtown, past the shops and hotels. It continued up the hill along the inner harbor, past the Snuggles Inn and my mother's house across the street. Then it looped around, following the contour of the harbor hill, passing the back harbor and Gus's, the marina, and the shipyard until it turned again and intersected itself across from the library at the only traffic light in town. Plenty of smaller roads branched off it, supplying access to almost all the residences in Busman's Harbor proper, but only Main Street got you in or out of town. So when Jamie had come into the restaurant, nose red from the fog and icy drizzle, to say there'd been an accident and two vehicles were blocking the intersection of Main and Main, I was surprised but not shocked. It had happened before.

"So then what?" Binder asked.

"The Caswells decided to order dessert after all. They split a brownie sundae."

He smiled. "And then—"

"Excuse me, Lieutenant." Officer Howland was at the kitchen door. "You're all needed."

Jamie, Flynn, and Binder jumped up. "We'll continue this at the station later," Binder said.

"Hey, wait," Gus called. "Can I open tomorrow?"

"We're not finished here," Binder said. "I'm taking the team with me now. We have something else we need to attend to, but they'll be back. If they finish today, and I think they will, you can open tomorrow as long as you can operate without using the walk-in."

"Where are you going?" I called as they all trooped out the kitchen door. I wasn't surprised when no one answered.

Chapter 5

For a minute, Gus, Chris, and I stared after the police. I couldn't imagine where they had gone, or what had been so important they'd left the crime scene during an active investigation.

Gus rose from the table. "If they're going to let me open tomorrow, I need to buy some food."

"You can use the refrigerator in my apartment for storage," I offered. "And I'll clean as much as I can out of the little one behind the bar."

"Thanky." Gus strode over to the counter and hefted the stack of homemade wooden boxes he used to transport Mrs. Gus's pies from their kitchen where she made them. "Want a pie?" He turned toward us, offering the boxes.

"Save them for tomorrow," I said.

Gus's beak nose wrinkled. "I don't serve day-old pie. Besides, what would Mrs. Gus do tomorrow morning?" After a recent illness, Mrs. Gus had cut down to making five pies a day, which made pieces harder to get, and therefore more precious. With this in mind, ignoring the vow I'd made after Thanksgiving dinner to eat lighter until Christmas, I asked if there was a pecan. When Gus said there was, I accepted it and thanked him.

Chris and I remained at the table after Gus left.

"I was the last one in the walk-in, wasn't I?" Chris said. "Around ten? I've told the cops that twice. I want to make sure it's what you remember."

"It is," I confirmed.

"And was the dead guy still sitting at the bar when I went in there?"

"Yes, but he left just after." I'd thought about little else all day. I was sure I was right. Unlike the rest of the crowd who'd driven to Gus's, the dead man had walked over the hill from the Snuggles. The accident at Main and Main didn't affect him. He was free to go, even if the rest of them were not.

"Where'd he go?" Chris asked.

"I thought he'd gone back to the Snuggles."

"And came back here and got himself killed in the walk-in?"

"We can't be sure of that," I said. "Maybe he was killed somewhere else and dumped in there." Maybe that's why Binder had taken the techs with him. Somewhere there was another crime scene. Maybe it wasn't even murder. Maybe the ME was wrong about the injection and, as I'd said to Jamie, when they did the autopsy they'd discover he'd died of a heart attack or a stroke. Which still didn't make sense. Why would he have been in our walk-in?

Chris took my hand. "We locked the doors when we went up to bed. There's no sign of a break-in.

That means Mr. Anonymous and possibly his killer were in the restaurant when we went upstairs."

I shuddered. Chris was right, but until he said it, I hadn't thought it all the way through, as he had, and come to the obvious conclusion.

"Did you actually see him go out the door?" Chris asked.

"I'm not sure. I can't remember. Did you?"

"No." Chris thought for a moment. "When was the last time you checked the bathrooms?"

The bathrooms. Because we still felt like guests in Gus's space, I was hypervigilant about inspecting the restrooms last thing at night before I went up to bed. But the previous night had dragged on and on, with our guests trapped in the restaurant by the accident. It was so late by the time we got everyone out, I'd staggered off to bed without looking in the washrooms.

I admitted this to Chris, who shrugged. "It doesn't matter, Julia. He couldn't have hidden there the whole time. We had guests who were using the restrooms right up until we closed."

He was right about that. I specifically remembered that the Bennetts, who had the farthest to drive, had used the facilities immediately before they left. That was almost three hours after I'd last seen the man at the bar who'd died in our walk-in.

"You can't lock your apartment," Chris pointed out.

We'd had this discussion before. "I've told you, Gus says the lock broke ages ago. Besides, what difference does it make? We lock the outside doors to the restaurant."

"Normally, no difference," Chris conceded. "Julia, face facts. We were locked in the building with a corpse, and possibly a killer."

"I get it. Don't keep saying it. It freaks me out."

Chris's features relaxed. "Okay."

"What were you going to do with your day off?" I asked. "Originally."

"Get some work done on my house. Then Sam's tonight for the game." As soon as his summer tenants had moved out of the cabin he'd bought from his parents, Chris had torn the second-floor walls back to the studs. It was a long, slow process building it up again. He paid for the upgrades, including the heating system, electricity, and plumbing, as he made money. The work all had to be done by the spring so he could rent out the cabin for the summer.

The "Sam" he'd referred to was Sam Rockmaker, bartender and part owner of Crowley's. Chris played poker with a group of guys at Sam's house every Tuesday.

"Do you want me to stay? Are you nervous about being here?" Chris asked.

"No. You go. I'm fine. The cops have been all over the building. This is probably the safest place in the harbor."

Chris stood and bent over to give me a fast smooch. Then he was out the door and I was alone in the empty restaurant.

* * *

I went upstairs to my apartment. Le Roi was at the top of the stairs, vocalizing in my direction, upset at the day's intrusions on his rigorous routine of napping, eating, and napping again. Even though he'd been an outdoor cat on predator-free, car-free Morrow Island, he'd taken to the life of an indoor town cat like a champ. We'd both felt instantly at home in the apartment over Gus's restaurant.

The place was a big studio, tucked under the eaves of the old warehouse that Gus's restaurant had once been. There was a high central ceiling and four dormered nooks, one on each side of the building. The one facing south contained my bed, still in the unmade state it had been in when first I, and then Chris, answered Gus's summons this morning. The east-facing nook contained the bathroom, the north-facing one the kitchen. The fourth was part of the main living space and held a giant, multipaned window facing west that framed a view of the back harbor. Outside, the boats belonging to the hardiest, most dedicated lobstermen were still in the water, but all the other slips were empty.

Now that feeling of home had gone, replaced by a creeping unease that tensed the back of my neck and pinched my shoulders. What if, as Chris had suggested, the stranger or his killer had hidden in my apartment while our guests dined and Chris and I worked downstairs? Had the murderer or victim sat on my couch, touched my stuff?

And then there'd been the cops this morning. They had searched the place too. I'd given them permission to do so when I signed the release. I shivered as I gazed at the rumpled bed. At least nothing embarrassing had been left out. But I wondered, had they been in my bathroom? Had they opened my drawers? They must have.

I went into the kitchen nook, preparing to clean out the refrigerator for Gus as I'd promised. The warehouse attic had been converted to living space during World War II. Gus and his family had moved out in the late 1950s, and nothing had been done to it since. The appliances were tiny and ancient. The freezer was a small metal box inside the refrigerator. If left unattended too long, it had to be defrosted with the hammer and chisel Gus kept in a toolbox behind the lunch counter in the restaurant.

As I'd remembered, there wasn't much in the old refrigerator. Chris and I had spent most of the previous weekend at my mom's, enjoying Thanksgiving with my family and our guests. Even without the holiday, it was hard to get motivated to buy food and cook with a restaurant right downstairs. I threw out some expired cartons of yogurt, the remains of a sub, and a few wilted stalks of celery. When I was done, I took the plastic bag out of the kitchen barrel, planning to take the garbage to the Dumpster behind the restaurant.

Gus didn't need to reopen right away for financial reasons. Unlike the Snowden Family Clambake, Gus's restaurant was on a secure footing. His house was paid for, his middle-aged children were prosperous, and Gus was the tightest of tightwads. I had to imagine that he and Mrs. Gus were pretty comfortable. But if he wasn't running the restaurant, I didn't think Gus would have the slightest idea what to do with himself.

But then, I was the pot getting all judgy about the kettle. When Chris and I had agreed to serve dinner at Gus's place, I'd assumed we'd do it seven days a week. After all, that's what Gus did. And that's what my family did at the Snowden Family Clambake during the tourist season.

But Chris had balked. "Julia, what part of 'off season' don't you get? This is when we spend time with friends, enjoy our hobbies, and take an occasional nap. That's why we work like dogs during high season."

As far as I knew, we worked like dogs during the high season to make money to survive the long winter and cold spring, but point taken. I'd always had workaholic tendencies. Long weekends away at boarding school without much to do except schoolwork, the pressure of business school, the crazy hours and relentless travel of my venture capital job had all reinforced my habits. But I had to admit, most of my workaholism came from inside me. I could have snuck off campus like my friends did at prep school, had more fun during college, and taken time during my work-related travel to do a little sightseeing, but that wasn't me. Maybe I wasn't that different from Gus.

"Besides," Chris had continued. "If we work seven days, when will I finish my house? When will I get my deer?"

That took me aback and made me reflect once again on the new life I was living. Throughout my sporadic dating life and short-lived relationships in Manhattan, I couldn't recall a single man telling me he needed time to bag his deer.

So we'd agreed. We would close Tuesdays and Wednesdays. Chris had returned to his life, his friends, and his off-season routine. I had nothing to return to.

I grabbed the trash bag, gave Le Roi a rub behind the ears, and headed for the stairs.

Chapter 6

Just as the Dumpster lid slammed, I heard male voices. I recognized Binder's baritone instantly, followed by Jamie's familiar cadence.

"Do you think . . . gone into the water?" Binder asked, though I couldn't make out the middle part.

I couldn't hear Jamie's answer either, but it sounded affirmative. I spotted them walking along the high bank of the back harbor. Jamie pointed into the water and said something I didn't catch. The deep, briny smell told me it was low tide. They'd be looking at exposed rock and even some of the harbor bottom. They were trailed by a scowling Sergeant Flynn, who stared into the water, hands in his coat pockets, saying nothing.

As I walked toward the three of them to see what they were up to, Binder caught sight of me. "Julia!" He said something to Jamie, who nodded and walked off in the opposite direction. "Let's continue our interview."

"Chris isn't here," I called back to him. He and Flynn were at the edge of the parking lot by then.

"No problem," Binder responded. "We'll catch him later."

I considered putting them off. Chris being there had been such a comfort at the earlier part of the interview. Plus, I valued his help in recalling what had happened. It was important to get it right, and I didn't completely trust myself on the details. I wondered if this reinforcement of my memory was exactly what Binder wanted to avoid, and if interviewing me separately was a strategy rather than a happenstance.

But a man was dead, and the person who'd killed him, quite possibly in the restaurant while Chris and I slept above, was still on the loose. I wanted that person caught as soon as possible. I agreed to the interview in the interest of keeping things moving.

I opened the back door, and Flynn and Binder passed through it. I offered them coffee and realized I hadn't eaten all day. I stared at the walk-in with the yellow crime scene tape across it, and then remembered Gus's pie. Binder accepted the offer of a slice. Flynn, of the toned body and slim waist, declined.

We settled into a booth and, though Flynn opened his notebook, we took time to chat. I'd been involved in three of their cases before this one. The first time had been the previous spring when the best man at a wedding was murdered on

Morrow Island. The other two had been during the clambake season.

My relationship with Binder had its ups and downs. Sometimes he seemed to value my contributions, even seeking me out to get a local take on things. Other times he went all "official business" and shut me out. Despite these bumps, I liked him and thought he was a good cop.

I thought Flynn was a good cop too, but his attitude toward me ran the gamut from annoyance to open hostility. He didn't want me involved in his cases. If he'd ever verbalized this directly, instead of giving me stony glances and sniping, I would have pointed out that I'd been instrumental in solving all three of them. He would have said, no doubt, that the police could have arrived there on their own. And who knows? Maybe they would have—just not as quickly.

I asked Binder about his wife and young boys. He reported all was well. They'd spent Thanksgiving with his in-laws in Eastport and he hadn't been called out once. He was the kind of man whose face glowed when he talked about his family. The pride he took in his work, which was considerable, would never come close to the pride he showed for his wife and sons.

Flynn was his usual reticent self. In answer to my very direct questions, and prodded by his boss, he admitted he was still dating Genevieve Pelletier, a renowned chef from Portland whom he'd met on a previous case. His ears glowed bright red and he didn't look at me as he spoke. His tone certainly didn't invite follow-up questions.

"Young Flynn here is trying for a transfer to Portland," Binder said. "I need to take advantage of his skills while I still have him."

"Probably won't come through," Flynn grumbled.

"And you, Julia," Binder said, "you've stayed in Busman's Harbor for the off-season and gone into the restaurant business."

"It was Gus's idea. He thought it was important for the community to have a gathering place in the evenings over the winter. Chris and I agreed to take it on."

Binder nodded, though he couldn't quite suppress a frown. He had his doubts about Chris. He'd once arrested him, and though Chris hadn't committed that crime, Binder's suspicions lingered. Not entirely without reason. I, too, had taken time to trust Chris, whose disappearances on his sailboat over the summer had nearly derailed us. But his pirate days were in the past.

Flynn picked up his pen and cleared his throat loudly, signaling his impatience with the coffee klatch. Jerry Binder was the more polished of the two, but I didn't doubt that I was to some degree being "handled" with this trading of personal disclosures. The kinder, gentler version of good cop, bad cop.

"So let's get back to it," Binder said. "You told us earlier the victim arrived around seven thirty."

"Yes," I confirmed.

Flynn consulted his notes from the morning. "He

sat at the bar here. You gave him a Wild Turkey. Then what?"

"Two more couples arrived for dinner. In quick succession. We got quite busy."

"The Smiths and the Walkers," Flynn read back. "Who came in first?"

"The Walkers." Almost as soon as I'd poured the stranger's drink, the street door had opened and Barry and Fran Walker clomped down the stairs into the restaurant. Fran, as always, carried an enormous pocketbook. It had made her look as if she were moving in instead of simply coming for dinner. She was bent over, partially weighed down by carrying it. Barry fussed behind her.

"Hurry up, Fran. We're late for our reservation."

At the bottom of the stairs that led into the restaurant, Fran straightened up and stared through the front room into the almost empty dining room. "I think they'll find room for us," she had said in her typical dry way.

Unlike the Caswells and the Bennetts, I'd known the Walkers all my life. Barry Walker had run the art supplies and frame store on Main Street since before I was born.

That evening, Barry had been, as always, shaggy and shambling. He was quite round, had a bald pate, and wore his sticky-outy gray hair in a style I always thought of as "a half Bozo." Fran, her flyaway hair tucked into an unsuccessful bun, looked exhausted. Even in the low light of the restaurant, the lines beneath her eyes were like caverns.

I had hung up their coats and prepared to lead

the Walkers to a table in the center of the dining room when the front door opened and another couple arrived.

"We're the Smiths," the man had said. "We have a reservation. Sorry we're late. The weather's so bad, I wasn't sure we should come."

By the time I'd greeted the Smiths, the Walkers had taken a booth in the third corner of the dining room.

"Welcome to Gus's Too. Let me seat you." I smiled my most gracious hostess smile.

"No, dear," Mrs. Smith had answered. "We'll take care of it." They had walked into the room, nodding to the Caswells and the Bennetts as they did, though not to the Walkers. Neither the Caswells nor the Bennetts acknowledged them. In fact, I was pretty sure I saw Caroline Caswell lean forward to study her wineglass in order to avoid the greeting. The Smiths had seated themselves in the remaining unoccupied corner booth. I had four couples seated as far from one another as Gus's dining room allowed.

"You're sure about that?" Binder said when I relayed this. "They deliberately sat far away from one another?"

"They did. What I'm not sure about is why they did it. I didn't think much about it at the time. I thought it was an example of the bus seat rule."

"The bus seat rule?" Flynn pulled his head up from his notes.

"From high school chemistry. Electrons fill up all the empty orbits around the nucleus before they start pairing up. Just like when you get on a bus, you head for an empty row, if there is one, before you take a seat with another passenger."

The cops still looked puzzled, so I tried again. "You know, it's like when guys line up at urinals—"

"Got it." Binder cut me off.

"Or so I'm told," I added. "I assumed the couples wanted to sit as far apart to have as much privacy as possible. In any case, I didn't have much time to think about it."

I'd taken drink orders from the Walkers and the Smiths and returned to the bar. The stranger sat there quietly, nursing his bourbon. I asked if he was ready to order.

"Can I just get a burger or something?" he asked.

While planning the restaurant, there'd been long menu discussions among Gus, Chris, and me. All afternoon, Gus served burgers, along with hot dogs, grilled cheese, lobster rolls, and fried clams. He was vehement he wanted something different for the restaurant at night. Chris and I agreed.

We'd settled on our limited menu: two appetizers, three entrees—meat, fish, and poultry—and two desserts. But would we grill a burger if someone asked? We decided, no, for now. Chris would be crazy busy in the kitchen without being a short order cook too.

"What did the victim eat?" Binder's question brought me out of my mental digression.

"Pea soup."

"That's all?" Flynn pressed.

"There were croutons in the soup, and I put a basket of rolls on the bar. I can't remember if he ate one."

"Did anyone else order the soup?" Binder asked.

"Quite a few people." The foggy, icy night made it an attractive option. "Barry Walker and Caroline Caswell ate it as their starter. Deborah Bennett had it, along with a salad, as her dinner."

"Excuse me." Binder moved out of the booth, jabbing at his cell phone as he went. Flynn got very interested in something in his notebook, and I fussed with the ketchup container on the table so we could avoid talking to one another, or looking at one another for that matter, while Binder was gone. When he returned, he said, "The crime scene techs will be back in a little while to take the soup for analysis."

Unconsciously, my gaze drifted toward the walk-in and its crisscross of crime scene tape. "But I thought the ME found an injection site."

"She did. But unless our victim was a drug addict, why would a healthy adult man let someone inject him? Perhaps he was subdued in some way. Slowed down, docile, or confused. How much of the Wild Turkey did he drink?"

I thought back, reconstructing the evening. "Three. Doubles." I hesitated. "I'm pretty sure."

"If he arrived at seven thirty and left at ten, as you believe, that's what—six ounces over two and a half hours. He was probably impaired but not enough to let someone shoot him up, unless he wanted it. We'll have the techs take the Wild Turkey. Did he have anything else to drink?"

"Water."

"Bottled or tap?"

"Tap. I filled his glass myself, from the spigot behind the bar."

"Ice?"

"Yes, from the bucket behind the bar."

"Any left?"

"I threw it in the bar sink at the end of the night."

Flynn scribbled furiously. Binder must have noticed my puckered brow. "Don't worry. We're doing this out of an abundance of caution. And I might as well warn you, when the techs come back to get the soup and the bourbon, they'll be searching through the rest of the food as well."

"Looking for poison?"

"Looking for a syringe. Gus found the victim alone, with no sign of a needle. If he injected himself, it's possible he hid it in one of the pots, even buried in Gus's hot dogs before he lost consciousness."

"Do you think that's what happened? He killed himself accidentally in Gus's walk-in?"

"Or his killer could have hidden the needle in the food."

"Oh." That scenario depressed me even more than the first one.

"Either way, if we find the syringe, we'll know a lot more about the manner and means of his death. So I hope we do."

There was a sharp knock at the kitchen door. When Binder opened it, Jamie stood outside. Binder leaned toward him and they held a whispered conversation. Flynn put away his pen and notepad as they spoke.

Binder turned back toward me. "I'm afraid we have to interrupt this again. We're needed urgently elsewhere. Is there anything else about last night you need to tell us?"

"No?" The word came out as a question, with a rising inflection at the end, because somewhere at the back of my murky, sleep-deprived mind, an unformed thought nagged.

Chapter 7

Binder and Flynn climbed into a cruiser driven by Officer Howland, who then sped out of Gus's little parking lot, though he didn't turn on the siren.

I looked at Jamie, who leaned against the doorjamb. "Want some coffee?" He seemed like he needed it.

"Thanks."

I thought he might fall asleep where he stood, propped against the doorway. Gus didn't stock anything as prosaic as a to-go cup. "If you wanted ta go," he'd say to the unwary inquirer, "whyja come heah in the fust place?" So I brought Jamie black coffee in a heavy ceramic mug.

"For goodness' sake, come in."

He looked around the little parking lot. "Okay, just for a minute."

"You look like I feel."

He dropped onto a stool at the counter. "You got, what, three hours' sleep last night?" he asked.

"Four. And I dozed for a while sitting up in a kitchen chair at my mother's. You?"

He yawned and stretched. "None. And I worked double shifts both Thanksgiving Day and Sunday. I was running on fumes as it was."

"A double shift on Thanksgiving? Why?"

"Guys have families, Julia." He said it with a finality that didn't invite conversation, but I could hear the echoing, unsaid, "And I don't."

"I thought you were going to Gina's family for Thanksgiving?" I'd returned to Busman's Harbor in March to discover that my old buddy Jamie had a long-simmering crush on me. I only had eyes for Chris, and the situation had gotten a little awkward, compounded by the time in June when he and I drunkenly, mistakenly, kissed. I was thrilled when Gina came on the scene in the fall, because her presence as Jamie's girlfriend had removed the last remaining tension between us.

"Nope," Jamie said. "That didn't work out. And it's not going to. Long term."

"I'm sorry."

He gave a casual whatcha-gonna-do shrug, a guy sloughing off emotion.

"Wait a minute," I said. "You went straight from the accident to the body in the walk-in? Why?" In the off-season, when the part-time employees were cut back, the Busman's Harbor police force consisted of seven sworn officers, including the chief, as well as a civilian receptionist and a few civilian 911 operators. But even given the size of the off-season force, there should have been better coverage.

"I'd finished what paperwork I could after the accident and was just leaving the station when Gus's call came in," Jamie said.

"But why did you answer it?"

He stared down at the counter. "I thought the two cases were related."

"The accident and the body? Related? How?" I couldn't imagine. The stranger, whomever he was, was sitting at our bar at the time of the accident. Vee Snugg had told us he'd come to town on the bus. How could a person who didn't have a car cause an accident at a time when he clearly hadn't been there, unless he was some sort of a time traveler?

"I'm going to tell you something, Julia, but you have to keep it to yourself. It's unofficial. I mean it. You can't tell your sister or your mother. Not even Chris."

I wasn't sure I wanted to agree to this. After a rough start communication-wise, Chris and I were at a point in our relationship where we told each other everything. Still, I was dying to know. I found myself nodding yes.

"I came this morning," Jamie said, "because I thought the body in Gus's refrigerator was the victim of the car crash." He paused, taking in the puzzled look on my face. "When I got to the scene of the accident last night, Ben Kramer was still in his pickup. Belted in, shaken up, but okay. But the car he hit, the Volvo, the driver's side door was open and the driver was gone."

"Left the scene?"

"I assumed. I've seen it before. The driver's intoxicated, so even if the accident's not their fault, they hide out until they figure they're at the legal limit. But from the beginning, that scenario didn't make sense. The car had Connecticut plates, and it was treacherous outside last night. Where would a person on foot go on a night like that? Your restaurant was the only place open on Main Street, but you're around the bend from the accident site. A driver couldn't see your lights." He drained his cup, and I got up to pour him some more.

"If whoever it was knew the area, if it was a summer person, then I thought, maybe it could have happened that way," Jamie continued. "Ben was certain he'd seen the driver go off in this direction. We searched all night but didn't find a trace. So when Gus called this morning to say there was a dead body in his walk-in, I assumed the driver made it to your place, but with some kind of internal injuries and disorientation, and wandered into your refrigerator and died."

"And you're sure that's not what happened? Have you got the time of the accident right?" Vee Snugg had said the stranger came on the bus, but maybe she was mistaken. Maybe the stranger had tried to drive to Gus's in the ice and fog, had an accident, abandoned his car, and came ahead anyway. It was hard to believe that the missing driver and the unidentified body were unrelated.

"Ben called us on his cell immediately after the accident happened. We've confirmed the time of the impact with several people who live in apartments over the stores near that corner. Besides, there's something else." Jamie squared his shoulders, sitting up straighter, and looked me in the eye. "Ben only got a glance at the driver, striding away from the scene, but he swears it was a woman."

Jamie was quiet for a few moments while I absorbed what he'd said. The body in the walk-in was indisputably a man. Yet it seemed so strange. A person unexpectedly missing, another unexpectedly found.

"The search is still on," I said. "That's why I hear helicopters." I'd been aware of the *wub-wub* of chopper blades all afternoon. Busman's Harbor had a Coast Guard station, so it wasn't an unusual sound.

"Yes. And the Warden Service just brought a dog."

I wondered what the dog, no doubt used to searches in the Maine woods, would make of all the smells in our little harborside town.

"We need to find the driver, of course, for her own safety," Jamie continued. "But we'll know who it is soon enough. We have the tag number and we've reached out to the state police in Connecticut. They'll get back to us quickly."

"Will you charge her?"

"Yes, I imagine. For leaving the scene. But the

accident wasn't her fault. Ben fully admits he lost control of the truck on the ice on the hill coming into the intersection and accidentally ran the light. She was just in the wrong place at the wrong time."

She certainly was.

Jamie drained his second cup and stood go to. "Thanks, Julia."

I walked him to the door. "Jamie, I know you can't talk to me about the investigation, but do the police think the killer was hiding here in the restaurant while Chris and I were asleep upstairs?"

He put a hand on my shoulder. "We'll know more soon—about when it happened and whether he was killed here or brought here. But you must realize that at some point, both the victim and the killer were in the building without your knowledge."

As soon as Jamie left, I went upstairs to my apartment and called Chris from my cell. I wasn't sure he'd pick up. If he was using one of his power tools at the cabin and had his noise-canceling headphones on, there was next to no chance. But he answered on the first ring.

"Hi. Everything okay?"

"Yes. Well, you know . . ."

"There was a dead guy in Gus's refrigerator this morning?"

"Yeah," I admitted. "There is that." The truth was, to calm my jitters, I needed to hear Chris's voice. Laying my head on his solid chest and listening to the steady beat of his heart would have been even better, but this was the best I could have at the moment.

"I'm just checking in before you take off for poker," I said, short-cutting my way through my emotion.

"Just got out of the shower. I'm headed out as soon as I get dressed."

A silence stretched between us.

"Julia, you're not calling to 'check in.' I can hear it in your voice."

He knew me even better than I thought. I took a deep breath. "I talked to Binder and Flynn again."

Chris was quiet for a moment. "How'd that go?"

"Okay, I guess. I wish you'd been there to check my memory."

"I'm sure it went fine. You remember what you remember. Binder and Flynn are experienced cops. They know how to filter what you say." I'd never heard Chris be so generous toward the state police. But then again, this time he was a witness, not a suspect. "I'm sure they'll interview me again too," he added.

I hadn't decided whether I was going to tell Chris what Jamie had told me about the missing driver. I'd promised I wouldn't. Jamie had named Chris specifically, thereby removing the "couple loophole"—the exemption that allowed you to pass a secret along to your significant other, unless the secret-teller included him or her by name as a person not to be told. I was lucky that Jamie occasionally dropped the cop persona and remembered our friendship. So instead of telling what I knew, I asked Chris a question. "What happened when you went out to look at the wreck?"

Last night, there had been some muttering after Jamie announced to our guests that they were stuck, but most of it had been good-natured. This was Maine, after all. These things happened. Everyone had ordered coffee or tea, and everyone except Deborah Bennett had eaten or shared one of our two desserts. My talented sister, Livvie, made all the sweets for Gus's Too. That night they were brownie sundaes with vanilla ice cream or Indian pudding. Out of deference to Gus and Mrs. Gus, we never served pie.

After the couples finished dessert and coffee, and time dragged on, they slowly made their way into the bar.

"My goodness, the stuffed chicken breast was terrific," Caroline had said as she walked past me, pixie eyes twinkling. "The lemon tarragon sauce elevates it to a whole other level."

I'd caught Chris's eye across the room and given him the thumbs-up. He grinned back, proud of himself, flashing a warm smile that enhanced the dimple at the center of his chin. My heart melted.

At first, when they had moved to the bar, the guests kept to their formation, sitting as far from one another as possible, which wasn't very far in the tiny space. Then slowly, they started to loosen up, coalescing around that favorite topic of both Mainers and retirees, the weather.

"Did you have trouble getting over here?" Henry Caswell asked Barry Walker. Henry was by far the friendliest man in the group, and it hadn't surprised me that he'd initiated the first bit of cross-group communication.

"None at all," Barry responded gruffly, as if Henry questioning his ability to navigate in bad weather was tantamount to questioning his manhood. I thought the conversation might die there, but then Barry expanded his answer. "If you think this is bad, you shoulda been here for the great ice storm in '98. Half the state had no power. We lost ours for ten days."

That had brought on a general rush of stories that might have been titled "Winter Storms I Have Known," with each of them trying to outdo the other.

Throughout this, the stranger at the bar had ignored the speakers seated at the little cafe tables behind him, occasionally glancing up at the game that played silently on the television. The weather discussion raged on, fueled by the after-dinner drinks I poured. Chris finished in the kitchen and came out to help me and mingle with the crowd.

Not long after, the stranger had gotten up and shrugged into his black parka. He paid his bill, nodded to Chris and me, and trundled out the door. Or so I'd thought at the time.

Then Barry Walker had stood and stretched.

"This is ridiculous," he harrumphed. "How long does it take to clear an accident in this town? I'm going out to see what's going on."

Phil Bennett jumped up. "I'll go with you."

I'd looked at overweight, shambling Barry and stick-up-his-rear-end Phil. Even indoors, Phil Bennett's long, skinny arms and legs seemed barely able to balance his rotund belly, like his center of gravity was off. They were the last two people I wanted slipping and sliding their way down the harbor hill. I looked at Chris, and he gave a slight nod.

"Hold up," he'd called. "I'm coming."

When the three of them went out the kitchen door, the cold air that swept into the bar seemed to dampen any hopeful spark of conversation. Caroline Caswell, normally so bubbly, had studied her manicure, while Deborah Bennett went off to the ladies' room. When she came back, she took her seat without acknowledging the others.

With all that had happened since, I wanted to know, without exactly coming out and asking, if Chris had seen any indication at the accident scene that one of the drivers was missing.

"Nothing remarkable," Chris said in answer to my question. "We went outside. The fog had moved out, but the roads were slick. I was worried about Barry. He slid all over the place, but we made it up the hill." Chris paused. "The moment we came over the top, past your mom's house and the Snuggles, we could see the lights from the vehicles at the corner. Ben Kramer's truck was still there, in the middle of the intersection, and the silver Volvo was pushed up against the telephone pole on the corner by Gordon's Jewelry. There were two cop cars, two tow trucks, and an ambulance, all lit up. It was a mess."

"And this was, what, more than two hours after Jamie first told us about the accident? I wonder why. . . ." I prompted. *Talk about leading the witness.*

"It took so long? I wondered too. But I didn't have two seconds to think about it, because at the top of the hill, Barry took a dive. His feet went out from under him and he slid right down as if he were on a luge. Phil and I took off after him. I was afraid we'd both go ass over teakettle."

"Oh, my gosh!"

"I know. When I caught up with them at the bottom of the hill, Phil was bent over Barry, saying, 'Buddy, buddy, you okay?' Barry groaned and said in a snippy tone, 'I'm fine.' Meanwhile, Jamie and Howland had come over and were trying to get us away from their accident scene."

"You were that close?"

"Barry practically slid under the Volvo. I pulled him out and up onto his feet. He's a big guy, and with the ice it wasn't easy. No doubt his backside's black and blue today. But he was fine, came up embarrassed and sputtering at Jamie and Howland about their incompetence, when were they going to clear the scene so he could go home, etcetera.

"Jamie took one look at Barry, smelled his breath, and told him he shouldn't be driving in the near term regardless. Then he pulled me aside and cautioned me about overserving. I said, 'Officer Dawes, it would be helpful to know when you expect to open the road so I know when to cut people off.' Jamie hemmed and hawed and said there had been complications. Finally he said he'd call or come over to the restaurant when it looked like they were wrapping up. Then he repeated his warning about overserving, which just pissed both me and Barry off.

"So that was it. Phil put an arm around Barry and we all made our way, slowly and carefully, up the hill back to the restaurant. You heard us report when we got back that there'd been 'complications' and the cops didn't know when the road would open."

"You didn't mention anything about Barry's fall when you got back to the restaurant."

"It didn't seem tactful. The only thing hurting worse than Barry's backside was his dignity. He had to be soaking wet. He must have been uncomfortable the rest of the evening."

"Was there any sign of what the complications at the accident site were?"

"Nope. Not injuries, I don't think, unless one ambulance had already left. The one that was there was idling. The crew stood outside it. Ben Kramer was out of his truck, walking around."

"And the other driver?"

"Didn't see him. Maybe he was injured. Anyway, why all this interest in the accident?"

"It seems odd to me that there was a serious accident and a guy murdered in our walk-in the same night. I think they must be connected."

"Julia." Chris sighed. "I can't imagine how. And maybe, just this one time, we should let the professionals handle it?"

Chapter 8

Chris said he had to hurry and get to poker, so we signed off. I didn't make any commitment not to get involved, nor did he expect me to. Murder had come straight to our doorstep, over our threshold, and into our home. Of course I would help out any way I could.

After we hung up, I sat on our broken-down couch and looked around the apartment. The big window framed a black sky, unbroken by stars or ambient light. The sun set early in December, especially when you were as far east in a time zone as coastal Maine. I let my thoughts wander. It had been a long, stress-filled day. Le Roi jumped up and settled beside me, purring loudly. He loved it when I was home and sitting still; it was such a rarity.

Suddenly I sat bolt upright, disturbing Le Roi, who meowed in protest. There it was. The fuzzy thing I'd felt was important but hadn't been able to remember. All four of the couples that had come to the restaurant the night before had paid with gift certificates!

Because they'd stayed so long and drunk lots of extra coffee and after-dinner drinks, they all gave me some cash or a credit card at the end of the night, so I'd forgotten, burying the coincidence somewhere in my sleep-deprived subconscious.

Gus had an ancient, gigantic cash register on which he rang up his sales. He didn't take credit cards, or checks for that matter. Chris and I were improvising. I ran credit cards through an app on my phone, and we kept cash in a cigar box that sat behind the bar. At the end of the night I hid it under my bed until I could get to the bank the next day to deposit whatever cash we weren't keeping to make change.

I got down on my knees and felt under the bed until I pulled out the wooden cigar box. The four gift certificates were still in there, and as I suspected, the serial numbers were in order. The certificates looked real, but then I'd designed them based on a popular template I'd found on the web. The only thing that was off was the expiration date. Maine law prohibited expiration dates on gift cards. Yet there was a date on each one—November 30. Yesterday. Henry Caswell was the only person who had mentioned the date, but all the couples thought that their certificates were about to expire.

Heart pounding, I went to my desk. I fired up my laptop and looked at the spreadsheet I'd created to track the gift certificates. Gift certificates represented a liability to a business. Once you accepted the money, you owed the goods and they were carried on your books as a debt, so it was important to know how many were out there and for what amounts.

We hadn't sold many. I'd started offering them only at the end of October. Sales had started slow but picked up as we got closer to Thanksgiving. I assumed it was because of the holidays. Gift certificates for a nice dinner were a great gift for an older parent or a couple on a tight budget who deserved a treat.

On my spreadsheet, I'd matched the purchaser with the serial number of the gift certificate. I'd created the gift certificates on my laptop. So as not to embarrass myself, I'd started the serial numbers at 100001 instead of 1. The four gift certificates I'd collected the night before had been sold during the first week of November as a part of a lot of five. That raised so many questions. First of all, who had bought them? I checked the app I used to process credit cards. It didn't store or provide much information, just told me the credit card had been approved and gave me a transaction number. Yet I must have written down the name of the person who bought them. I had to have mailed the certificates to the purchaser somehow. I searched through the notebook I kept next to my computer, looking for the information. Nothing. Then I searched my e-mails and found nothing. I must have written the name and address on a scrap of paper and thrown it away.

I checked my phone. If the buyer hadn't e-mailed, he or she must have called. But again, we were improvising, using my cell phone for reservations and other calls to Gus's Too. As a result, I'd become even more attentive than usual about checking messages and deleting the ones I had dealt with.

As I'd feared, there were no calls on my phone from unknown numbers. I couldn't find what I needed, because I'd thrown out a scrap of paper and cleaned out my voice mail box. Hoist by my own anal-retentive petard, as it were.

I called Lieutenant Binder but was sent straight to voice mail. I left a terse message about discovering something odd.

After thinking about it for a moment, I took most of the cash the customers had given me the night before and moved it to my wallet. I'd stop at the ATM to deposit it the next time I went out. I left the cigar box with the gift certificates in it on my desk, next to my laptop. That way I would be certain to remember to take them to the police station in the morning.

I went back to the couch, but exhausted as I was, I couldn't settle. I realized I had to eat something for dinner. My refrigerator was cleared out for Gus as I'd promised, and the one downstairs was barricaded by crime scene tape. Over a mostly lazy weekend, we'd finished off the last bits of Thanksgiving turkey at my mother's house. Her larder was as bare as my own. The supermarket closed at six in the off-season. It was almost seven.

I resigned myself to the only alternative left to me, unless I wanted to take a long drive off the peninsula, which I most certainly did not. I had to go to Hole in the Wall Pizza, the most depressing food emporium in the Western world. Since my return, I'd discovered by dint of experimentation that their Greek salad was passable—if you didn't mind limp lettuce and picked your way around the pinkish tomatoes, which were as hard as baseballs and about as tasteless. As long as you didn't order any "extras" like grilled chicken on the salad, your meal was likely to be edible. I'd made that mistake once, and whatever it was on that salad, it wasn't chicken.

I called in my order. The owner had a passel of adult children who all seemed to work in unpredictable shifts. Each one had a unique spin on the Greek salad, and I wondered what I would get. Then I went downstairs and walked out into the parking lot, headed to my mom's house to pick up my car, which I kept in her garage.

Just as I passed the Dumpster, my sister, Livvie, cruised into the parking lot in her ancient minivan. "You ready?" she called.

"Ready for what?"

She pantomimed an exaggerated sigh. "For the Sit'n'Knit. Don't tell me you forgot."

I had. I had completely forgotten the Sit'n'Knit. "It's been a crazy day," I answered.

"So I've heard."

News of the body in the walk-in would be all over town. But that wasn't the only reason I'd forgotten the Sit'n'Knit. Livvie had decided if I was going to stay in Busman's Harbor permanently, I needed to make friends, and she'd put herself in charge of the operation. I wasn't so sure. I had a new business and a new boyfriend, and I could have immersed myself entirely in those endeavors. But Livvie didn't think that was healthy, and when Livvie had strong opinions, things usually went her way.

I stood outside her car, looking at her in the light of the dash. My rebellious little sister had grown into a gorgeous twenty-eight-year-old woman, with a strong face, chiseled cheekbones, a straight nose, and long auburn hair. She was expecting her second child in February, almost ten years to the day after she'd given birth to her first. While I'd gone on to prep school, college, business school, and a job in Manhattan, Livvie had stayed in Busman's Harbor, married her high school sweetheart and raised a child.

I'd always been the good girl and she the wild one, but in the decade since the birth of my beloved niece, Page, somehow our roles had reversed. Now I was dating the bad boy with a past and she was the stable wife and mother. In that time, our ages had reversed as well. Now she was the older, wiser sister and had taken to bossing me around. Or at least trying.

I wasn't so sure about the Sit'n'Knit. It was conceived as counterprogramming to Sam Rockmaker's poker night and was roughly composed of the wives and girlfriends of the men who played in the game. For the most part, the women were married and had children, and the talk tended toward colic and daycare. I wasn't bored by it, but despite Livvie's best intentions, it made me feel even more like an outsider.

I started to make my excuses. "I don't think I can go tonight," I said.

"Get in the car."

"No, really. I'm so terrible at the knitting."

"It's not about the knitting, Julia."

"I haven't eaten. I called a Greek salad into Hole in the Wall."

"We'll pick it up on the way."

Game. Set. Match. I still wasn't used to losing to my sister. I went back to my apartment and grabbed the bag that contained my knitting things. As I climbed into Livvie's minivan, I said, "What I'm really worried about is everyone grilling me about the body in the walk-in."

"It's not always about you, Julia," Livvie said, stepping on the gas.

After we picked up the salad, we drove halfway up the peninsula. Livvie turned off the highway and bumped carefully down a dark lane toward the home of this week's hostess. I was glad I wasn't trying to find the place on my own. Finally, we turned into a circular drive and saw warm lights shining from every window of a large, Cape Cod–style house.

When we got out of the car, I caught one of my
favorite aromas—wood burning in a fireplace nearby.

We entered through a breezeway between the
house proper and the garage into a spacious mud-
room. Following Livvie's lead, I left my work boots
in a line of similar footwear and padded into the
house in my socks.

As soon as I entered the kitchen, I realized the
house was newly built, not an old Cape. What I'd
taken as the second floor was actually an illusion.
The rooms on the main floor soared to the roof-
line, full of windows and skylights that must have
made the house bright even on a winter day.

Most of the knitters were already there, drinking
mulled wine from blue mugs around the kitchen
island. The evening's hostess, Kendra Carter,
greeted me warmly. Then she took the pitiful to-go
container of Greek salad and deftly emptied it into
a green-trimmed soup bowl. As she did this, I apol-
ogized for not eating before I came.

"Don't even think about it. You've had a tough
day, I know."

Kendra led us into a spacious great room dominated by a fireplace, which contained a roaring fire.
There was plenty of seating, so everyone found a
spot and rooted in their knitting bags, while I sat
outside the circle and focused on my salad. Kendra
took a seat in a comfy-looking chair by the fireplace
and removed a portion of a delicate, white shawl
from her canvas bag. She had curly brown hair she
wore pulled back in a low ponytail and had a mag-
nificent smile that crinkled upward to her rosy

cheeks and chocolate brown eyes. She and Livvie had been close friends at Busman's Harbor High School, but each had gone her own way—Livvie to marriage and pregnancy, though not, as she would cheerfully tell you, in that order; Kendra to university and then a PhD in marine biology. Along the way, she'd acquired a husband and two kids, and now she'd returned to work at the oceanography lab on Westclaw Point, site of some of the best jobs in town. She crossed one long, lean leg over another and began to knit. She'd been back in town only for a year, yet she appeared perfectly at ease in her surroundings and with these women. I envied her easy integration into Busman's Harbor, which seemed in particular contrast to my own.

I finished my salad, took the bowl to the kitchen, rinsed it, and put it in the dishwasher. In the beautiful room, I looked at the childish drawings on the bulletin board and marveled that friendly, calm Kendra seemed to have it all—job, family, happy home.

When I got back to the great room, all eyes were on me.

"Spill," Livvie commanded. "What happened at Gus's this morning?"

Traitor. What happened to "It's not always about you, Julia"?

I gave them the shorthand version, the one that had to be all over town already. A stranger—no, I didn't recognize him or know his name—had died in Gus's walk-in. The ME had questions about the death, so the state police were in town investigating.

"You mean he was murdered," someone clarified.

"Maybe. Probably. The police are waiting for lab tests."

"So this murderer was in the restaurant last night, after everyone left?" Kendra asked, her pretty brow wrinkled.

I didn't answer. I truly didn't know, but I was sure everyone took my silence as a yes. I decided to turn the tables and start asking questions of my own before the evening turned into an interrogation.

"Do any of you know the Bennetts, Phil and Deborah? They live on Eastclaw Point," I asked.

"Sure," Kendra answered. "Were they in the restaurant last night?"

"Yes." I didn't see any harm in answering.

A few people nodded. Marley Bletcher, former middle-school class clown and one of the few other singles in the group, pulled back the skin on her face that same way I'd done when talking to Chris, imitating Deborah's plastic surgery. "She comes into Hannaford's all the time." Marley was a checkout clerk at our local chain supermarket.

"Their home was on the Garden Club's house tour last summer," someone added. "It's amazing. Gorgeous. Huge. She's a decorator."

"And what about him?" I asked.

"Retired," Kendra answered. "I think he was something in Big Pharma."

"He's a big farmah?" Marley asked. "Because he doesn't seem like a farmah to me."

"He was an executive with a large pharmaceutical company," Kendra corrected gently.

"When did they start staying in town year-round?" I asked.

"This is their first winter," Kendra answered. "They have two boys, mid-thirties, a little older than us." She looked at me. "They're close to Chris's age. Maybe he knows them?"

Summer kids? I doubted it. I shook my head.

"Anyway," Kendra continued, "he's retired and they're here full-time. They completely did over that house. Still, it's an isolated place to live in the winter. All the neighbors are gone for miles out to the point."

"What about Henry and Caroline Caswell?" I asked. "Anyone know them?"

"The tennis players? They're vicious for old people. They absolutely crushed me and my husband," Kendra answered.

I could see Henry and Caroline as good tennis players. Although the pixieish Caswells were both petite, they looked like they were in great shape. "Do you know where they're from, or anything about them?"

"Nope. He was a medical doctor, but other than that, nothing," Marley said.

Really? Henry was a doctor? That surprised me. While it was true some retirees shed their former identities like a lobster sheds its shell, it was rare when a doctor didn't work his preretirement profession into the conversation somehow.

"Do you know what kind of doctor?" I asked.

They all shook their heads.

Everyone in the group knew Fran and Barry Walker,

she of the giant pocketbook, he of the Bozo hair. Marley said Fran Walker worked as an aid at a nursing home. That surprised me, because she was more of an age to be cutting back, not taking on new responsibilities. She'd always worked alongside Barry at Walker's Art Supplies and Frame Shop. I wondered if the nursing home was instead of or in addition to her responsibilities at the store.

"I hear their daughter's back in town," someone said. Quinn Walker had been one of Livvie's and my favorite babysitters when we were young.

"She's divorced," Marley informed us. One certainly could stay on top of things working at the only market on the peninsula. "She and her kids are living with Barry and Fran."

"How old are those kids now?" Livvie asked. Quinn had a boy and a girl.

"Middle school."

The moms in the group sighed, an acknowledgment of the challenges of living with adolescents. Maybe that was the reason Fran had looked so exhausted the night before.

Nobody knew much about the Smiths, which didn't surprise me. They had bought the Fogged Inn, a B&B at the edge of Main Street, just as you entered town. Experienced residents knew not to invest too much friendship in new B&B owners. They came to town full of romantic dreams, but as I knew from a lifetime of observing Fee and Vee at the Snuggles, inns were an enormous amount of work. In Maine, the average B&B proprietor lasted less than two years, so new owners had to prove they were in it for the long haul before the locals put any work into getting to know them. Somebody in the group said her cousin's ex-husband's sister had done chamber work for the Smiths over the summer and reported they were "weird." I took that as the usual Busman's assessment of outsiders in the early going.

The evening wore on and the conversation drifted to other topics. I applied myself to my knitting project, allegedly a pair of socks for Chris, though I'd dropped so many stitches on the first one it looked more like I was knitting a small, gray funnel cloud.

Chapter 9

I awoke in the morning to the sound of Gus stomping up the stairs to my apartment. When I returned from the Sit'n'Knit, I'd found my refrigerator filled with eggs, bacon, and milk. Gus had taken advantage of my offer.

I snuggled deep under the covers and played possum. I thought it would be less embarrassing both for Gus and me. Chris stirred beside me. He'd arrived at midnight after his poker game broke up. He didn't always drive down the peninsula after his game. Often he slept at his cabin. But he must have known I'd be uneasy in the apartment by myself.

I hated that uneasiness but couldn't deny it. The studio had felt like home from the moment I'd come up the stairs with Gus six weeks earlier. I hated and resented this person, whomever he was, who'd murdered a man and taken that from me.

Gus tramped back down the stairs, and I edged closer to Chris's body heat. The big window in the west-facing dormer framed a black sky, unbroken by even the slight hint of sunlight. It was tempting to stay in bed, but I knew Gus would be mobbed with people curious about the events of the day before and he'd be back upstairs soon for more supplies. I put my feet on the cold, rough floorboards and headed for the bathroom. By the time I got out, Chris was up. As soon as we were dressed, we climbed down the stairs into the restaurant.

As I'd expected, every table, booth, and counter stool was occupied. People milled in the entrance area, waiting for a spot to open up. Chris spoke to Gus, then went back up the apartment stairs to get more food. I picked up a full carafe of coffee, put another one on to brew, and walked through the front room and the dining room refilling mugs.

The talk of the town was the dead man and the possible reasons for his death. The news about the injection site hadn't got out, so the speculation was wild. Aside from the usual suspects—heart attack, stroke, drug overdose—there was talk about cyanide, ricin, and terrorist attacks. The speculation about the victim's identity was even wilder and ran from a wanted fugitive to "Joan's brother's wife's cousin." In a small town, some people would never admit there was a human on earth they couldn't find a personal connection to.

I tried to keep my head low and keep moving, but it was inevitable people would ask me questions.

"Didja have a hostage situation here in the restaurant when I came calling yesterday morning, darlin'?" Bard Ramsey's voice boomed across the dining room, quieting conversation at the tables

around him. "Because that's what I had to figure
when you wouldn't let me and the boys in for
breakfast."

"Nothing like that," I responded.

"Then what was it like?"

"There was a man who died here in the restaurant," I said, telling him something I was sure he
already knew. "The cause of death wasn't immediately clear, so the ME is involved. That's all I know."

"He didn't just die 'in the restaurant.'" Bard
pointed toward the walk-in, festooned with crime
scene tape. "Who was he and how did he get into
Gus's big icebox?" As I suspected, Bard knew all the
details.

"I don't know," I answered truthfully. Bard gave
me his most skeptical look, and I moved away as fast
as I could.

When I grabbed the next pot, I saw Chris had
joined Gus behind the counter and was helping
him keep up with the overflowing crowd. Gus was
offering a limited menu of eggs and pancakes to
accommodate his compromised food storage. I
watched my two favorite men for a moment, holding my breath. Gus was unreservedly a solo act, but
they alternated at the prep station, the big grill, and
the counter like a well-oiled machine. I picked up a
couple of orders and delivered them to keep the
machine humming.

Things finally slowed down after ten. In the off-
season, lots of people had nowhere to rush off to,
and trading gossip at Gus's was more fun than
sitting at home. Gus poured mugs of coffee for

Chris and me and came around the counter to sit with us.

"You people left the kitchen door unlocked last night," he groused.

I looked at Chris, who'd been the last one in.

"No way. I'm sure I locked it."

"It was unlocked when I came in this morning," Gus insisted.

It seemed to me more likely that Chris had locked the door as he said. He knew how unsettled I was about having a corpse discovered in the building, and he would have been extra careful. From inside the restaurant, locking the kitchen door was a simple matter of turning the latch. From the outside, it had to be locked with a key. For years, only Gus and Mrs. Gus had possessed keys. Now Chris and I were entrusted with two additional copies.

I didn't like that the door had been unlocked. Not one bit. Not when someone had probably—no, almost definitely—been murdered in the building two nights before. Chris opened his green eyes wide to signal that his thoughts were in the same direction.

I didn't say anything to Gus. There was no point in freaking him out too. He had a healthy belief in Chris's and my youthful carelessness. "We're sorry, Gus," I said to cut off further discussion. "It won't happen again."

Across the counter, Chris frowned at my disloyalty, but he had to know appeasement was the right strategy.

* * *

I agreed to watch the restaurant while Gus and Chris went off to the supermarket to buy supplies for lunch. As I sat at the end of the counter finishing my coffee, Jamie came in. I poured him a cup without even asking. He accepted it gratefully and took the stool next to mine.

"Did you manage to get some sleep last night?" I asked.

"Nine hours," he answered. "Slept through my alarm. Missed roll call, so the chief sent a patrol car by my place to make sure I wasn't dead."

"I'm sure that wasn't embarrassing."

He smiled. "Not a bit."

"Did you find out who your missing driver is?"

Jamie shook his head. "The owners were easily located by the Connecticut state police, but they're a retired couple in Costa Rica for the winter. The keys were in the car, which was in the attached garage. There were no signs of a break-in, so the local cops are interviewing everyone who has keys to the house, which looks like a housekeeper, a neighbor, and the alarm company. Their son is in college in upstate New York, but he's not missing and swears he hasn't used the car in weeks."

"Frustrating."

"Yup."

I glanced at the walk-in. "How are Binder and Flynn doing?"

"Don't know. They're in Augusta for the autopsy."

"Are they coming to town today? I have something I need to tell them."

"I imagine it depends. If they identify the body

while they're up in Augusta, that could take them off in other directions. Unless, of course, the victim has local connections."

"What about the couples in our restaurant that night? Did Binder and Flynn talk to them?"

Jamie swiveled his stool to look at me. "Yesterday. All of them. Why do you ask?"

I blushed and stammered. "Because late last night, I remembered something that could be important."

"Out with it." His voice was stern, but he smiled to let me know he wasn't really angry.

"I can't believe I didn't realize this sooner. It's just that, it was such a crazy day yesterday, and—"

"Julia, how bad can this be?"

It wasn't bad at all. I just felt stupid. "I realized last evening that every couple in the restaurant Monday night paid, or at least partially paid, for their meal with a gift certificate that had been altered to add a phony expiration date."

"Okay," Jamie said. "Why is that important?"

"Could it really be a coincidence? I've sold less than fifty."

"Are you suggesting someone orchestrated a gathering of those particular people? They all said in their interviews they have no ties to the victim and no connection to one another."

"I don't think it's a coincidence," I said stubbornly. "Somebody added those expiration dates."

"Okay," Jamie said. "Give me the gift certificates and I'll make sure Lieutenant Binder knows about them."

"Back in a jiff." I ran upstairs and opened the cigar box on my desk. The gift certificates were gone! I riffled through the small amount of cash and change I'd left in it. Nothing. Where could they be? I swore, ransacking the items neatly stacked on my desk. I scattered papers, opened folders. Still nothing.

"Everything all right up there?" Jamie called up the stairs.

"No," I answered in a voice that brought him running. "I can't find the gift certificates!"

"It's okay, Julia." Jamie laid a hand on my arm. "I'm sure you will. I don't even know if Binder and Flynn will be back in town today. There's time."

"But they have to be here." Frustration brought tears to my eyes and a quaver to my voice. "I think someone took them."

"Took them?" I couldn't blame his skepticism. "Is anything else missing?"

My laptop and the cigar box, with the cash I'd left to make change in it, sat right on my desk. "No. I don't think so. But Gus said the door was unlocked when he came in this morning."

That got his attention. "Julia, you have to lock your doors." Door locking wasn't common in Busman's Harbor.

"We did lock them. That's the point."

"You did, personally?"

"No, Chris did, when he came back after Sam Rockmaker's poker game."

Jamie rolled his eyes. "Julia—"

"I know," I said. "You're going to say it was late. Chris had a few beers. But he wouldn't—" Chris was careful about stuff that was important to him. He was careful about me.

"It's okay." Jamie tried to calm me. "Tell me this. Did the victim pay with a gift certificate?"

"No," I admitted in a small voice.

"So it's unlikely there's a connection."

"Maybe. The certificates were bought in a lot of five, but the fifth one hasn't been redeemed. I have the spreadsheet that shows the day they were sold and the transaction number. Can Binder use that to get the credit card company to tell him who bought them?"

"Sure. Do you have the address where you sent them?"

"No. I must have thrown it away. I'm sorry I can't remember it." Selling five gift certificates wasn't an everyday occurrence at Gus's Too. I had a vague memory of the transaction, which had taken place in early November, but no memory of the details.

Jamie shook his head. The police department required him to keep his hair short, but to me he would always be my old friend, with the floppy blond hair, peeling nose, and sky blue eyes. "The credit card info should be enough. E-mail it to me."

While he stood watching, I e-mailed the spreadsheet to his official Busman's Harbor PD address, and then he disappeared down the stairs.

Chapter 10

When Gus and Chris returned from shopping, I helped them carry the refrigerated items up to my apartment. Le Roi fussed at the intrusion. He still wasn't keen on Chris, and he viewed the sudden appearance of Gus as beyond the pale.

When we got back downstairs, Gus turned to us and said, "Time for you two to go. I'll be fine here." We both protested, but Gus said firmly, "I'm sure you have things to do. Gus's is first and always a one-man operation. Now scat."

Chris said, "I do have summer houses to check on." One of his myriad jobs, an extension of his landscaping service, was tending to empty houses over the winter. With the recent ice and cold snap, he needed to make sure there weren't any plumbing issues or tree damage. When Gus went back to the grill, Chris turned to me. "What are you up to?"

I told him the sad saga of the gift certificates. I

didn't say specifically that I thought they'd been stolen. I didn't want to discuss it in front of Gus.

"That doesn't sound like you, to lose something important like that," Chris said.

"I keep thinking about that guy in the walk-in, going over and over what everyone said and did that night. I'm convinced the couples in the restaurant were brought there that night for a reason, even though they all said they didn't know the dead guy or each other when they talked to the cops. While Binder and Flynn are in Augusta today, I want to check a few things out," I said.

"That's the spirit," Gus shouted from the other side of the room. "Solve this mystery, get rid of that damn yellow tape." He gestured toward the walk-in. "Life goes back to normal."

Chris didn't repeat his caution about leaving things to the professionals. He took off, and I went upstairs. I couldn't easily discover who bought the gift certificates, or who stole them for that matter, if they had, indeed, been stolen, but I could certainly find out how the couples who used them had come by them. I shrugged into my L.L.Bean winter coat and headed for the door.

I went to my mom's and picked up my car, a maroon '71 Chevy Caprice. It was what Mainers called a "winter beater," a disposable wreck to be ditched as soon as it needed a major repair. As always, I muttered a little prayer of gratitude when it started. The heater worked sporadically at best. Sometimes it required miles and miles of driving to come up to temperature. Other times it spewed foul-smelling, superheated air. I pulled out of the garage, drove down Main Street, then headed out of town and up the peninsula.

Ten minutes later, I turned off the highway onto the access road for Busman's Harbor Hospital, passed the hospital, and kept going. The Baywater Community for Active Adults was just a few miles farther down the road, perched on a site that gave most of its homes a good view of Townsend Bay. I slowed as I approached the gatehouse, but the skinny wooden barrier was in the up position. So many retirees from other places came to Maine looking for "gated communities." It was easier for developers to install these silly structures than to ask the obvious question, "Who do you want to keep out?"

The houses in the community were side-by-side duplexes, single story with huge garages that fronted on the road. There were about a hundred of them, all painted in bright pastels more reminiscent of the tropics than the rugged Maine coast. I crawled along in the Caprice until I spotted the Caswells' address, 15 Lupine Road. Of the couples who'd used the gift certificates, I knew the Walkers best, but I'd instinctively headed for the Caswells' house first. Caroline and Henry, with their pixie looks and twinkling eyes, seemed so friendly.

Caroline looked a little puzzled after she answered

the bell, but rallied immediately and greeted me graciously. "Julia, please come in."

We passed through a hallway into a great room that combined living room, dining room, and kitchen. The design was modern, but the Caswells' furniture was traditional. It must have come from their preretirement family home, wherever that had been.

"Henry's in his study," Caroline said. "Let me just call him. Hen-RY! Julia Snowden's come calling."

She offered coffee, which I accepted, and the three of us gathered around the glass table where they must eat their informal meals. Through the sliding door, I spotted a full bird feeder on the deck, moving with the wind, ready for winter visitors.

"I assume you're here to talk about what happened," Henry said, once we'd settled in.

"Yes," I confirmed. "That poor man. What Chris and I can't figure out is how he got in the walk-in. I wondered if you remembered anything."

Henry's bright blue eyes met his wife's brown ones. "The police were here yesterday asking questions. And Caroline and I have talked too, trying to figure it out. It's unsettling. We were with him that night, and now he's dead."

"Had you ever seen the man before?"

"Never," Henry answered. "Have the police figured out who he was?"

Caroline brought steaming cups of coffee to the table, and I took a sip. It was strong and tasty, warming me from the inside out. Although the Caswells' home was new and much tighter than the usual drafty Busman's Harbor dwelling, I was still chilled through from my car ride.

"Not that I know of. Lieutenant Binder and Sergeant Flynn are in Augusta today at the autopsy, so I haven't spoken to them," I answered. "Did you notice anything in particular about the man who died?"

"Sat at the bar by himself. Wasn't sociable. Is that what you mean? We told all this to the police," Henry said.

So they hadn't noticed the scar and the prosthetic ear. Even when they'd moved into the bar, they'd sat behind him. His dark hair was long and curly. Maybe Chris and I were the only ones who'd noticed, since we faced him from behind the bar. I asked the question that had brought me there. "Just one more thing. You paid partially that night with a gift certificate. Where did you get it?"

"It came in the mail last week. I assumed it was a promotion to get people to try the restaurant." Henry looked at me. "It wasn't?"

"I didn't mail that gift certificate to you."

"I thought it was funny the expiration date was so soon," he said.

"Last week was the short week with the Thanksgiving holiday, and we didn't make it to your place," Caroline added. "But when we got home from our daughter's and there was no food in the house, your restaurant seemed like the perfect solution. We really had a lovely meal. You're doing a great job.

Of course, I would have been happy to have left a little earlier."

"Do you know any of the other diners who were there Monday night? I noticed you all talking in the bar."

"I don't really know any of those people," Caroline answered. "We were trapped together, and it seemed polite to chat a little, but I don't remember the conversation getting more intimate than the weather." Beside her, Henry nodded his agreement.

That was my memory too. There didn't seem to be much more to say. My next stop was going to be the Bennetts way out on Eastclaw Point. "Do you mind if I use your bathroom?" I asked.

"Surely, come along. The powder room is right through there." Caroline directed me to an area off the kitchen where a long hallway led to a guest room, study, and a full guest bath. I used the facilities quickly and started back up the hall when something in the study caught my eye. Over the desk was a framed diploma for Henry Caswell from the Yale School of Medicine. So the women at the Sit'n'Knit had been right. He was a doctor. Yet I was sure I'd heard people address him as "Mr. Caswell." I had even done it myself, and he never corrected me.

I thought about remarking on the diploma, but I'd sort of been snooping and couldn't figure out how to bring it up. I went back to the great room, where Caroline met me and walked me to the front door. I pulled on my coat, thanked her, and went on my way.

Chapter 11

It was a bit of a drive back down the peninsula toward town and then on out onto Eastclaw Point. Busman's Harbor was shaped like the top portion of a lobster lounging in the sea. The head of the lobster formed the town, and the claws, called Eastclaw and Westclaw Point, reached out to embrace the big harbor, leaving just enough of a channel for sizable boats to enter and exit.

When I was little, all the houses on the points were summer homes. A few were kept open until Christmas or New Year's for family gatherings, but they were exceptions. Most of the imposing "cottages" were unheated. In the old days, the town didn't even bother to plow the road. But slowly, over the course of my lifetime, more than a few homes were converted to year-round residences. There were still long stretches of road where the houses, set off on little lanes or down long driveways, were obviously empty. I thought it would be a tough life, alone out here through a Maine winter, without the comforts and companionship of town.

Toward the end of Eastclaw Point, the road split, each spur going off to one of the spits of land that gave the point its clawlike shape. Just past the fork, I spotted a sign that said BENNETT and turned into a pea gravel drive. I was aware of a house looming off to the left as I pulled in, but it was the view in front of me that grabbed my attention. Waves crashed on boulders at the end of a big lawn, sending spray into the air. Across the water, two islands rose up—tiny uninhabited Craigie Island and Dinkum's Light beyond. The sea smoke off the water made them look like mirages. I stood, captivated for a moment, and then approached the front door.

Deborah Bennett opened it before I knocked. She must have heard the Caprice come up the drive. When she greeted me, her tone was a bit overeager, confirming my suspicion that it must be lonely out here at the end of the road.

"Ms. Snowden, so nice to see you again so soon."

"Please, it's Julia."

"And I'm Deborah." She put a hand on my elbow and drew me inside. "Let me take your coat."

The mask of her plastic surgery always threw me. Her face wasn't ugly, but it wasn't human, either, and that alone was enough to repel. She hung my coat in a closet off the big entrance hallway and led me into the living room. Walking ahead of me, she was a lean, fit figure in black slacks and a pearl gray sweater. Whatever she'd looked like before the surgery, I guessed she'd been pretty.

The living room was gorgeously decorated, formal as the large room demanded but in the colors of the beach. French doors opened onto a stone porch that faced the view I'd just been amazed by. Deborah was a fabulous decorator, as the room attested, but her interiors couldn't compete with the exterior, and didn't try.

She offered me coffee or tea. I asked for water, and she led me through the high-ceilinged formal dining room into an enormous, brand-new kitchen.

"This place is beautiful," I said.

"Thank you. It was a long, hard slog to get here. Phil and I have owned the house for more than thirty years, but a little over a year ago we started a major overhaul so we could live here full-time when he retired."

"Maine can be tough in the winter," I said. It had been sixteen years since I'd spent a full winter in Maine. When I'd arrived back the previous March, it had been still more than technically winter. As a result, I'd suffered some of the inconvenience, but not the sheer duration, of month after month of too short days, long dark nights, low temperatures, and a variety of pelting precipitations.

"We're going to get out for a couple of months in Palm Beach," she answered, like she'd heard re-marks about the challenges of Maine winters many times before. "Would you like a tour?"

I replied enthusiastically. She walked me through room after room. Since the house had water on three sides, every one of the six large bedrooms had a sea view, along with a private bath. On the landing, she pointed upstairs to the third floor. "Phil's studio. We won't disturb him."

I nodded to show I understood, and we walked down the grand staircase.

"This was an old family summer house when we bought it, and we left it that way for years," Deborah said. "We wanted a place where the whole family could gather, our sons and their friends, and later, their wives and the grandchildren." We returned to the kitchen, where my glass of water still sat on the big island. Deborah and I perched on stools, and she asked, "Tell me, Julia, why are you here?"

I'd been expecting the question. In fact, I'd been expecting it sooner. "I'm concerned about the man who died in our refrigerator," I said. "As far as I know, the police still haven't identified him. I came to see if you or your husband remembered anything about him at all. Anything that would help."

"The police were here yesterday. We told them all we knew." She put me off, but her body language was open and inviting. I found it easier to read her body than her mask of a face.

I tried again. "I feel so badly for his family."

She glanced at the digital clock on the microwave. "Phil will be coming down any minute for his lunch. Perhaps you'll stay and we'll talk?"

No sooner had she finished the sentence than we heard Phil's footsteps on the stairs, descending from the third floor. When he entered the kitchen, his shirt was dabbled with colorful flecks of paint and he smelled vaguely of paint thinner.

I rose from my stool. "Mr. Bennett, Julia Snowden."

"You must call him Phil," Deborah said.

"I didn't know you painted, Phil."

"You must have seen his work throughout the house," Deborah said. "The oils."

I had seen them. And wondered about them, because they weren't the dramatic seascapes I would have expected in a house like this. They were portraits. Portraits of ordinary people—farmers, cleaners, lobstermen. They were somehow hyperrealistic, so that I could see every whisker and wrinkle, every darker fleck of color in the iris of an eye. But mostly they seemed to speak through the canvas with a kind of truth, not merely about the subject's profession or circumstances but about his or her character.

Deborah put bowls of chopped radicchio, tomatoes, scallions, and fresh jalapeños on the island, along with a plate of corn tortillas. Then she deftly cooked a piece of white fish on the professional range.

While she worked, I asked Phil about his trek to visit the accident scene with Chris and Barry Walker. "Did the man at the bar leave the restaurant before you, Chris, and Barry went out to see the wreck?"

Phil leaned back on his stool, his brow wiggling behind his glasses with the effort to recall. "I think so. Yes, he left before us."

"Did you see him out on the street, maybe gawking at the accident?" I tried to think of reasons, on a cold, icy night, why the stranger hadn't gone right back to the Snuggles. The corner of Main and Main was just down the hill from the inn, and maybe the bright lights from the emergency vehicles had attracted his attention.

"No, nothing like that. Barry Walker fell and slid down the hill. There was a lot of commotion, and I'm not certain I would have noticed if the poor man had been there, but I certainly didn't see him."

"Do you know any of the other couples who were at the restaurant Monday night?" I asked.

Phil looked over at Deborah, who stood with her back to us, in the sound cocoon created by the stove vent and sizzling fish. "I've been in Barry Walker's art supplies store a few times."

"That's it?"

"Yes."

Deborah put the fish on the table and pulled a bowl of creamy white sauce from the refrigerator. She handed each of us a cloth napkin and sat down to eat. I copied their motions as they wordlessly layered the fish, veggies, and sauce on the tortilla. As soon as Deborah took a bite, I rolled mine up and dug in.

"This is fantastic," I said. And it was. The crunch of the veggies, the light taste of the fish, and the savory sauce combined to make a delicious meal.

"It's hard to get fresh vegetables here in the winter," Deborah said.

I nodded, my mouth full. *It's only December. You ain't seen nothin' yet.*

"Phil likes a proper lunch," Deborah added.

Phil Bennett showed none of his wife's friendly manner. He'd answered my questions fully yet formally. Deborah was warmer. Anxious to be helpful, she dredged up every detail she could from that night, and frequently punctuated her conversation with remarks like "That poor man" and "It's awful that his family may be looking for him, not knowing what's happened." As lunch went on, I found myself less distracted by her face.

As to the gift certificate, it had come in the mail, just as the Caswells' had. "I was surprised by how soon the expiration date was," Phil said, "but I figured you wanted people to try out the restaurant sooner than later because it was new." A business rationale made sense to a former Big Pharma executive like Phil.

"Do you still have the envelope?" I asked. "Was there anything else in it?"

Phil knit his eyebrows together over his spectacles. "You mean you didn't send it?"

"I haven't done any sort of promotion like that."

Behind the mask, the color drained from Deborah's face. "That's unsettling."

"I'm sure there's a logical explanation," Phil reassured her. He turned to me. "I think the envelope and insert might be in the wastebasket in my study. It's on the way out. I'll walk you. We've spent enough time on this."

Phil had dismissed me as if I were a bothersome employee. I didn't like it, but I had to admit I'd gotten what I came for.

They got off their bar stools and stood side by side. Despite Phil's spare tire, they were both tall and straight-backed, with a regal bearing. If the Caswells were pixies, the Bennetts reminded me of a pair of Afghan hounds.

I said good-bye to Deborah, and Phil led me to his study, which was off the front hall. The room was as formal and as lovely as the rest of the house. He fished a number ten envelope out of the trash and handed it to me, then walked me to the door.

"Julia, I understand your concern about the man who died in your restaurant, but I have to ask you not to come bothering Deborah again. She's not as strong as she looks. She's suffered from panic attacks for years. We have them under control with medication, but stress is the worst thing for her."

I said, "Of course, I understand," as he firmly guided me out the front door and closed it behind me.

Chapter 12

I sat in the Caprice while I examined the envelope Phil had given me and the card I found inside it. The envelope was handwritten, addressed to "Mr. and Mrs. Bennett." No return address. The stamp said, "Pre-sorted First Class," which I knew from doing commercial mailings for the Snowden Family Clambake Company required no postmark. Whether the person who had mailed the gift certificates used the pre-sorted service to disguise the mailing location or simply to keep up the ruse of it being a part of a mass mailing, I couldn't know.

The insert was an envelope-sized card with a description of the restaurant and our limited, ever-changing menu, along with an address, hours, phone number, and e-mail. I had designed these cards and always included them when I mailed out gift certificates. When I'd sent the certificates to the unknown purchaser, I'd undoubtedly included five of these cards.

It seemed clear that the sender had deliberately enticed the Bennetts and the Caswells to the restaurant, and probably the Walkers and Smiths as well. But why? I knew of no connection between them, and though they'd chatted politely about the weather, nothing indicated the couples were any more than acquaintances. Phil said he'd been in the Walkers' art supplies store "a couple of times," which made sense given he was a painter.

Did any of this connect the couples to the dead man? And what about the fifth gift certificate? Was another party supposed to be there who hadn't taken the bait?

I wondered about Phil Bennett's caution not to disturb Deborah again. I was familiar with panic attacks. I'd suffered from them since my teens, though it had been five months since I'd had one. Mine were brought on by conflicts between duty and emotion, when my head insisted I do something my heart resisted, or vice versa. Somewhere, buried deep in a drawer, I had an amber vial of Valium pills, prescribed by a doctor, to be taken if I was in a situation that might bring on an attack. I assumed this was what Phil meant when he said Deborah's attacks were controlled by medication. I was sure this strategy worked well for people whose triggers were airplanes or heights or tight spaces—things that could be anticipated—but my attacks had never been predictable. Five months was the longest I'd gone without one in years. Staying in

Busman's Harbor and loving Chris must have agreed with me on some biological level.

I turned these thoughts over as I bumped back to town along already-potholed Eastclaw Point Road. It was barely December and my teeth rattled as the Caprice, with its complete lack of shock absorption, found every nook and cranny. The heater continued to balk. By the time I got to town, I was freezing and my jaw hurt.

I cruised by our ugly brick fire-department-town-offices-police-complex. If Binder's official car was there, I would stop and tell him about the gift certificates. There were no state police vehicles in the parking lot, so I kept going.

I pulled my car into my mother's garage and took a brisk walk down the hill toward the center of town. Walker's Art Supplies and Frame Shop was in the first block past the corner of Main and Main, right next to Gleason's Hardware.

I had loved the place when I was a child. The Walkers kept a full supply of children's craft items like pipe cleaners, tongue depressors, and pot-holder loops, along with the adult offerings of oil paint, watercolors, and canvases. On Morrow Island, where my family lived in the summer, there was no TV, movies, video games or indoor diversions other than books. My parents were eager to keep Livvie and me occupied, especially on rainy days. Every year before we moved out to the island, we stopped at Walker's and loaded up on the marvelous craft items in the store. It was like Christmas in June.

A bell over the door jingled as I entered. Barry was bent over his worktable, which occupied a central position in the double storefront. He was cutting a mat to frame a watercolor painting of vibrant spring flowers in a blue vase. He didn't look up when I entered, which didn't surprise me. Barry was a little deaf.

I cleared my throat loudly and called, "Hello!"

Barry straightened up slowly, like he was still hurting from his tumble down the hill two nights ago, as Chris had predicted. "Julia Snowden, as I live and breathe. Thinking of taking up art as a hobby now that you're home? There are some great classes at the Y. Mine, for example."

I shook my head. "No, not today."

"Then what brings you to my fine establishment?"

"I want to ask you something about the other night in the restaurant."

Barry put down his X-acto knife and looked at me. He was a tall man, heavy and jowly. As always, the hair that ringed his bald head stuck out as if he'd had slight contact with an electrical socket. His clothes were baggy and wrinkled, his shoes worn and paint spattered. There was no way around it— Barry Walker was a slob, and in his later years had given up any pretense otherwise.

"Is Fran here?" She usually worked alongside her husband, running the retail side of the business while he cut the frames.

"Nope. Too slow in the winter to keep two of us busy. Last couple winters, she's worked over at the Cranberry Convalescent Home."

So once again, my informants at the Sit'n'Knit had been right. I looked around the store. It had always been charmingly disheveled, like its proprietor, but now it seemed dusty and dingy, missing Fran's touch. The big plate glass windows needed washing and filtered the weak December afternoon light through a haze of dirt. I thought of the store as successful. Artists were the first tourists ever to come to Maine, drawn by the dramatic vistas and bright, flat light. In the summer, it was normal for me to come out of my mom's and practically stumble over someone sitting on the sidewalk, painting a picture of the house. In fact, if a few days went by and no one set up an easel out front, we began to feel a little neglected. Barry cheerfully met the artists' needs. In the summer, the store was crowded, but there'd always been enough business for him to stay open all winter. Artists who'd moved permanently to Maine and retirees like Phil Bennett kept it busy. I wondered why things had changed.

Barry's own paintings lined the back wall. They were abstract, dramatic. Thick applications of acrylic piled on wood in slashes of color. I'd loved his work since I was a child. The paintings never made me think, but they always made me feel. For the first time, as an adult, I wondered about them. They weren't the kind of art that would be bought by vacationing tourists. Did Barry make his life harder by persisting in this form? If he'd painted lighthouses and waves crashing on rocks, surely he would have sold more.

"I hear Quinn's home," I said.

Barry nodded his shaggy head. "She is indeed. Husband trouble, I'm afraid. Still, it's great to have her and the grandchildren in the house."

"I want to ask a few questions about the other night," I said, getting down to business.

"The police were here yesterday. I told them all I could." Barry sat on a stool beside his workbench and gestured for me to take another. "But fire away."

"When you went out with Chris and Phil Bennett to look at the wreck, did you happen to see the stranger then?"

"Nope." Barry told the same story about their little adventure that Chris and Phil Bennett had, though he left out the part about sliding down the hill on his backside. "It was slippery out as the dickens," was all he said about it.

I asked another question, even though I knew the probable answer. "You paid that night with a gift certificate. Where did you get it?"

"No idea. The Mrs. had it. I can ask her if you want me to."

"No, that's okay." I'd have to make a point to talk to Fran later. "Can you think of some reason or some person who would want to gather you and Fran, the Caswells, the Bennetts, and the Smiths at the restaurant on the same evening?"

Barry answered easily, without a sign of worry or stress. "Why would someone do that? I don't really know any of those people. Phil Bennett's been in the store buying canvases a couple of times recently, but other than that . . ." His voice trailed off. "Julia, what's this about? When Fran and I talked to the police yesterday, they didn't seem particularly interested in what we had to say. I had the impression they were checking us off a list of obligatory interviews."

I didn't want to tell Barry I thought someone had lured him and his wife to the restaurant on the same night there'd been a murder there. I wasn't sure, for one thing, and there were too many open questions—who, why, and was it in any way connected to the stranger and his death, for a few. So instead, I told a different kind of truth.

"I've been uncomfortable about what happened that night. Someone was murdered right downstairs while I was sleeping, and the police have no idea who did it. It's taken a bit of the wind out of my sails. I was so excited about running the restaurant, but now . . ."

Barry put one of his big, paint-flecked hands over mine on the worktable. "I'm sorry, Julia, this has upset you. I'm sure the police will figure it out soon."

"Thanks, Barry. I appreciate it."

"Sure you don't need any art supplies before you go?"

I managed to get out of Walker's without buying anything. A failed knitting project was all the crafting I could handle. I stood for a moment on the sidewalk in the fading late afternoon light, squared my shoulders and continued about a half a mile down Main Street toward the imposing Victorian facade of the Fogged Inn.

Twice I almost turned around and went back to my apartment. I'd left visiting the Smiths until last, because of all the couples, I knew them the least. Which is to say I didn't know them at all.

I climbed onto the Fogged Inn's wide front porch. It was empty of furniture because of the season, but I imagined it was a delightful place to sit and read or simply stare at the boats in the harbor. A sign beside the front door said, WELCOME, and below that a list: NO CHILDREN. NO PETS. NO CHECKS. NO SOLICITATION. NO ACCOMMODATION WITHOUT PRIOR RESERVATION.

For a place meant to be welcoming, the long list of "no's" had the opposite effect. I took a deep breath and rang the bell. Footsteps echoed inside and the door opened.

"Hullo." It was Mr. Smith, looking a little fuzzy, like I'd woken him from a nap.

"Whoizzit?" A female voice bellowed from upstairs.

"Why it's . . ."

"Julia Snowden," I supplied.

"Julia Snowden," he shouted back. "You know, from the restaurant."

"Whazhewant?"

He peered at me expectantly. He was a strikingly handsome older man with long white hair that reminded me of a lion's mane. He wore gray slacks and a blue shirt with a black belt around his trim waist.

"To talk about the night before last," I supplied.

He turned to yell this, but there was a creaking on the stairs and Mrs. Smith appeared behind him. "The police have already been here."

"I understand. This is more something I'm doing on my own."

"Well then, you better come in." Mrs. Smith gestured me inside.

Mr. Smith moved away from the door so I could enter, inadvertently backing into his wife. *"Watchwhereyergoing!"* she barked.

As the three of us stood in the front hallway, I looked through the broad archway into the living room. It was filled with heavy antiques—ponderous chairs, Tiffany lamps, and an uncomfortable-looking sofa. This wasn't the Old Family Money Beach House Charm that Deborah Bennett had so successfully achieved at her place, or the comfortable, lived-in use of family pieces at the Snuggles. This was in-your-face antiquey-ness.

In the hallway hung another list of prohibitions. GAME ROOM CLOSES AT 9:00. NO NOISE AFTER 10:00. BREAKFAST SERVED PROMPTLY AT 8:00, NO EXCEPTIONS. NO WIFI, NO TV, NO FOOD SERVED AFTER BREAKFAST. Well, that would certainly make you feel at home.

"Sit down. You'll have some tea," Sheila Smith said, leaving no room for argument. "Michael, get us some tea. And cookies. The shortbreads. From the tin by the stove." She pointed me toward one of the deep, mahogany-trimmed chairs and settled herself in the other. She wasn't as attractive as her husband. Her mousy gray hair was worn in an old-fashioned pageboy. She was thin, even a little frail looking. I wondered if she was older than her handsome spouse.

"So, how long have you run the restaurant?" she asked. "Is the hunky chef your husband?"

I shrank from the questions, especially since to the extent I'd envisioned the conversation, I was the one doing the asking. Figuring it was better to give a little to get a little, I answered. "Five weeks. Chris is my boyfriend."

"How long have you been together? Do you live together? How did you meet?"

"Since the summer. Not officially. We actually met when I was in seventh grade and he was a junior in high school, but I hadn't seen him for years until I moved back to town last March." I recited my answer with a "Just the facts, ma'am" delivery, hoping she'd get the hint and move off my personal life. Ironic, I understood, because I was there to probe into hers.

She leaned in confidentially, though she didn't lower her voice. "So hard to work with loved ones, isn't it?"

Michael Smith chose that moment to enter with the tea things. It was awkward timing but saved me having to answer. Sheila fixed me a cup and handed it to me. She'd evidently decided I took cream, no sugar. She did the same for Michael and finally for herself. Then she passed the shortbreads in my direction. In the interests of appearing cooperative, I took one.

"We order these from Scotland," she said. "So expensive. That cookie you're eating costs more than a dollar. So enjoy it." She put the plate back down without taking a cookie or offering one to Michael.

It was too late to put it back, so I did as she commanded. "Delicious," I said, which it was. Though I would have said so regardless of how it tasted. Then I seized the initiative, figuring maybe that way I could change the dynamic of the conversation. "How long have you run the inn?"

"Oh my," Sheila answered. "We bought it last fall, but it had to undergo extensive renovations. We opened over Memorial Day weekend."

I tried to picture the house in earlier times. I had a vague memory of flaking white paint and sagging porches. The inn was right at the entrance to our little downtown, which should have been a great location, but over the years it had a For Sale sign on its small front lawn more often than not. Owners died, went broke, or gave up the business. It was one of those places that never seemed to take hold. In earlier times, people might have said it was cursed.

In June, I'd visited every hotel, motel, and B&B in the harbor, passing out Snowden Family Clambake brochures for them to give to guests, but somehow I had missed the Fogged Inn. I was surprised I hadn't heard it had reopened, the harbor grapevine being what it was.

Of course, I said none of this to the Smiths. Instead, I asked, "What brought you to Busman's Harbor?"

"Michael has always wanted to run a bed-and-breakfast—to live in a big sea captain's home overlooking a harbor. So when we retired and this inn came on the market, he thought it was our destiny to own it. We sold our place in Westchester County outside New York City and, well, here we are. It's been challenging, let me tell you. A constant struggle. The traveling public isn't what it used to be. But we are living his dream. Our dream," she corrected.

Michael cleared his throat. "I think you had some questions for us about the man who died?" It was the first time he'd spoken since Mrs. Smith had joined us.

"Yes, thank you. Did you speak to him that night? Do you have any ideas who he might have been?"

"The poor man," Michael murmured.

"No idea," Sheila said breezily. "None at all. Didn't talk to him."

"Did you happen to notice what time he left?"

"Absolutely not," Sheila answered for both of them. "We told the state police all this."

I continued, undeterred. "You paid for your meal with a gift certificate. Where did you get it?"

"Came in the mail," Michael answered. "Introductory offer, it said. I'd cooked us Thanksgiving dinner. It was just the two of us. We'd been living off turkey in one form or another for days. A meal out sounded like just the thing, even though the roads were treacherous. We didn't have to go far."

It was true. Though the Fogged Inn was on the other side of Main and Main, it was only a mile and a half or so from Gus's restaurant.

"Do you still have the envelope the gift certificate came in?"

"Heavens, no," Sheila answered. "We don't keep our trash. Out it goes right away with the recycling to the dump."

Sheila was as ruthlessly efficient as I was. I hoped I didn't resemble her in other ways. The conversation was getting me nowhere. I tried one last question. "I noticed as the evening went on, you were chatting with the other couples. Are you friends or acquaintances of the Bennetts, the Caswells, or the Walkers?"

"Certainly not," Sheila answered. "It was just . . . we were all stuck there . . . and, well, one has to be polite."

Michael walked me to the door and said goodbye. I climbed down the wide steps and continued out to the sidewalk. When I turned and looked back at the Fogged Inn, he stood, long white lion's mane surrounding his face, framed by the window in the door, watching me go.

Chapter 13

I walked back down Main Street, chewing on what I'd learned. Which was to say, nothing new, except that I hoped I'd never spend the night in a B&B like the Fogged Inn. If the beds were as uncomfortable as the chairs, it would be like spending a night on the rack.

On the way past the police station, I noticed Lieutenant Binder's official car in the parking lot. I pushed open the heavy glass door to the building and stepped inside.

"Is he in?" I asked the civilian receptionist, tilting my head toward the door of the large multipurpose room that Binder and Flynn used when they were in town.

"On the phone."

"I'll wait." Through the door I heard the low rumble of a male voice, and then silence as he listened to the person on the other end. Then the voice spoke again.

The voice stopped and the receptionist glanced

at the lights on her console. "You can go in now," she directed.

Binder sat, laptop open, behind a folding table set up to accommodate the state cops on a temporary basis. "Well, speak of the devil and she appears." He stood and gestured to the folding chair across from him.

"What does that mean?"

"I just got off the phone with one of your many fans. You've been bothering people with questions about the man who died in your walk-in."

Phil Bennett. It had to be. He'd warned me off Deborah and then he'd called Binder to complain.

"Who was it?" *As if I didn't know.*

"I'd rather not say. What are you up to? It alarms me you've bothered so many people, you can't figure out which of them complained." He let that sink in. "Anyway, what brings you in?"

"Jamie—Officer Dawes—said the autopsy was this morning. Any results?"

"If I tell you, will you stop pestering folks and let us do our job?"

I didn't respond. That depended in large part on how this conversation went.

Binder sighed. "The initial screens are back. That was the ME on the phone just now. Our victim had enough diazepam in his system to subdue him but not enough to kill him." Diazepam was the generic name for Valium, I knew from my little-used prescription.

"Were there any signs of sedatives in his room?"

Jamie had said the search at the Snuggles turned up no drugs.

"Not in his room at the inn. Not on his person."

"So someone might have given him the sedative in order to subdue him, so they could then give him the injection?"

"That's the theory. Now we wait for more test results, to see what he might have been injected with."

Phil Bennett had told me Deborah took medication for panic attacks. Did the police know about this? That brought me up short. Did I actually suspect that one of the diners was a murderer? Not really, was the answer. But I was certain, based on the gift certificates, that someone had brought those specific eight people to the restaurant that night. Why, or what the connection was to the murder, I didn't know, but I thought it was worth finding out.

"What did the medical examiner say about the dead man's scar?" I asked.

"She thinks whatever caused it happened a long time ago, when he was a kid. To try to find information about a kid injured like that, years ago, when we have no idea what part of the country . . . Doesn't make sense." Binder shook his head. "If he's a legit guy, with a job and a wife or a girlfriend or kids, someone will report him missing. Then the scar will make it easier to be sure he's a match."

"And if he's not a 'legit guy'?"

"Then some law enforcement agency somewhere will have run into him. Did he have an accent?"

"No. Not a Maine accent, not a foreign accent."

Binder shifted in his seat. "Okay, I've told you what I know. Time for you to tell me what you've been doing."

I hesitated for a moment, wondering where to start. Binder had known me for a while now. There was not much chance that he'd think I was crazy, but I had a slightly crazy tale to tell.

I took a deep breath. "Someone deliberately gathered those four couples—the Caswells, the Bennetts, the Walkers, and the Smiths—in our restaurant on the night of the murder." I explained about the gift certificate each of the couples had received.

"It seems to me, someone is trying to steal from you," Binder said when I finished.

"No, the certificates were all paid for. Someone charged them to a credit card. The only thing added was the expiration date."

Binder fiddled with his laptop. "Let's see. The Caswells are retirees from Maryland. They've been here for two years, live in that active adult community. The Bennetts have had a house on Eastclaw Point for thirty years, but last winter and spring they renovated it and moved up here from Connecticut full-time this summer. The Walkers have been in town forever. He owns the art supplies store on Main Street. She works at the Cranberry Convalescent Home. Finally," he continued, "we have the Smiths. They're from Mamaroneck in Westchester County, New York. Bought the Fogged Inn last November. Started running it as a bed-and-breakfast

over Memorial Day this year." He looked up from
the laptop. "You've apparently been out questioning
people. Did you learn anything more than we did?"

I thought over my visits with each of the couples.
"No," I admitted. "I get it. No obvious connection.
And since we don't know who the dead guy is,
there's no obvious connection to him, either. But
it's it a little hard to believe that the unusual things
that happened that night are completely unrelated.
A group was gathered in our restaurant. An accident trapped them there. A stranger who came into
the restaurant was murdered. That can't be a coincidence." *The driver of the car in the accident that night
has disappeared,* I added in my head, because Jamie
had sworn me to secrecy.

"It can be," Binder said, "and it probably is. One
thing you learn early in law enforcement is that coincidence is alive and well and far more common
than people think." He paused. "By the way, we
took down the crime scene tape this afternoon and
gave Gus the go-ahead to use the walk-in. He was
cleaning it with bleach before the officers left the
restaurant."

"Thank you for clearing that up quickly." Much
more quickly than when there'd been a murder on
Morrow Island last spring and he'd shut down the
Snowden Family Clambake, already teetering on
the brink of financial ruin, for days and days.

He shrugged. "The walk-in has told us everything it has to tell." He glanced at his laptop screen,
as if anxious to get back to it. "I'll send someone
over to pick the gift certificates up, along with the

credit card information. We can get to the bottom of what happened more quickly than you can."

I explained that the gift certificates were missing and I thought they might have been stolen.

Binder looked amused. "You think someone came into your apartment, in the middle of the night, while you were there and took the gift certificates, and only the gift certificates?"

It sounded ridiculous when I heard someone else say it. I felt my face redden. "Yes."

"Can I assume Mr. Durand was asleep in your apartment as well when you allege this happened?"

Okay, now it truly did sound crazy. "Yes."

Binder took pity on me. "Relax, Julia. You probably mislaid them. Did the victim pay with a gift certificate?"

The exact thing Jamie had asked me. "Er, no."

"Then it probably doesn't matter. Give me what information you have on the credit card and don't worry about it."

"I e-mailed it to Officer Dawes."

"Then you've done all you can. I'll be sure to catch up with him. Our best strategy for figuring out who killed our victim is to figure out who he is and why someone would want to murder him. I'll follow up on everything you've given me, and I thank you for bringing it to my attention, but you have to let me do things in my own time, in my sequence. Okay?"

When I didn't immediately agree, he continued. "Julia, I'm not fooling around. Do I need to remind you that the perpetrator of this murder has not been identified or captured, and this person may have been inside the building where you live and work? This isn't a joke."

Binder and I had had our differences in the past, but he'd never warned me off like this. His words shook me. And I didn't want to tell him about the continuous sense of unease I had in my own home, because that would only make it worse.

"And be sure to lock your doors," he added.

"I hear you." I gave him the envelope, flyer, and card I'd collected from the Bennetts. He took them solemnly and walked me to the door.

As I walked out of the town building, my cell phone rang. Mom.

"Hullo, Julia. I'm calling to invite you and Chris to dinner tonight. Fee and Vee will be here." My mother lowered her voice, even though she was probably alone in her kitchen. "The poor dears are upset by what happened to that man who was supposed to stay at their inn. You know, that man who was killed—"

"In my home," I finished. "Believe me, I get it."

"So will you come?"

"Who's cooking?" I tried not to sound anxious, but my mother was a terrible cook. I was happy to spend the evening in comfortable companionship with the Snugg sisters if that's what they needed, but I wasn't sure it was worth the potential damage to my taste buds.

Fortunately, Mom took my question the right way.

She laughed. "Don't worry. Livvie and Page are on the way. Your sister's helping me with dinner."

"Well, in that case, I'm in. Let me call Chris and see what he's up to."

"Great," Mom said. "Six o'clock? See you then."

I called Chris right away. "Julia, if you're going to your mom's, do you mind if I stay here and do some more work on the cabin? I lost almost all of yesterday." If he couldn't rent out the cabin by summer, the whole underpinnings of his economic existence would be threatened.

"Sure. You stay there. See you later."

"Yup. For sure."

I arrived back at the restaurant with an hour or so to kill before I was due at Mom's. Gus was gone for the day, the door locked, lights out. I flipped the lights on and was grateful to see the walk-in divested of its crime scene tape.

I locked the kitchen door behind me carefully, climbed the stairs to my place, and fetched my laptop. When I had moved into the apartment, I'd paid for cable and Internet. There'd been a big discussion with the cable company and with Gus. Chris and I wanted a TV in the bar, for Monday night football and Sunday evenings. Gus was already opposed to the bar; the idea of a TV gave him apoplexy. "I won't turn my establishment into some doctor's waiting room with talking heads blabbing on about the Cardonians."

It took me a moment to figure out he meant the Kardashians. I was surprised he even got that close. Eventually, we negotiated a truce, whereby we got the TV and I promised to hide the remote in my apartment while Gus was in the building. Internet was even more of an issue. We needed it to run credit cards for our restaurant, and since cell service out at the end of the world was just too iffy, we needed Wi-Fi. Plus, I wanted it for my apartment. You can take a girl out of Manhattan, but only so far.

"No Internet!" Gus fumed. "Absolutely not. That's the last thing I need, people sitting here all day checking their brokerage accounts and writing the great American novel. Never!"

Again, we reached a compromise. We would get Internet and Wi-Fi, but I wouldn't tell anyone the password.

"No one," Gus emphasized.

The cable company became convinced we were going to offer connectivity to all our patrons and wanted to charge us an exorbitant business rate. When the cable guy showed up, I let him spend five minutes on his own with Gus. He emerged shaking his head and said he'd be happy to tell the company to charge me the residential rate.

Sitting on my couch, my computer in my lap, I web-searched my way through the couples who'd been at the restaurant two nights before. I was sure someone had brought that group of people together deliberately, and if that was true, there had to be a connection.

I looked up Dr. Henry Caswell first. There were lots of websites ready to tell me his specialty (anesthesiology), but the sites didn't offer the ratings

from patients I'd become accustomed to seeing
for doctors. Possibly because his patients were
mostly unconscious. He'd worked for the previous
twenty years at Johns Hopkins Hospital. Some of
the websites noted his retirement, but most did
not. I looked for, but couldn't find, anything
controversial—a news report about a malpractice
suit, for example.

There was much less information online about
his wife, Caroline. She was a stalwart of her garden
club in their Maryland suburb and was active with
the botanical garden in Busman's Harbor. Perhaps
that was her local substitute for having her own
garden, something that wouldn't be possible at the
Baywater Community.

There was tons of information on the web about
Phil Bennett. He'd been the chief financial officer
of a huge pharmaceutical company until an even
bigger European conglomerate had purchased it a
year before. I read enough to realize the Bennetts
were rich. Not comfortably retired, like the Caswells,
but truly wealthy. Deborah had told me they were
getting away to Palm Beach for a couple of months.
What she hadn't said was that they owned a house
there and an apartment in a New York City co-op
building in addition to their Busman's Harbor
"summer cottage." They'd sold their house in
Greenwich, Connecticut, before they'd moved up
the harbor, and the listing photos were still available online. The house looked like a palace and was
beautifully decorated, as I would have expected.

I thought I'd find a website for Deborah Bennett's

interior decorating business. What little people seemed to know about her always included the information that she was a "professional" interior designer. But there was scant mention of her on the web, and I wondered if all the homes she decorated were her own.

I looked briefly for information about the Walkers, and what I found confirmed what I already knew. The art supplies shop had a terrible website. It looked like someone had persuaded Barry he needed a "web presence" and he'd gone along, but with no idea what he was trying to accomplish. The local paper, which had back issues available online only for the past five years, told me that Barry had been president of the Chamber of Commerce two years ago. Fran was active in the Congregational Church. Nothing I hadn't known. Nothing that connected them to the Bennetts or the Caswells.

A Sheila Smith had recently retired after seventeen years as a federal judge for the Southern District of New York, presiding over civil cases. That fit with what she'd said about moving from Westchester County. I found a formal photograph of her in her judge's robes, her face peering out under her bangs, stolid and grim. When I'd sat in front of her, I'd certainly felt judged. I was glad I'd never been involved in a case that would have brought me before her bench.

I searched for "Michael Smith," but even adding "Mamaroneck," it was hopeless. The name was too common to yield any reliable search results.

I sat back to consider what I knew. Four couples, linked by age. All had lived in different places in the northeast United States. The Bennetts were rich and the Caswells well off. The Walkers appeared to struggle financially. I couldn't begin to guess about the Smiths. I assumed they were comfortable, though with our short tourist season and the amount of fixing up the Fogged Inn had required, I doubted they were making any money as B&B owners.

No obvious connection. But I was sure there had to be one. I just had to find it.

Chapter 14

I locked up the restaurant and headed to Mom's. Livvie and Page were already there when I arrived, and the place smelled like heaven. Livvie's meatloaf was in the oven along with baked potatoes, and broccoli was cut and ready to go in the pot.

I gave my pregnant sister a hug. "Where's Sonny?"

"Beat. I told him I'd bring a plate of food home for him."

Most of the lobster boats in Busman's Harbor were out of the water, tucked away in the lobsterman's side yards, but Livvie's husband, Sonny, was still hard at work every day on his father's boat, the *Abby*. Lobster prices rose ever higher in the winter, due to low supply and high demand, especially from France, where Maine lobster had become a traditional part of the Christmas Eve meal. Bard, Sonny's dad, was recovering from rotator cuff surgery and Sonny's younger brother was in treatment for an addiction to painkillers. So it was left to Sonny, despite an inquiry of his own, to haul traps until the weather finally forced the *Abby* out of the water sometime after the New Year.

"What can I do?" I asked.

"Help Page with the salad," Livvie answered.

I sat down at the kitchen table next to my soon-to-be ten-year-old niece, who took a sharp knife to some carrots like a pro.

"How's school?" I asked.

"Same as when you asked me on Sunday. And on Saturday. And on Thanksgiving Day before that."

What else are you supposed to ask kids? "So you would say it's—"

"—the same. Yes, it is." Page turned back to her chopping, humming happily as she did.

Mom came through the swinging door from the dining room. "Hullo, Julia."

In spite of the schedule she'd kept lately, Mom looked great. Her petite frame was encased in a red cashmere sweater and a pair of navy slacks. Her shortish, thick blond hair was well cut, and she wore just a hint of makeup. This was quite a turn-around for my mother, who'd gone through five rough years after my father's death. Her look, which had always been casual, had declined from "carefree" to "don't care" during the years of her mourning. The "little job" at Linens and Pantries agreed with her.

The Snugg sisters arrived, taking off layers of coats and scarves in the front hall. Livvie took the meatloaf out of the oven, and we gathered at the table.

"Delicious," Vee pronounced after her first bite of meatloaf, some of the roses returning to her cheeks. "Just like I taught you."

Livvie had learned to cook in self-defense after enduring a decade of my mother's attempts to turn herself from a privileged, motherless girl raised by a revolving-door series of housekeepers into a Yankee housewife. One of the places Livvie learned her skills was in Vee's kitchen, and Vee's meatloaf was one of our favorites.

"Wonderful," Fee confirmed.

While Page was at the table, the conversation stayed light, but throughout the meal I felt the weight of words unsaid, emotions unexpressed. As soon as Page was excused to do her homework, the subject of the stranger and his murder came up.

"It's so upsetting," Fee said, rubbing her fingers bent by arthritis. "The state police have been back again. That Lieutenant Binder was around, without his handsome sergeant." The sisters shared a crush on Flynn. "He kept asking about the stranger. The man we think was called Justin."

"Or Jason," Vee put in.

"Or Jackson." Fee crinkled her napkin impatiently. "Why can't we remember? But then, we barely spoke to him. Lieutenant Binder clearly thinks we're ninnies. He kept asking, 'When the man made the reservation, where did he say he was calling from?' 'When he arrived, where did he say he'd come from?'"

"What the lieutenant doesn't understand," Vee said, "is that innkeepers take their cues from the guest. If he wants to talk, so be it. But if he's getting away to have time alone, we're not going to force ourselves on him."

"Speaking of innkeeping, do either of you know the Smiths who bought the Fogged Inn last year?" I asked.

"Goodness, yes," Fee answered. She paused as though trying to figure out how to put the next part delicately.

"Out with it," my mother said. "We're among friends."

"We've heard nothing but complaints about the place. When they first opened, I tried to be neighborly. If we were booked up, I'd refer guests over there. I figured I would help them get on their feet. But they found one reason or another to reject every single person I sent them. No children. Indeed," Fee said.

"When you've been in the business long enough, you learn that guests are self-selecting. The parents who choose a B&B for their family know their kids can live without in-room televisions or a pool. We've never had a problem with young people," Vee added.

"Have you met the new owners?" I asked.

"The Smiths? Just at the post office," Vee said. "I said hello. She didn't seem to know who I was."

That was an enormous breach of protocol. Savvy inn owners would have introduced themselves at all the other B&Bs in town before opening. The hospitality industry lived and died by referrals. Not only did innkeepers refer guests to other inns when they were full, they were also sometimes tasked with finding rooms in multiple B&Bs for big parties in town to celebrate weddings or other events.

"That place will be up for sale by a year from now, just like always," Fee said. "Mark my words."

"Do you know the Caswells, Caroline and Henry?" I asked.

Mom, Livvie, and Vee all looked blank, but Fee wrinkled her brow. "The tennis players? I see them quite often when I walk MacCavendish." MacCavendish, called Mackie, was the latest in the sisters' long line of Scottish terriers. Their last one had passed away peacefully of old age just before the hectic summer season began. Vee had held the line over the summer, but in the fall Fee prevailed, and Mackie, a five-year-old rescue, had joined their family. For all the warmth and hospitality Fee exuded with her B&B guests, she was really most at home with her dogs.

"So you know the Caswells?" I persisted.

"No. Just to say hello." Fee paused. "They're quite new, I think."

The Caswells needed an additional two decades in the harbor not to be considered "new."

"Yet there is something so familiar about her face,"

Fee said. "Every time I run into her, I'm sure we've met before. Where are they from?"

"Maryland."

Fee shook her head. "Then that's not it."

The conversation drifted on to other things. The sisters excused themselves and Mom, Livvie, and I gathered in the kitchen to clean up.

"Did you know Jamie took a double shift on Thanksgiving because he had no place to go?" Out of old habit, we'd formed an assembly line—Livvie washing, Mom drying, and me putting away the clean dishes. Every time we did it, I missed my dad, who should have been there, joking and laughing as he cleared the table and put away the leftovers. Without us ever discussing it, I had added his duties to my own, but the hole remained in our family.

"Jamie knows he's welcome here," Mom said. "Or he should."

For years, we'd had Thanksgiving at our house with Mom, me, and Livvie's little family, plus Fee and Vee, Bard and Kyle Ramsey, and Jamie and his parents. Jamie's three older siblings were so much older, his mother called him the period at the end of the sentence. "More like an exclamation mark," his father joked. "Surprise!"

Jamie's older brother and two sisters had gone off to college and then moved out of state, establishing careers and raising families of their own.

Jamie had stayed in town, coping with much older parents who depended on him. This year, they'd gone to Florida to spend the winter with one of his sisters. As far as I knew, Jamie was still rattling around their empty house next door.

"I thought he was spending Thanksgiving with that Gina," Livvie said, stepping away from the sink, the last of the dishes done.

"He told me that's not happening anymore."

Livvie sighed. "Too bad."

"He didn't want to talk about it," I added.

"I'm sure."

Mom hung her dishtowel on the stove handle. "We can't let him spend the winter mooning around in that big house. Julia, you need to talk to him."

Livvie crinkled her eyes at me to show she understood it wouldn't be that easy. Jamie and I hadn't been capable of resuming our easy friendship since I got back to town. Partially, that was my fault. I'd been so crazed trying to get the Snowden Family Clambake back on its feet when I first got home, I hadn't even called him. Then things just got weird between Jamie and me after that kiss.

"I guess I should," I responded to my mother, making no promises. I didn't know how to recapture the easy comfort Jamie and I had as kids.

When I got back to my apartment, I went to my refrigerator, thinking I'd help Gus out and, oh-by-the-way, keep him from stomping through my apartment in the early morning hours by moving his remaining food back down to the walk-in. But when I opened the door, the fridge was empty. Gus must have been by to drop off food downstairs and cleared it out himself.

Chris arrived soon after me, and we had a chance to catch up with each other. We snuggled while he talked about his projects at the cabin. As I listened to his description of the work he'd done, the problems he encountered, and the solutions he found, I reveled in the easy domesticity of our conversation. Even though I was thirty, I hadn't ever had a relationship like this.

After five months, my heart still pounded and my knees turned to jelly whenever Chris walked into a room. My favorite thing was to catch a glimpse of him while he did something mundane—buttoning a shirt, chopping vegetables in the restaurant, or getting out of his truck—and had no idea I was watching. When that happened, my need to touch him was so great that sometimes I couldn't stop myself from reaching out to feel his forearm or his stubbly cheek. I knew this desperate, physical yearning couldn't last forever, or so I'd been told, but it hadn't quieted yet, or even diminished.

As a couple, we still had a lot to work out. We had problems with possessive pronouns. Was it my apartment or ours? Though he stayed almost every night, most of Chris's stuff remained at the cabin, so it was "my" apartment. But Gus's Too was definitely "our" restaurant. We were both all in.

When I talked about my day, Chris listened carefully, without interruption. Despite his statement about letting the professionals handle it, he'd never been one to tell me what to do or to caution me not to get involved.

"I think the four couples in the restaurant that night are somehow connected, and someone— maybe one of them, maybe someone else—wanted them there."

"I think you're right," Chris agreed. "Remember I told you when Barry fell, Phil said, 'Buddy, are you all right?' All day today, that phrase circled in my brain. It wasn't what Phil said, it was the way he said it. Like 'buddy' wasn't an expression, but was Barry's name."

"So you think that in the moment, when it looked like Barry might be hurt, Phil forgot himself and called Barry by an old nickname?"

"Exactly."

Phil had said he'd been in Barry's store "a couple of times." Hardly the type of relationship that led to intimacy and nicknames.

"They have a connection," Chris said. "You're right about that."

I said, tentatively, "I think the gift certificates were stolen."

"What? Out of this apartment?"

"I can't figure out how else they disappeared."

Chris took my hand. "Think about what you're

saying, Julia. Someone came in, while you and I were both asleep, and took one very specific item, nothing else, out of a very specific place, the cigar box."

His touch gave me the courage to say what I was thinking, crazy as it was. "I know it's nuts, but it's the only thing that makes sense. Think how little sleep we got the night before last. And yesterday was a stressful day. We were exhausted." I warmed to my argument. "You were out late at Sam's. Everyone who's been in the restaurant knows about the cigar box. I keep it behind the bar and I'm always putting money in it, taking change out. Last night, I left the cigar box out on the desk in the apartment instead of putting it under the bed like I usually do."

Chris took his hand back and rubbed his dimpled chin. "Anyone who's ever come to the restaurant might know about the cigar box, but only twelve people knew the gift certificates were in it. One of them is dead. One's a cop. One is you. One is me. That leaves the four couples who were guests that night. Do you really think one of those people broke in here and stole them?"

"I'm almost sure of it."

"I'm putting a lock at the bottom of the apartment stairs tomorrow."

I took that as a statement of support. "Thank you. For the lock and for believing in me. Please, let's not tell Gus. It will only upset him and raise the issue of the unlocked kitchen door again. Let's be super-careful about locking it going forward, so we can be absolutely sure."

Chris didn't fight me, or repeat that he was sure he'd locked the door last night. What Jamie had implied was true. It had been late and Chris had more than likely had a few beers at the poker game. Had he fumbled the latch, thinking it had caught when it hadn't? I wasn't going to raise the possibility. I had Chris's support. We were on the same team. That was all I needed.

"If you get it, why doesn't Lieutenant Binder get it?" I asked.

"Get what?"

"All of it," I said. "Someone gathered these particular couples at the restaurant. And whoever it was is now covering up by stealing the evidence. Whoever it was wanted those four couples, plus someone else, to be there. One gift certificate was never redeemed."

Chris knit his brow. "The cops have bigger problems to deal with. They don't know who this dead guy is. They have the missing driver from the accident at Main and Main. If I were them, I'd be trying to figure out the murder victim's identity as the path to figuring out who'd want to kill him. You would too."

"You know about the missing driver?" A weight lifted off my shoulders. Jamie had asked me not to tell Chris, and I hadn't.

"Julia, everyone in town knows."

I should have figured. At least I was out from under my promise to Jamie.

Chapter 15

The next morning I was awakened by the reassuring sounds of clunking and banging and the smell of bacon frying coming from downstairs. It was wonderful to wake up to a relatively normal day. Of course that also meant Gus's Too would be open for dinner.

Chris rolled out of bed not long after me and was immediately on the phone with a supplier. In the background as I dressed, I heard him dickering about the price of scallops. They were in season—draggers were out along the Maine coast—but most of the catch would go to fish markets and restaurants throughout the northeast. It would be challenging to fill our relatively tiny order at a reasonable cost. Gratefully, I left him to it and headed down to Gus's.

Gus was busy, but in a normal Thursday sort of way, not like it had been the morning before. With the crime scene tape gone, the gawking opportunity was over. Gus worked like a demon behind the counter filling orders. I wandered back and poured myself a cup of coffee.

Across the dining room I saw a familiar hand in the air waving me over. "Yoo-hoo," Fee Snugg called. I took my coffee and sat down in the sisters' booth. Vee's plate was piled with Gus's scrumptious blueberry pancakes, while Vee attacked two eggs over easy with a piece of toast. It was wonderful to see these two women, who worked so hard giving breakfast to tourists all summer, enjoying themselves at Gus's.

"I'm glad I caught you," Fee said. "After we talked last night, I couldn't stop thinking about where I've seen that Caroline Caswell before. It drove me crazy. And then it came to me. At the yacht club."

"The Caswells are members of the yacht club?"

"No. Or I don't know," Fee clarified. "I'm not talking about now. She's in one of those old photos of the yacht club dances that line the hallway. I'd recognize her anywhere." She hesitated. "Is it helpful I've remembered?"

"It could be." If Caroline wasn't really a newcomer to Busman's Harbor, perhaps she had connections in town I didn't know about. "Thanks. I'll go over after breakfast and check it out."

Gus appeared at the edge of the booth to take my order.

"Was the kitchen door locked when you came in this morning?" I asked.

"Ayuh. Thanky. Whaddya want for breakfast?"

"Oatmeal, maple syrup, raisins. Thanks."

"Comin' up."

After we finished breakfast, I went back to my apartment. Chris completed a call with another supplier while Le Roi sat on the coffee table, regarding him with suspicion. Le Roi's attitude was that he was the apartment's original tenant. Chris was an interloper.

"I'm off to pick up supplies, and I'll take the lock off the door downstairs to see if I can replace it or get parts. The seafood and produce trucks will be delivering this afternoon," Chris said. "Can you be here as soon as Gus closes to help with prep?"

With all our do-ahead food gone, thrown out as a result of the police search, prep would be especially challenging.

"Sure."

"Where're you off to now?"

"The yacht club."

Chris tilted his head. "A little off-season for that?"

"Something I want to look into."

He grinned. "Be careful."

"Always am. Gus said to thank you for locking the door."

"Always do," Chris said, and I knew enough to leave the subject alone.

The Busman's Harbor Yacht Club sounded a lot more hoity-toity than it was. Not far from Gus's on the working side of Busman's Harbor, mostly it was a place to moor pleasure boats. Although some of the yachts there in the summer were pretty spectacular, most of the vessels were fairly modest sailboats and motorboats. The club also kept a small fleet of sailboats, and their school was where almost every kid in the community, summer and local, learned to sail. In the summer, I loved watching the parade of little yellow boats as the students followed each other around the harbor like ducklings.

The clubhouse itself was a ramshackle affair with a room full of wooden lockers for stowing boat-related gear at one end of a long hallway and a community room, which had all the charm of a drafty elementary school gym, at the other. The front door was locked, as I expected. Nothing worth stealing was stored over the winter, but the members didn't want teenagers using their empty building as a hangout.

I went in search of Bud Barbour, who owned a small boat repair business just down from the yacht club and who picked up extra money as its caretaker.

Bud's repair shop was locked up tight, riding out the quiet time until spring when boats were readied for the water. I climbed onto his deck and rapped on the back door. Morgan, his black lab, barked a noisy greeting from inside. In the background I heard explosions and gunfire. Old Bud was a dedicated video gamer.

"Coming!"

I waited in the cold while Bud killed off a few more bad guys and finally made his way to the door.

"Howdy, Julia. What brings you here on this dreary day?"

"I need the key to the yacht club."

Bud pursed his lips behind his Santa Claus beard. "What fer?"

I'd learned in similar circumstances that when I was as specific and truthful as possible, people didn't ask as many questions as you might expect. "I need to take a look at one of the photos in the hallway."

If someone had said that to me, I certainly would have wanted to know why, but evidently my activities were not as interesting to Bud as I imagined.

"I'll get the key for you." He shuffled into the dark innards of the house and reappeared with a key chained to an enormous wooden tag that said YACHT CLUB. "You be sure to bring this back, Julia Snowden," Bud said as he handed it to me. "I know where you live."

Didn't everybody?

I walked the key back to the yacht club and unlocked the outside door. The electricity had been turned off for the season, but in the first room, the locker room, there were plenty of windows to provide light, even on a gray day. The floor-to-ceiling wooden lockers were three feet wide and three feet deep to accommodate the oars, outboard motors, life vests, and other boating paraphernalia kept there. I admired the polished oak of the lockers. The yacht club might not be fancy or showy, but it was quality built.

The long hallway was reasonably light at each end due to the windows in the locker room and community room, but the middle was completely in shadow. The walls were lined with photographs, one after another, each at eye level. I realized too late I should have asked Fee for more details about the photo of Caroline she remembered.

The images of the yacht club dances were in chronological order up one side of the long hall and down the other. So the ones nearest the locker room door were way too old on one wall and too new on the opposite side to have Caroline in them. The yacht club dance was a right of passage for summer families, a special treat, only for the college-age kids. It was originally billed as a cotillion, a coming-of-age ritual. In the early years, by tradition, the girls wore white dresses, the boys dinner jackets.

On my right, the young adults of 1890 stared solemnly into the camera. The girls' dresses had high necklines and tight waists. On my left, last year's crop of rowdies hammed it up, the girls in short dresses, the boys' jackets cast aside, ties loose. At some point, the white dress tradition had gone away and the girls' shifts were awash in vibrant summer colors.

I kept walking slowly down the hallway, which grew increasingly dark, squinting at the photos as I went. The solemn-faced Victorians turned into sleek Edwardians and then smiling flappers. Photos were no longer formal portraits. The collegians of the 1920s weren't afraid to show they were having fun. They held champagne glasses, despite Prohibition, and smoldering cigarettes in long holders. Then came the toned-down years of the Depression followed by the war years. For the first time, there

were an unequal number of women and men in the
pictures. There weren't enough men left at home
to go around. During World War II, the girls' sleek
dresses and wavy hair made them look old beyond
their years. An entire generation that had to grow
up too quickly. Most of them were smoking, too,
just like in the twenties and thirties.

As I reached the end of the hall, light streamed
in through the windows in the community room.
I turned around and started back the other way. I
looked at the photos on the opposite wall with interest, watching the changing fashions, wondering
about the people. I was sure I must have looked
into the eyes of several of my ancestors. But I'd also
done some quick math. I knew Caroline was a
recent retiree, so I could figure out more or less
how old she was. The kids in the photos immediately after World War II still looked purposeful and
adult, many of the men still in uniform. Then there
was another shift, and in came big skirts and poufy
hair and giggles at the camera. I slowed down as I
reached the sixties, ticking up the years. And then,
there she was. Front and center in the photograph
for 1967, so I couldn't miss her. Fee was right—
Caroline had aged but was otherwise unchanged.
I slipped the photo off its single hook and carried
it back to the better light in the community room
so I could examine it.

Caroline was in the first row in the front, ele-
gantly arranged on the floor. Her hair was boy-short
even then, alone among the big hairdos of the
other girls. If they were going for Katherine Ross in

The Graduate, Caroline was Mia Farrow in *Rosemary's Baby,* though without the haunted look. She stared into the camera, bright-eyed, confident, happy.

I looked at the rest of the photo, searching the faces to see if any of the others who'd been in the restaurant that night were there too. I was astonished. They all were!

Henry was next to Caroline on the floor, her arm through his. His hair and brows were dark, his lean face not yet pixie-like. In a dinner jacket and skinny bow tie, he glowered, his features a map of simmering anger. His hostile expression didn't seem at all like the Henry I knew.

The others sat in chairs or stood around them. After Caroline, Phil Bennett was the most recognizable, with his long skinny legs and arms. Slowly, Michael and Sheila Smith came into focus, mainly because Sheila's thin figure and hairstyle of bangs and curls were unchanged. Even back then, Michael had mane of flowing hair, though whether it was light blond or prematurely white, I couldn't tell from the black-and-white photograph.

Though both Sheila and Michael were in the picture, Sheila was standing next to Phil Bennett, his arm around her, and Michael was with . . . Fran Walker! It took a few moments for me to decide the young woman was really Fran. She was sleek and trim, every hair in her bouffant artfully arranged. With her overlarge features, she should have been ugly, but she was gorgeous.

Barry Walker was also in the photo. Like the other men, he was dressed in a dinner jacket, but he looked uncomfortable in his clothes. His long hair touched his collar and looked dark blond or light brown. I tried to remember back to my childhood. What color had Barry's hair been? I couldn't come up with it. Barry stood close to a pretty woman I didn't recognize.

It took a long time for me to believe Deborah Bennett was in the photograph. I had assumed her plastic surgery had been an attempt to recapture the beauty of her youth, but the woman in the photo looked so different. She was stunning, for sure. The young woman in the photo had a beauty that jumped out of the frame. But her cheekbones were somehow differently shaped than Deborah's, and instead of Deborah's cascade of light blond hair, this woman's dark hair was an elaborate construction that swept back and up, and then hung down into a flip. But as I stood in the cold, empty community room, studying the photo, I became convinced from her height and carriage and beautiful legs that the woman was Deborah. She stood with a man I was sure I didn't know. He was in a U.S. Navy dress uniform, and the photographer had caught him laughing.

In the center of the photo were two other people I didn't recognize, obviously another couple, her hand on his arm. They looked young and happy, the center of a charmed life. As in the other photos from that era, most of them held a lit cigarette and many held cocktail glasses.

Was one of the people in the photo whom I didn't recognize the intended recipient of the fifth gift certificate? Was the couple in the center still together? Had the person who mailed the gift certificates hoped to stage a reunion?

As I made my way to the door, I stopped again and stared at the photo from 1959. Vee Snugg was at the center, her mouth open, caught in the act of tossing out a witty bon mot the others reacted to. Fee was there, too, dressed in a shapeless shift, her arm through the arm of her date, who, like all the other men, stared at the glamorous Vee. Fee thought of herself, even described herself, as homely, but I saw a shy woman with a sweet face and a comfortable figure. Neither sister had married. Vee had spent her childbearing years in love with a married man who would never leave his wife. I wondered about Fee. Had any man ever been in love with her? What if she hadn't been the sister of the charismatic Vee?

I tucked the 1967 photo under my arm and kept walking until I reached the locker room and exited through the front door, locking it behind me.

Chapter 16

I wasn't sure how long I could keep the key before Bud came looking for it. I figured, let him come after me. I walked out of the back harbor with the photo and the key in hand. I kept the office where I ran the clambake business in the front room on the second floor of my mother's house. Dad had operated the business from there for twenty-five years. With its bulky metal file cabinets, heavy oak desk, and view out the window to the Snowden Family Clambake kiosk on the public pier, the office made me feel like I carried on an important tradition.

At my desk, I turned the wooden frame of the photo upside down, poking at the brads that held its back in place. When they proved too stiff for me to move, I used a scissors to pry them open. I glanced at my cell phone on the desk surface. No call from Bud yet.

When the frame opened, I slid the photo out, put it in my printer–scanner–photo-copier, and pressed the start button. The machine chugged along while I shifted nervously from foot to foot, mentally urging it to go, go, go. For my trouble, I got a passable copy. I put the photo back in the frame and put it and the copy into an L.L.Bean tote bag I had stowed in the room. I took the tote bag with me when I left the house.

I hurried back to the yacht club, unlocked the door, and returned the original photo to its place. As I left, I noticed the images from later years along the row. The photograph I'd returned to the wall of the group from 1967 marked the gateway to a turbulent time. In the next photo, girls with straight hair parted down the middle, pale lipstick, and simple shifts with hemlines skimming their thighs stared into the camera. Boys, with jackets off and ties loosened, made faces.

Then there was a four-year gap in the photos. I suspected there had been no interest in fusty yacht club dances on the part of the young people during the end of the sixties and early seventies. Starting in 1972, the photos returned. They were in color, though everything was slightly yellowed. The color photos hadn't held up as well as the black and white. The white dresses for the girls were gone by then, and most of the boys were long-haired, dressed in blazers and khakis. Smoking in the photos seemed to have gone out of fashion, too, though I had no doubt people did it, tobacco and other things, just no longer for the camera.

In 1977, I found my mother, standing two feet away from her date, looking miserable. She was already in love with my father, the local boy who'd delivered groceries to her house on Morrow Island in his skiff. No doubt her widowed father had forced her to go to the dance, probably with some poor kid deemed "appropriate." I felt sorry for the girl standing alone, and even a little sorry for her poor, unaware date.

In 2005, I found me, looking almost as unhappy as my mother. As the offspring of a summer person and a townie, I'd never felt like I fit in. My parents hadn't made me participate in many of the summer people's rituals, but they'd insisted on this one, for reasons I couldn't remember anymore. When her time came, Livvie got out of the whole thing by being Livvie. And being married. And the mother of a two-year-old.

I left the building, locked the door behind me, and went back to Bud's. He looked suspiciously at my tote bag and growled, "What tookya so long?" when I handed the key to him.

"Sorry!" I called, and lit out for the police station.

There were no state police vehicles in the parking lot. "Is Lieutenant Binder in?" I asked the civilian receptionist.

"In Augusta with Sergeant Flynn. Back tomorrow."

I wondered what was keeping them there. "Officer Dawes?"

"On patrol. Can I take a message?"

"No, thanks. I want to talk to one of them in person. I'll come back later."

I walked up the hill as far as the Snuggles. Fee deserved to know she'd been right about the photo.

Their Scottish terrier ran to meet me, with a tail wag that involved his entire rear half. I squatted, petting him. "Hello, Mackie." He rolled over, exposing his belly.

"Come in, come in. Your mother's here," Vee said, leading the way to the kitchen.

Fee and my mother were seated at the kitchen table. On it was a teapot, a sugar bowl, and a creamer.

"Not at work?" I asked my mother.

"I go in at one and work until close." The long holiday shopping season would be a marathon for Mom. Not that she was afraid of hard work. Like my dad, she'd worked her tail off at the Snowden Family Clambake for twenty-five years.

I sat down and gratefully accepted a cup of tea. The Snugg sisters served coffee to their B&B guests but didn't touch the stuff themselves.

I put the copy of the yacht club photo on the kitchen table. "You were right," I told Fee. "It is Caroline Caswell."

"And is that," Vee said, pointing, "Franny Walker? Chapman, she was then. My word, she was beautiful. This photo brings it all back."

"Not just Fran Walker," I said. "It's all of the couples who were in the restaurant that night. Henry Caswell. Phil Bennett. Deborah. Barry. The Smiths." I pointed to each one as I named them.

"Well, I'll be." Fee was astounded, even though she'd been the one who remembered the photo.

"Did you know them?" I asked.

One by one, the women shook their heads. "Not really," Fee said.

Fee and Vee were almost ten years older than the group in the photo; my mother was ten years younger. I could see why none of them had much of a recollection of this particular group of teenagers.

Then Vee said, "Rabble Point Road."

"Yes!" my mother exclaimed. "They're the Rabble Point set!"

"Rabble Point set?" I asked.

"They were a group of families that summered on Rabble Point Road, out near the end of Eastclaw Point," Fee said. "It was a summer colony, with a tennis court, beach access, and a deep-water dock. The families were all very close, as I remember. Parties every night. Now that I see them in the photo, looking so young, I know this group. They were the children, the older children, the first group born after the war."

"Except for Franny," Vee said. "Funny, I don't remember her being part of that group. Her parents certainly didn't live on Rabble Point Road. Her dad worked in maintenance for our father on the golf course, and her mom worked as a housecleaner and took in laundry."

The Snugg sisters' father had been brought from England to serve as the golf pro and manage Busman's Harbor Golf Club. As a result, they lived in the same half-in, half-out world I did. Their father was well respected and they lived surrounded by summer people, but at the end of the day, he was their employee.

"Well, she was certainly with the group that night," Mom said, pointing to Fran.

"What happened to Rabble Point?" I asked. "I've never heard of it."

"It's gone," Fee said. "The cottages were bull-dozed years ago."

"Bulldozed? Why?"

"I don't know. It happens with summer families. Children grow and move to the other side of the country or around the world. Too many heirs in-herit to share the place. They sell up. At least, that's the usual," Fee answered. "My word, it's been a long time since I've been out to the end of Eastclaw Point." Their duties at the Snuggles kept the sisters tethered to the B&B in good weather.

"Do you recognize the couple in the center of the photo?" I asked. "Or the man in uniform? Or the woman with Barry Walker?"

All three of them shook their heads. "I can't dredge up a name from my old memory banks," Fee said. "I can tell you only that they look familiar. I'm sure they were part of that Rabble Point group."

Mom stood. "Thank you for the lovely tea. I've got to get to work."

I drained my cup and stood too. "Thank you, ladies. And Fee, thanks for remembering Caroline in this photo."

"Yes," Fee said, "but now that you know, what will you do?"

Ah, that was the question.

* * *

I stood on the Snuggles' porch for a moment, zipping up my coat against the cold. Across the street, I saw Mom pull out of the driveway in her ancient Mercedes and head to work.

Lieutenant Binder had warned me off the case, told me there might be a dangerous killer on the loose. But from the moment I'd remembered the gift certificates, I'd been convinced there was a connection among the diners. The yacht club photo gave me proof. Binder was a good cop and his approach of identifying the victim and then tracking his associates might eventually work. It was true, as he said, that just because someone brought those people to the restaurant that evening didn't mean any of them had a connection to the victim, or the killer. On the other hand, I was increasingly sure there was and I wanted to prove it, but how?

Clearly, whatever I did, I had to stay away from the Bennetts. I was sure it was Phil who complained to Binder.

I collected my car from Mom's garage and headed toward the Baywater Community for Active Adults. Besides Deborah Bennett, the Caswells had been the most welcoming to me when I stopped by the day before.

They'd also lied. Those adorable pixies had lied. Or Caroline had while Henry sat there. "I don't really know any of those people," she'd said of the others.

I pulled into Baywater, driving carefully over the speed bumps. Since my last visit, someone had tacked up a wreath on the unused gatehouse, getting ready for the holiday to come. There was a small group of dog walkers in the road, collars up against the wind. I edged by them and stopped in front of the Caswell house.

Caroline answered my knock. "Hello, Julia. I wasn't expecting to see you again so soon."

"I know. I apologize for dropping by. Is this an okay time? I have a few follow-up questions from yesterday."

She stepped back from the door so I could enter, but her face was uncertain. "Henry's at the gym. He just left, so he'll be a while. That is, if you wanted to speak to both of us."

I was happy to talk to Caroline alone. I don't know why, but I sensed that made it more likely she would open up to me.

"Come," she said. "We'll sit . . . over there." It seemed that after two years in the open-concept house, Caroline still had trouble putting names to spaces. She sat me again at the table near the kitchen where we'd been the day before.

"Coffee?"

I was awash in the tea the Snugg sisters had given me, but I thought it best to say yes. When Caroline finally sat, I took my copy of the yacht club photo out of my tote bag and handed it to her.

"Oh." She was clearly surprised. Moments ticked by before she spoke again. Then the round "O" of her mouth relaxed into a small smile. "I haven't seen this for years. We were so young."

"My neighbors, Fee and Vee Snugg, said something about the Rabble Point set."

"That is what they called us. I suppose it fit. We were all close in age, the oldest kids in the group, the original baby boomers."

She turned the photo in her hands. "When I was growing up, we came to the cottages at Rabble Point every summer, year after golden year. On that private lane we ran completely free, in and out of each other's houses all day long. The grown-ups drank, smoked, played bridge, and argued about politics, but we were utterly carefree. We played tennis and swam at the little beach across the road. The water was freezing, but you'd never get one of us to admit it. I don't think there was a group of children anywhere as completely happy as we were." Her voice was thick with emotion. She looked at the photo, and then looked away.

I gave her a moment to compose herself. "And you were all members of the yacht club?"

"All of us kids learned to sail there. And later, when some of us could finally drive, we hung out there all the time, leaving the moms and the little kids back at Rabble Point. Except Franny Chapman, of course. She didn't summer at Rabble Point or belong to the yacht club. Her mom cleaned for the Lowes and often brought her along to play with us when she was little. She grew up to be so beautiful and smart and funny. Each of the boys had a crush on her at one time or another."

Beautiful and smart and funny. The Fran Walker I knew, the bent-over woman with the giant pocketbook, seemed defeated by life.

"Caroline, when I was here yesterday, you said

you didn't know the other people in the restaurant the night of the murder. And yet here you all are in the photograph."

She chewed on her lip. "I said I didn't really know them. And truly, I don't. We were all in college when this photo was taken in. We grew apart, followed different paths in life, lived in different states." She looked at me to see if I believed her. I kept my expression neutral. Evidently that wasn't good enough, because she continued. "I haven't talked to any of these people except Henry in more than forty years. Honestly, when they came into the restaurant, I didn't even recognize Fran and Barry. I didn't know they were a couple for one thing. And they've let themselves get so old. And Deborah." Caroline shuddered. "You'd think all that plastic surgery would make a person look younger, more recognizable, but the person I saw that night didn't resemble the Deborah I knew at all."

I pointed at the man in uniform who stood next to Deborah Bennett. "Who is he?"

"Oh, poor Dan Johnson." Caroline sighed. "He was a couple of years older than the rest of us, finished with university by the time this was taken and an ensign in the navy. He died in Vietnam less than three months later."

"And then Deborah married Phil?"

"More or less." Caroline squirmed in her seat. "Eventually."

"Eventually?"

"Yes. She was sad for a time. Then she married Phil." Caroline was curt, like she didn't expect me to understand. "Henry left college and joined the navy that fall."

The U.S. Navy? He must have barely made the height requirement. And if he'd dropped out of college to join the service, how did he become a doctor?

Caroline fell silent. I gave her the time to gather herself. Then she exhaled noisily and took a sip of her coffee. "I'm sorry. These are difficult memories for me."

"Who are they?" I indicated the smiling couple at the center of the photograph.

"Howell Lowe and Madeleine Sparks. They were engaged when this photo was taken, not yet married. They were our king and queen. The smartest, most likely to succeed. Howell's father owned Rabble Point Road. The rest of our cottages were on land leased from him."

"And this woman?" I pointed to the person standing next to Barry Walker.

"Madeleine's sister, Enid Sparks."

I turned to face her. "Caroline, remember the gift certificate I asked about yesterday? I didn't send it to you. Someone else did, and that person also sent gift certificates to the Walkers, the Bennetts, and the Smiths. There was one more certificate purchased. I think it was sent to one of these people, to gather all of you at Gus's, too."

Caroline blinked rapidly. "But whatever for?"

"I don't know."

"And you think it had something to do with the man who was murdered?"

"I don't know that either, but I aim to find out."

"I am very sorry to tell you that no one could have tried to lure Howell and Madeleine to your restaurant. They're both dead."

I was shocked. In a short time their vibrant faces in the photo had made them real for me. "Goodness. How?"

"Together. In an accident." Her features softened, and her voice became hoarse. "They were very young when it happened. They missed it all. Raising a family, building a career. The joy of grandchildren. It's so sad."

"And Enid?" I prompted.

"I lost touch with Enid after Madeleine died, just as I lost touch with everyone else in this picture. I honestly don't know if she's alive or dead."

"And you didn't think it was remarkable to find all these other people at the restaurant?"

"I've told you. We lost touch. For us, Julia, it wasn't like it is for you. We didn't have e-mail or Facebook or other social media to stay in touch. Long-distance calls were expensive and reserved for special occasions and emergencies. It was a different time. I exchanged Christmas cards with Sheila for a few years after Madeleine and Howell died, but her life was so full of disappointments, I came to feel my happy letters about our girls and how well Henry's navy career was going were cruel. I stopped sending them and she never got back in touch."

Caroline looked down at the tabletop. "I'm sorry I lied to you. I knew this ancient friendship had nothing to do with the death of that man, and it would . . . complicate things. That's why I didn't tell you."

"Or the police. You didn't tell the police either."

"Or the police either," she whispered.

"You've got to tell Lieutenant Binder and Sergeant Flynn all of this. Today."

"We will," she finally said. "I promise."

Chapter 17

I left the Caswells and climbed back into the Caprice. Caroline had confirmed she knew the other people in the photograph forty years before, but she'd denied knowing them today. I wasn't sure if I believed her, though that part of her story had a ring of truth. I was certain of one thing: She wasn't going to call Lieutenant Binder today or any other day.

What to do next? I wanted to see Rabble Point Road for myself. Surely that wouldn't upset anybody. I hadn't asked Fee exactly where it was, so I looked for it on the map app on my phone. As I suspected, it didn't show up. In fact, Eastclaw Point Road itself petered out where it forked, and thereafter it was designated "Insignificant Road" by the satellite that sent my phone its information.

I started the car and headed toward Eastclaw Point Road. When I reached it, I drove slowly, checking the names on the mailboxes and signposts to my left and right. Fortunately, it was a time of year when there was next to no traffic, so there were no impatient drivers fuming behind me. The vegetation had died back, making the signs easier to read. At the fork in the road, I took the spur toward the Bennetts' house and slowed down even more. Eastclaw Point Road was met by private roads and long, winding driveways. I got all the way to the end of the road, where steel gray waves crashed up over boulders; turned around; and started back.

This time, at the fork I went the other way, practically crawling. No car had passed me the entire time. I was almost at the end of the road when I spotted a wooden sign. It was so weathered, at first it appeared to be blank, but when I was almost on top of it, it came into focus. RABBLE POINT ROAD. PRIVATE WAY.

I turned my car onto the road and bumped down it. It was more potholes than asphalt. As Fee had said, there were no buildings, just low scrub, now devoid of leaves, and a few pine trees bent by years of wind. It was hard to imagine the thriving summer colony Caroline had described. I stopped the car about halfway down the road so I could get out to explore. The wind slapped my cheeks and I hurriedly pulled up the zip of my coat to my throat.

At first, it appeared there was nothing to see as I walked along the road. But then I spotted a break in the natural landscape. I thought I was seeing tumbled-down New England stonewalls, but the rock piles were spread apart, not continuous.

I went to the edge of one and pushed the dry brush aside with my boot. It was the corner of an old foundation. Only two sides still stood, but I imagined it had supported a sizable summer cottage. I continued down the road, zigzagging across it to look at the remains of foundations on either side. They weren't deep enough to be true cellars. Summer cottages wouldn't have had them, but in Maine, where the earth froze and thawed and froze again, you had to dig down to build up.

By the time the road terminated in a barely distinguishable cul-de-sac, I'd counted a dozen foundations, six on each side of the road. I tried to envision Rabble Point as Caroline had described it, lined by houses, each one set back and a bit askew to maximize everybody's view of the ocean. I pictured the adults moving from house to house, patio to deck, drinking and smoking, while the kids ran free along the lane. Fee had said there was a tennis court. I searched the scrub for it but couldn't find the remains.

A gust of wind came up, so fierce it nearly knocked me backward. I did a little jig to stay on my feet, and looked up. On the other side of the scrub, a manicured lawn stretched, dry and dead now, but obviously well kept. Beyond that loomed the backside of a house. Three-stories tall, with shingled sides and a stone foundation.

The Bennetts' house.

I recognized the French doors leading to the lawn. The ruined foundations of Rabble Point

Road were in the Bennetts' backyard, one of the reasons their home had views to the water in three directions. What hadn't been apparent when I'd entered the house from the other side was that the facade facing Rabble Point Road was the original front of the house. The Bennetts lived in the old Lowe house, the home of the owners of Rabble Point Road.

What did this mean, if anything? I thought about asking Deborah Bennett, who'd been so warm and accommodating, but didn't want Phil to call Binder again. I stood, absorbing the atmosphere, willing the road to tell me something. But it didn't.

I walked back to the Caprice, climbed in, and cursed its broken heater once again.

Bumping down the broken road, I hoped the Caprice wouldn't bottom out before I hit hardtop. I drove back toward town with more questions than answers, unsure of what my trip out to the end of nowhere had taught me.

As I approached the fork in the road, I was astonished to see Deborah Bennett flagging me down. She had on a headscarf and an outsized pair of sunglasses despite the gloomy day, but it was impossible to mistake the trim figure under the well-tailored coat. I tapped the brakes and stopped. I'd seen no cars during the whole journey, so I didn't bother pulling to the side of the road. I lowered the window.

"Julia, thank you for stopping." She came up to

the driver's side door and ducked so we met at eye level.

"No problem, Deborah. Can I help you with something?" I wanted to talk to her about the photo, but I remembered Binder's warning about Phil.

"Caroline called to say you'd come by asking questions about that old photo from the yacht club." My face must have betrayed my surprise. Caroline had just told me she hadn't spoken to Deborah, or anyone in the photo besides Henry, for years. How did she even have the Bennetts' number?

"We're in the book," Deborah said, as if she'd read my mind.

The phone book. We stared at each other for a moment across a generational divide. It would never occur to me that the Bennetts' number was in the phone book, or that they had a landline, for that matter. But if they'd kept the old number from the days when the shingled beauty was their summer house, they would be in the book. The question remained, Why had Caroline called?

"Caroline told me you hadn't spoken in years." Had she called everyone in the photo?

Deborah nodded, her headscarf moving up and down. "That's true. She called me because she was concerned about how I might react to seeing the picture without a little warning. I spotted you out on Rabble Point from my bedroom window and thought I'd be proactive. Pretty desolate out there, no? Listen, it's freezing," she said. "Do you want to come back to the house?"

I hesitated for a moment.

"Phil's not home," Deborah assured me. She went around to the passenger side and got in. I drove us the short distance down the other fork to the long gravel driveway. "Phil told me he'd asked you not to bother me," Deborah said. "They're all so worried about my feelings. Honestly, I'm not as much of a hothouse flower as everyone thinks."

She opened the front door and we trooped inside. The ground had been frozen out on Rabble Point, but I still worried about my boots. "Do you want me to . . . ?" I pointed at my feet.

"No, no, no. Don't worry, you won't hurt anything. The house may be all dressed up for the ball, but at its heart, it's still an indestructible summer place."

I followed her into the kitchen.

"Hot chocolate?"

My nose was tingly from my ramble on Rabble Point. "Yes, please."

I sat at the island while Deborah heated the milk. I'd brought my tote bag inside and itched to take the photo out. "Why is Caroline so worried you'll react badly to the photo?" I asked.

"Do you have it?" Deborah turned from stirring the chocolate on the stove.

"Yes." I slid the copy out of the bag. She turned off the burner, came to the island, and looked at it.

"Look at us, all so young," she said. "Smoking like chimneys. We thought it made us look older and sophisticated. But we weren't like the generation before us who'd endured the Depression and war. They were born grown up."

Deborah's manner was laid back, untroubled. As always, it was impossible to read her face, but her voice told me that, if anything, she was amused by the photo, not freaked out. What had Caroline been so worried about that she'd called a woman she hadn't spoken to in decades?

"When this photo was taken, the world was already changing. We were isolated in our little summer colony in Maine, but by the time we got back to our college campuses in the fall, the world was in flames. We had no idea." She fingered the photocopy thoughtfully. "Poor, lovely Dan was dead before Christmas."

"And then you began dating Phil?"

"Not right away. It was much more complicated."

She turned away to pour the hot chocolate into sleek white mugs. When I brought the cup to my lips, the steam tickled my recently numb nose.

"It would be hard for members of your generation to imagine how completely our coming of age was dominated by the Vietnam War. We didn't have a professional military that went off and fought for us. The consequences of our war were all around us. Having a draft was what finally turned the public against it and brought it to an end. A real end." She looked at my solemn face. "I do admire your generation. You've managed not to blame your contemporaries who are fighting in your unpopular wars. You've kept the blame on the

old men who sent them there, where it belongs."
She took a sip of the cocoa, then sighed. "My generation tore ourselves in two. We blamed each other for everything that happened. In many ways, we're still fighting that war today, trapped in the same old arguments."

"Is that why they're concerned about you seeing the photo?" I asked. "Because Caroline thinks it will make you sad to see Dan?"

"It does make me sad. Yes, for Dan and for Madeleine and Howell too. They missed out on so much." Her sentiments echoed Caroline's. She fell silent, lost in thought.

"Caroline said her summers on Rabble Point Road were the happiest of her life. She made it sound wonderful. Friendly grown-ups getting together for meals, a roving gang of kids," I said.

Deborah looked up. "Did she? I suppose that's what I remember as a little kid. But I have other memories, too, from when I was more aware. Lots of drinking and smoking. Inappropriate flirting among the adults. And more. Not all the dads could spend the whole summer. They were at work in far-off cities. Caroline's dad was a colonel in the army, stationed in DC. The fathers came up for long weekends when they could, and for most of August. Except Henry's dad, who was an academic, and Barry's who was a landscape artist. That's why Barry's family came to Maine. And Howell's, of course, because his dad was so rich he didn't need to work."

She took the photocopy in her graceful hands. "By the time this picture was taken, my parents were separated. The family came up for the summer without my father."

"So your memories aren't so happy?"

"The memories should be happy, but they're tainted by all that came after. The breakup of my family, Dan's death, then Madeleine's and Howell's."

"What happened to Rabble Point?"

"The cottages were always on land the families leased from Howell's father. He decided not to renew our leases, which meant he had to buy back the cottages at market rates, which he was easily able to do. They were never worth much anyway, because we didn't own the land. Once he'd bought them all back, he knocked them down and carted away the debris."

"Why did he do that? Did it have anything to do with Howell and Madeleine's deaths?"

"Maybe. Probably. It happened right after. Or maybe he wanted to improve his view. I don't know what was in his mind."

"But you bought this house from him," I said.

She didn't seem surprised I'd figured out her home was once the Lowes'. "Not from him. He died that summer, six months after his son. We bought the property from a trust ten years later. We never dealt with anyone but the lawyers. The house was so neglected. The poor thing was in a losing battle with the Atlantic Ocean."

I knew what she meant. My mother's house

wasn't on a point like this one, but even in the more protected harbor, she had one side of it painted every year in a regular rotation, like the Golden Gate Bridge.

"I couldn't let this house go to ruin. Since I'd been a child, I'd loved its beautiful bones. I think it's the reason I fell in love with old architecture and became a designer." She paused, staring into her mug. "And maybe, a part of me was nostalgic for Rabble Point too. Like Caroline."

"And you didn't recognize the others that night in the restaurant?"

"I did. Or some of them. Caroline looks exactly the same, doesn't she? And Sheila. Michael looks older, but he's still so handsome, with that white mane of hair. It took me a while to recognize Fran and Barry Walker. They've both aged so badly, and I didn't know they were together. Once in a while, I would hear something about the others through mutual friends, but Fran and Barry had fallen off the radar completely." She shifted on her stool. "Since we were all clearly trapped in your restaurant, the only polite thing to do was to make small talk, but I have to tell you, I never hoped or wanted to see any of those people again."

"If Caroline wasn't concerned about your reaction to the photo because of seeing Dan, why didn't she want you to see it?"

Deborah pointed to herself in the picture. "Do you see me here? I was beautiful. I didn't appreciate it then, but I knew how others reacted. I had no idea how fleeting it would be." She swallowed hard, and her eyes glowed with unwept tears. She looked away from me but kept talking. "In 1980, I was in a car accident. I was driving. I had my seat belt on, but it wasn't latched properly and I was thrown through the windshield, ejected from the car." She looked back at me. "It's taken ten excruciating surgeries for me to look as I do now. Have you noticed, there are no old photos in this house, none from before my accident?"

I thought about the tour of the house she'd given me the day before. There were photos everywhere, arranged on tables and bookshelves. But they were almost entirely of her boys, their graduations, their weddings, candid and formal shots of their little children. Nothing old. Certainly nothing from before 1980. And of the portraits Phil Bennett had painted that hung all over the house, not one was of his wife. At any age.

"Everyone is terrified for me to see what I used to look like, to understand what I've lost. But I would have lost my looks by now anyway. I'm grateful for the face my surgeons were able to give me. Unlike Dan, Madeleine, and Howell, I got to raise a family, pursue a profession, travel the world, see thousands of beautiful sunrises and thousands of starry nights. Phil and I have had a lucky, lucky life. We really have."

I could tell she meant what she said. She and Phil did seem to have a lucky life. They'd been blessed with family and buckets of money—and all that it could provide.

Did that make up for the loss of her beauty? Deborah had lived her life as if it did.

We finished our cocoa and she saw me to the door. I was grateful to get out before Phil returned.

Chapter 18

While I was on a roll, I shrugged off Binder's warning and drove back into town to the Fogged Inn. Caroline and Deborah had confirmed the identities of the people in the photo. There seemed to be no doubt as to who they were. But hearing recollections about the past might help me put the pieces together.

When I rang the bell, the door flew open so quickly, I was sure Sheila must have seen me approaching.

"It's you," she said.

"Can I come in?"

She shrugged. "Suit yourself. I assume you're here about the blasted photo." So Caroline had called her too.

She led me through a swinging door into an old-fashioned kitchen. The inn's extensive renovations didn't extend to this room that guests would never visit. The cabinets were metal painted a dull beige color, the countertops faded Formica. The wallpaper was covered in garish brown roses. Sheila sat at the dinged-up maple kitchen table and gestured for me to join her. "Michael's in Portland for the day."

I pulled the copy of the photo out of my tote bag.

"Ah, there it is." Sheila didn't sound sad or nostalgic. Her voice was tinged with anger.

"You're with Phil Bennett in this picture."

"We were dating back then. He was my first and only boyfriend. After college we were married for three years. We had a huge reception at the Inn & Resort at Westclaw Point." She paused, reading my face. "I see nobody told you that. Deborah and Phil always pretended it never happened, like it could be wiped away with a giant eraser. Life doesn't work that way. At least, my life doesn't."

I was dying to know what had happened. I could imagine a number of reasons a woman's husband would wind up married to one of her childhood friends, but all of them would be painful. I couldn't think of a way to ask.

"That night at the restaurant, you acted as if you didn't know Phil," I said. It was one thing not to recognize the others, who had all aged. Or Deborah after her face was rebuilt. But not to recognize a former husband? I couldn't believe it.

"I didn't know what to do," Sheila said. "I didn't even know he lived in the area. Last I heard, they were in Connecticut. I truly didn't recognize Deborah. I was halfway into the dining room before I saw Phil. Michael saw him at the same moment, spun me around, and marched me to the opposite corner. The meal was endless. And then to be stuck there by the accident. It was torture. All I wanted was to go home to my bed."

I pointed to the photo. "Your husband Michael is with Fran Walker."

"That ran its course. He was in law school in Connecticut. She stayed in Maine. The truth is, all the boys had crushes on her at one time or another, but it wasn't going to last. She was a high school graduate. We were all from professional families."

My parents had made it work. My father had waited out the years my mother was in college. But perhaps that was part of what made their relationship so extraordinary. "Why did you and Michael tell me, and tell the police, that you didn't know the others?"

"We don't know them. Not anymore." Almost exactly what Caroline had said but even less believable. As a former federal judge, surely Sheila would know the consequences of lying to the police. She must have had a strong motivation for shading the truth. I wanted to know what it was.

"Do you know the man who was murdered in my restaurant?"

"Absolutely not. I'm certain I'd never seen him before that night."

I wondered if that was true. After all, the last time I'd seen her she'd denied knowing people she'd grown up with. "Why did you move back to Busman's Harbor?"

"I didn't want to, but the last few years of my

husband's professional life were disappointing. He fell out of love with the law. He talked more and more about coming back here to Maine, owning a B&B. I thought it was a fantasy. But then his firm forced him to retire and he started making trips up here, looking in earnest. This place came on the market. I begged him to find an inn in another town, one without so much history for us. But he'd fallen in love with this house. I was eligible to retire too. I put in my notice. I wasn't ready, but Michael had supported my career and me over the years. It was my turn to support him." So she wasn't older than Michael, as I'd suspected. They must be close in age. Yet he looked younger, more vital. She looked dried up.

"But you hate it here," I said. She'd never tried hard to disguise it.

"I do. I came down to breakfast every morning this summer to find my dining room full of hungry strangers. That's a special kind of hell, let me tell you. No privacy. No part of the house that's entirely my own. I couldn't wait for the season to end. But now that the horrid summer is over, this town is so tiny, I don't know what to do with myself." She plucked a paper napkin from a holder on the table and shredded it as she talked. "I just want to go home. But this is Michael's dream. And we've sunk all our money into this place. I no longer have another home to go to. I am well and truly stuck."

I didn't know what to say. I'd spent plenty of time agonizing about whether to stay in Busman's

Harbor or leave. This woman didn't need platitudes from me.

We stumbled through the rest of the conversation. I put the copy of the photo back in the tote bag and she saw me out. I was amazed at the intimacy of her confession of unhappiness to me, a relative stranger. I didn't feel warm and fuzzy toward her, but I could tell she was surely lacking for friends. I wondered if this was me in the future, friendless and bitter in a small town.

In a luxury of the off-season, I parked right in front of Walker's Art Supplies and Frame Shop. Through the smudged front windows, I saw Barry's head with its wild Bozo hair bent over the worktable. His daughter, Quinn, was on the other side of the shop, organizing shelves. I pushed open the door, listening for the jingle of the bell.

"Hi, Julia!" In her early forties, Quinn still had a bouncy, youthful energy. She was attractive, and now that I'd seen the photo of the young Fran, I could see a little bit of her mother around her mouth. But Fran was dark, and Quinn quite fair, a Nordic warrior princess, which normally disguised any resemblance.

"Hi, Quinn. Are you working in the shop again?" Quinn had been a fixture in the store when I was young.

"Doing some inventory for Dad. Can we help you?"

I wanted to talk to Barry about the past, and I

doubted he'd do that with Quinn present. I couldn't figure a way to ask her to leave, so I bought some pens and a six-pack of lined paper pads for the clambake office.

"Thanks, Julia!" Quinn said. "Great to see you."

I was thankful to see Fran's beat-up sedan in the Walker driveway when I pulled up in front of their house. When Fran came to the door, she was dressed in two layers of sweaters, a cardigan over a pullover. She waved me over the threshold, and I stepped into the front hall. The inside of the house wasn't much warmer than the outside.

Unlike Sheila Smith and Deborah Bennett, Fran gave no sign that she'd been expecting me. I wondered why Caroline would have called Deborah and Sheila, but not Fran.

She led me into the dark living room and offered me a seat on their threadbare couch.

"I saw Quinn," I said. "She looks great."

"Looks better now that her awful husband's out of the picture."

What do I say to that? I pulled the photocopy out of the tote. "I came to ask you about this."

She picked a pair of reading glasses up off a side table and put them on. "Well, look at that. There we all are."

"The Rabble Point set."

"The Rabble Point set and the cleaning lady's

daughter," she corrected. "Look at me, all dressed up, thinking I was all that."

"You're with Michael Smith in this photo."

"Barry came along much later. Michael and I were hot and heavy back when this picture was taken. Look at him. That hair. My word."

"He still has it."

"Not quite like he did in his glory days, but yes, he still has the hair. I about died when I saw him the other night."

"So you recognized him?"

"Right away." She continued to look at the old photograph. Her feelings about the past were harder to read than Caroline's nostalgia, Deborah's sadness, or Sheila's anger. I couldn't tell what Fran felt. Clearly, I was dealing with a real Mainer, not one of those emotional types From Away.

"What happened with you and Michael?" I asked.

"Distance, I guess. I stayed in Maine while he went to law school. But perhaps it was never meant to be."

"Yesterday, Barry told me he didn't know anyone in the restaurant that night, except Phil Bennett, who had come into the store a couple of times."

She looked up sharply. "Barry told you Phil Bennett came into the store?"

"Yes. But what I want to understand is why you and Barry both lied to the police about knowing these people."

Fran's lined face relaxed. "We didn't want to be involved. Barry's a little paranoid. He likes to smoke a doobie from time to time, and you know how the cops around here are about that."

My eyebrows shot up.

"Don't be so shocked," Fran responded. "We're old. We're not dead." I laughed and she did, too, patting my hand as she did. "Poor Julia. So easy to get a reaction."

By then, I was thoroughly confused. Was she having me on? That would be so like her sense of humor. Or was she serious? Did she and Barry still sit around smoking joints in their living room?

Fran took the reading classes off, making a further mess of her always untidy bun. When she laughed, the wrinkles in her brow turned to laugh lines and the years fell away. For the first time, I glimpsed the smart, funny woman from the photo.

"Fran, are you okay? Because the last couple of times I've seen you, you've looked exhausted."

"It's nothing, dear. I haven't been sleeping well. One of the many indignities of old age, you'll discover."

It was an unlikely explanation, but I didn't argue. I took her through the same conversation I'd had with the others. Her answers were unilluminating. She had no idea who the stranger who'd died in the walk-in might be.

I heard the whoosh of air brakes, and through the front window I caught sight of a yellow school bus. The sound of children's chatter filled the air outside.

"Quinn's children," Fran said, pointing to a boy and a girl who'd split off from the rest of the group.

"I'd rather not discuss this when they get to the house." There were footsteps on the porch, and then the children tumbled inside. They were healthy-looking blondes like their mother. At their grandmother's command, they each shook my hand and asked me politely how I was. The boy's voice broke, moving from high-pitched to honk in a single sentence. "Fruit and milk in the kitchen," Fran said. They didn't have to be told twice.

I thanked her and put my hand out for the photocopy. I glanced at it as I tucked it into the bag. Something about it was bugging me, but I couldn't figure out what. Then I realized that if the kids were home from school, I was overdue at Gus's. I ran down the porch steps to my car.

Chapter 19

As I drove back downtown, I thought about what I'd learned. Deborah had lived through two traumatic events, the loss of Dan Johnson in Vietnam and the destruction of her face in a car accident. I had to agree with her assertion that she wasn't a fragile flower. She seemed like a strong woman who knew who she was, and who'd overcome her challenges to build a fulfilling life.

Deborah had had a catastrophic automobile accident, and Caroline had said Madeleine and Howell Lowe died in an accident. It seemed like more than a fair share of tragedy to be visited on a small group of friends. I wondered if the accidents were connected, or even one event. Had Deborah been driving the car when the Lowes died?

I left the Caprice in my mother's garage and walked toward the restaurant. Chris was probably already doing prep work for this evening. As I came over the rise just before Gus's parking lot, my heart skipped a beat. The medical examiner's van was back in Gus's parking lot, along with a fire truck and an ambulance.

What is this about?

I ran the rest of the way down the hill. When I got closer, it was obvious the activity wasn't inside the restaurant but in the water. I waited impatiently, shifting from foot to foot, while Jamie conferred with the medical examiner, heads close together.

The harbormaster and three firemen brought up something on a stretcher from the rocky wall of the harbor. It was already encased in a plastic bag, but I could tell from its size and shape it was a body. I guessed that Jamie had found his missing driver. The body bag was loaded into the ME's van. She said something to Jamie, and then she and a driver got in the van and pulled out of the parking lot.

Jamie spotted me and came over.

"Your accident victim, I assume."

"Looks like it. She must have been disoriented after the accident. Taken a header into the water."

"We're a ways from the corner of Main and Main."

"The amount of time she's been in the water, she could have floated from anywhere. People smarter than me will figure out the currents and the tides and where she likely went in."

"Did you find out who she was?"

"No pocketbook or anything, though it could be in the harbor too. And her coat is somewhere. Ben Kramer described it as green on the night he saw her leave the accident, but it's come off her. Now

that we know where she was, we'll bring in divers."
He pulled out his phone. "Meanwhile, I've sent a
general description to the Connecticut State Police
and to the Hoopers, the couple in Costa Rica, to
maybe jog their memories about someone like her
who would have access to their car."

"Who spotted the body?"

"Kids, walking home from the school bus. It was
an early release day at Busman's Elementary. The
tide was low and she'd fetched up on the rocks."

I shivered. "How old were these kids?"

"Pair of boys, age ten," Jamie answered, mouth set.

"Not something you and I ever saw walking home."

He relaxed. "We would have thought it was a
grand adventure."

"We would not have." I looked at my old friend.
We had so much shared history. Walking to and
from the school bus every day, the summers he
spent working with my family at the clambake, the
holidays he'd spent at our house. Aside from Chris
and Livvie, he was the easiest person for me to talk
to in town. If he was looking for a soul mate in
Busman's Harbor, he was fishing in a small pond.
I couldn't be that person, but I wished him only
the best.

"We should hang out more," I said.

If he thought my remark was out of the blue, he
didn't show it. "I'd like that." He smiled. "There's
more news. Binder and Flynn finally got the full
autopsy results on their victim today. Cause of death,
insulin overdose."

"I'm betting he wasn't diabetic."

"Nope. It looks like whoever did murder him gave him the diazepam to lower his resistance and then injected him with the insulin."

"So the crime isn't solved."

"It isn't. But this is a huge leap forward."

The ambulance and fire truck pulled out of the lot. Chris stuck his head out of Gus's kitchen door and waved. Jamie and I both had to get to work.

As I entered through the kitchen door, Gus was cleaning the hulking grill. "They gone?" he growled, using his shoulder to indicate the parking lot.

"Just finishing."

"Took them long enough. Just what I need, another dead body."

Chris came out of the walk-in, a stainless steel pan of root vegetables in his hands. "There you are."

"Yes, sorry. Almost ready to work. I just need a minute."

"You've got some time." Chris glanced at the old man, clearly wishing he'd hurry along. I could imagine their conversation prior to my arrival. Chris offering to help Gus, with a secondary agenda of moving him out of the way. Gus refusing, stubbornly clinging to his routine, secure in the knowledge that he, and only he, knew how to truly clean his restaurant.

I took the tote bag upstairs and put it on the bed. Le Roi came running and rubbed his cheek against it. I hung up my coat and swapped my outdoor boots for sneakers. If I was lucky, I'd get time to run upstairs and change before dinner service.

I fed Le Roi and thought about where to put the photocopy. I was still bothered by the disappearance of the gift certificates. Lieutenant Binder was convinced I'd mislaid them, but I was sure I hadn't. And even if I had, why hadn't they turned up? After thinking about it for far too long, I put the tote bag, the photocopy still in it, on the top shelf in the closet alcove. The copy, after all, was less important than the gift certificates. The original still hung in the hallway of the yacht club.

"'Night now," Gus called from below. "Take care of yourselves."

"Bye!" I hurried down the stairs.

Chris heard the door close behind me at the bottom. "I didn't get to put the lock in," he told me as I came into the kitchen. "I took the old one to Gleason's Hardware. They laughed when they saw it, it's so old. The said the whole knob mechanism had to be replaced to get us a modern lock, which will mean putting a new hole in the door. It's a big deal. I bought a dead bolt for the top of the door on the inside, but I didn't want to install it while Gus was hanging around. I thought it would raise all sorts of questions. Then he got distracted by the fuss in the parking lot and didn't leave. So we'll have to go one more night without a lock."

I kissed him on the cheek. "No worries. We'll be extra careful to lock the restaurant doors."

"Always am." Chris pulled the vegetables out of the bin. "We're under the gun here. You're the sous chef. You up for it?"

"What does a sous chef do again?" I teased.

"Whatever the chef wants her to." His usual response.

"And what does the chef want her to do?" I asked in what I imagined was my sultriest, sexiest voice.

"Right now? Peel and chop vegetables."

Drat. Though I did get a kiss that made my heart pound and my knees weak.

I heard a vehicle door slam in the parking lot, and my brother-in-law Sonny Ramsey entered through the kitchen door.

"What's going on now?" He jerked his head toward Jamie's cruiser, the only official vehicle still parked on the other side of the lot.

"They found a body," Chris told him.

"The driver missing from the accident?"

"Who else?" Chris answered. "What do you have for me?"

I stepped out of the way, knowing what was coming.

"Lobsters," Sonny said. "Just out of the water. Saved you half a dozen."

"Thanks. How much?"

"Seven dollars a pound."

"Seven dollars!" Chris yowled like a cat that had its tail stepped on.

Sonny shrugged. "It's coming on winter. Prices are high. Bugs are hard to find and there aren't many boats out. You'd pay fifty dollars a pound for lobster meat this time of year down in Boston."

Chris grimaced. "And I'd be charging thirty bucks an entree if I was down in Boston. Let's get real. What's the lobster pound paying you?"

"Five," Sonny admitted. It was easy enough for Chris to check the catch price.

"I'll match it."

Sonny drew himself up to his full height, six foot two of bull-necked, barrel-chested, redheaded man. "You should pay a premium for a small number, delivered direct, by an injured man."

Chris put his hands on his hips and also stood tall, matching Sonny in height if not in weight. "You should give me a discount. You're married to Julia's sister."

Sonny shot me a look like I was the root of all his troubles. "Five dollars a pound. Done."

"Done."

Honestly, why did they have to go through this routine every single time? It had to be a guy thing.

Sonny left. Chris already had a big pot of water on to boil. "What are those going to be?" I asked.

"Your family's recipe for corn and lobster chowder."

"Yum."

"Do we have any reservations for tonight?"

"Just two," I answered. "I can't figure out if the commotion out there today will attract a bigger crowd or drive people away."

"Great. At least we know what to prepare for."

At four o'clock there was a sharp rap on the kitchen door. Livvie arrived with the desserts.

"Thanks." I helped her carry in three chocolate-frosted chocolate cakes and a pan of creamy rice pudding.

"Gotta run," she said. "Picking up Page at swim team."

I went upstairs and changed, then made sure I had both the salad station and the bar set up so I could easily serve. Before I unlocked the door to the dining room, Chris handed me a steaming bowl of chowder. "Eat while you have the chance. Have you eaten at all today?"

I thought back over the day. I'd been served endless drinks—coffee, tea, hot chocolate—but hadn't eaten a thing. "Not since breakfast."

He passed me a chunk of crusty bread and said again, "Eat."

I dipped the spoon into the soup. It was Grandmother Snowden's Depression-era recipe, meant to stretch plentiful and inexpensive lobster meat as far as it would go. Chris made it now as a hearty dish with big chunks of lobster. The lobster meat, corn, onions, and cream combined to create a sweet and savory delight.

"Wait," Chris said, and garnished it with crunchy corn nuts.

"Man, this is good."

Chris flashed his handsome, full-faced smile, proud of his work. "Push it tonight. We've got lots."

It turned out we were flooded with customers.

People sat at nearly every table and the bar was full. Even nights when we'd had plenty of time to prep, we weren't staffed for this number of people. I ran my legs off, which in some ways was good, because I had a plausible excuse for not lingering when people asked questions about either the body in the walk-in or the body in the harbor, or both.

I was surprised to see both Deborah and Phil Bennett and Barry and Fran Walker. Though it seemed like weeks, they'd just been in the restaurant three nights before. I was grateful Chris changed the menu daily. Fran and Barry were on their first course when Deborah and Phil wandered in.

"I couldn't face cooking tonight." Deborah was friendly as always. Phil trailed behind her, wearing his usual look of mild annoyance at the inevitable shortcomings of others. They didn't stop to say hello to the Walkers, whose own local friends stopped by their table all evening. Barry regaled them with the story of the stranger at our bar. "Didn't talk to any of us. Didn't say anything. You could have knocked me over with a feather when I heard he'd been murdered."

Binder and Flynn came in and sat at the bar when we were at the peak of business. "You're back." I pushed bottles of Sam Adams over to them, along with a couple of menus.

"We came to show the world we weren't afraid to eat here," Binder said. "We thought you might have a problem due to the recent unpleasantness." The corners of his mouth turned up. "Evidently not."

"People are ghouls," Flynn said.

"I don't think so," I responded. "They just need a place to digest the latest news."

When I delivered their chowder, Binder leaned toward me. "Julia, we've been back in town less than an hour and we've had another complaint about you barging around asking uncomfortable questions."

Phil Bennett. I'd been so busy, I hadn't seen him approach the detectives. "That wasn't my fault," I protested. "Deborah Bennett waylaid me out on their road."

Binder looked genuinely confused. "Julia, what are you talking about?"

"I'm talking about Phil Bennett, and I'm telling you I haven't been bothering his wife."

"It wasn't Bennett who complained." *Who then? Barry Walker?* "It was Michael Smith."

"Michael Smith? He isn't even in the restaurant."

"We ran into him on the walk outside." Binder paused so that could sink in. "And what were you doing out by the Bennetts' house anyway?"

"I visited Rabble Point Road." I leaned across the bar. "Wait 'til you see what I discovered this morning." Out of the corner of my eye, I saw a diner waving frantically for his check. "I'm busy right now. Can you stick around until things quiet down?"

Binder dug into his soup. "We're off duty. We're in town tonight so we can get an early start tomorrow. Come by the station in the morning."

Apparently even state cops understood the principle of not working eighteen hours a day during the off-season better than I did.

Chapter 20

We were so slammed, it was eleven at night when Chris and I headed upstairs to my apartment. Before we did, I watched as Chris slowly and carefully locked the kitchen door, listening for the click of the latch. I'd locked the street door an hour earlier when the last guest left. Chris had watched me do it.

"I didn't even have a chance to show you what I found today," I said. I could tell from his movements he was still keyed up from the success of the evening.

"Let me jump in the shower, then you show me."

Half an hour later we were on my couch, both bundled in sweats against the cold air seeping in through the big front window. And it was only the first week of December. This was but a preview of what was to come.

Chris was still coming down off the evening's success. "That was amazing. And on a Thursday. Do you think we can draw that kind of crowd every night? Maybe we should hire another server."

"I'm still in wait-and-see mode. Binder thought the crowd was curious about the activity in the parking lot this afternoon. Flynn called them ghouls."

"Really? Is that what you overheard as you were serving people?"

I considered. "No. I mean everyone was talking about the murder, and the body in the harbor, but I think that's natural. It didn't feel like we'd turned into a scene-of-the-crime museum or anything. Not like yesterday morning. Nobody asked to tour the walk-in, did they?"

"Nope." He laughed. "So tell me about your day."

Where to start? I told him about my conversation with Fee and Vee and how that led to the discovery of the photo.

"And they're all in it? That's incredible."

"All of them. I'll show you." I fetched my tote bag off the top shelf in the closet alcove and pulled out the photocopy.

"Amazing," Chris said as he studied it. "Have you noticed how Michael Smith looks familiar? Like we've seen him before all this?"

"Is that it? I knew there was something in this photo that was bugging me. Maybe it's just that he looks the same today?"

Chris squinted at the photo. "No, that's not it. I don't know what it is. Just a feeling."

"He complained to Binder that I talked to Sheila."

"Just because you had a conversation with her?"

"Yup." And Phil Bennett had warned me not to talk to Deborah. Lots of overprotective husbands in that group. "I'll take the photocopy over to the police station first thing in the morning." I returned the photo to the tote and left it front and center on the coffee table so I could grab it and go.

"Good plan." Chris stretched. "I need to sleep."

"Me too," I said.

"It's not here!" I turned the tote inside out and upside down and shook it. I felt a little sick. "How can it be gone?"

"What's gone?" Though it was still dark out, Chris was fully dressed, ready for an early morning pickup with his cab.

"The copy of the yacht club photo! How can it be missing? I showed it to you last night."

"Are you sure you put it back in the tote?" Chris riffled through the stuff on the coffee table, his voice rising with alarm. "Maybe we left it out."

"I'm positive I put it back in this tote bag and left the tote on the coffee table. It's gone. Someone has been coming into the apartment."

He looked like he wasn't buying it. I almost couldn't blame him. "Who even knew you had the photo in that bag?"

"I showed it to Caroline Caswell, Deborah Bennett, Sheila Smith, and Fran Walker," I answered. "And Fee and Vee. And my mother."

"That's it?"

"I suppose each of the women in the photo probably told their husbands. Sheila definitely told Michael, because he complained to the cops about me bothering her. Binder said Michael was lingering on the street outside the restaurant last night. Do you think he could have snuck up here and taken it?"

Chris shook his head. "You showed me the photograph after we locked the doors." He paused. "Do you really think one of the people in the restaurant the night of the murder took the photo somehow? How would a person even get in here?"

I didn't answer. I didn't know what I thought. "What I don't get is why anyone would take it. It's a copy. The original is still hanging in the yacht club. What does getting rid of one copy accomplish?"

"Did you hear anything in the night?" Chris asked.

"I went right to sleep." I shivered, imagining someone creeping into the room where we slept.

Chris nodded. "We were so busy last night, I was exhausted. Once I closed my eyes, I was dead to the world."

"Don't say that!"

"It's an expression. It doesn't mean anything." He looked at my stricken face, put an arm around me, and drew me to him. "I'll put on that deadbolt today."

"Thank you. And I think it's time to tell Gus what's going on. It's just too creepy."

Chris let me go and nodded his agreement. "Yes. Tell Gus."

"Last night Binder said he and Flynn are getting an early start this morning. I'll go to the station first thing. Luckily the original photo is still at the yacht club."

At least I hoped it was.

Chapter 21

Chris took off to pick up his fare, and I went downstairs in search of coffee. Gus was in the restaurant getting ready to open. He'd turned on the lights, and the warm scene made me feel better instantly.

Gus grunted softly when I took the tray of maple syrup dispensers and set them on the tables. Mrs. Gus's pies were still in their wooden boxes, so after I finished distributing syrup, I reverently opened the boxes and put each one on a shelf in the glass case, my mouth watering in delicious anticipation as I did. Apple, pumpkin, chocolate peanut butter, pecan. I went behind the counter and poured a cup of coffee from the pot Gus had already made. "Want a cup?"

"Why not? We have time." Gus came around the counter and sat next to me. "You and your boyfriend left the kitchen door unlocked again last night."

The hair on the back of my neck stood up. "We

didn't. I'm certain. Chris locked it while I watched him, to make triple sure." One time might have been carelessness—Chris's not locking the door or my mislaying the gift certificates—but two times was two too many. "Gus, someone's come into my apartment twice and taken things."

His blue eyes opened wide, black pupils contracting. "Taken things. What things?"

The answer to that was only going to lead to more questions, so I said, "Nothing valuable."

His look was skeptical, which I didn't take personally, because that was one of his most common looks.

"Chris and I have locked the door every night, I swear. I think the kitchen door is unlatched in the morning because whoever is coming in doesn't have a key, so they can't lock it from the outside when they leave." I paused to make sure he understood. He nodded for me to go on. "Is there any other way into the restaurant besides the front door and the kitchen door?"

Gus's expressive features rearranged themselves from annoyed to surprised to comprehending. "Did I ever tell you what this building was before it was a restaurant?" he asked.

"You told me it was a warehouse. Why?"

Gus went behind the counter and grabbed a powerful flashlight and a putty knife out of his toolbox. "So I never told you what was stored here in the old days?" He headed behind the newly installed bar. I followed. He felt around with his foot. "Here it is."

"Here what is? I don't see anything."

"Patience. This was meant to be hidden. They knew how to build things back when it was put in."

He bent over and used the putty knife to pry open a trapdoor. I peered into the murky darkness, listening to the surf lapping on the harbor rocks.

"During Prohibition, like lots of warehouses along the Maine coast, this building was used to store alcohol smuggled in from Canada until it could be trucked to the railroad and shipped to Boston and New York City. This place used to be filled top to bottom and side to side with illegal booze."

I stared into the darkness. "Where does it go?"

"That's the interesting part. Come see." Gus dropped down into the hole below.

"Be careful!" No one except Mrs. Gus knew how old Gus was, but for certain he wasn't young. The boulder below looked slippery. I followed him. The trap door slammed closed behind me, echoing off the surface of the rock.

Gus ducked under the floor joists of the building, walking between the pilings.

I looked around. Through the opening between the restaurant floor and the giant boulder on which it stood, dawn gave the sky a rosy glow. The only way out, that I could see, was straight over the boulder and into the harbor. At high tide you'd get soaked. At low tide, you'd either break a bone on the rocks or get stuck in the muck at the bottom of the harbor. "Now what?" I asked.

"C'mon." Gus was spry, I had to give him that, and in a sort of hunched-over duck walk, he made straight for the place where the boulder met the bank that carried the road above. And disappeared.

"Gus!"

"Right here," he called, sticking his head back out of the opening in the rock wall and shining the flashlight under his chin. If it was an attempt to reassure me, it didn't work.

"What is this?"

"Mostly it's a natural cave, although there's a manmade part at the other end. C'mon," he repeated.

I followed him into the dank, dark opening. I put my hands out. The cave was narrow. I could touch both sides. "Gus?"

"Right here." He flicked the flashlight ahead of him in the tunnel. "Keep coming."

I could hear the surf outside, but otherwise the cave was like a cocoon. I'd never been claustrophobic, but there was always a first time. I took a step and ran into Gus.

"Easy. We're almost there."

As we moved along, the sides of the cave turned from rock to earth with wooden supports every few feet.

"Wait a minute. Stay where you are." Gus pointed the flashlight at a stepladder that stood near the earthen wall at the end of the tunnel. "This'un is new," Gus said, examining the ladder. "Someone's been down here recently."

He put a foot on the bottom rung and climbed up. I hovered below him, staying close for my own comfort and to spot him in case he fell. He pushed open a door overhead, and dim light entered the tunnel. Gus was up and out of the hole. I followed.

I emerged through the floor of locker 10B in the Busman's Harbor Yacht Club. I couldn't quite believe it. "Did we just get here through the floor of a locker?"

"Ayuh." Gus gestured, taking in the big space. "Most of the booze that came into my building went south, where the money was, but the yacht club always charged a cut. During Prohibition, they needed booze for their members. There's only one thing a rich man desires more than a big boat, and that's Canadian booze with the label still on it." He laughed at his own witticism, and I did too.

"Who knows about the tunnel?"

"Fewer of us every year, I'd guess, but still plenty of people. It used to be a right of passage for the yacht club kids, making some poor teenager walk through the tunnel. A couple of times a group of them found their way into my place. Made a terrible mess and drank all my tonics." Tonic was the old New England word for soda or pop. "I made them seal it up at this end."

"It looks like someone unsealed it."

"Ayuh."

"Why isn't the end at your restaurant secured?"

"'Twas. I think Chris must have taken off the board I nailed over it when he installed the bar. As you saw, the opening is well concealed. The board probably got in his way and he couldn't see any purpose to it, so he took it out."

"Maybe." It made as much sense as anything. "While we're here, I need to check on something." I sprinted down the hallway. As I feared, there was an empty spot where the photo from the 1967 yacht club dance had hung. My heart sank.

"Hurry up! I gotta open in five minutes," Gus called.

I returned to the locker room, dejected.

"What's wrong?" Gus asked. "You look like your best friend died." Without waiting for an answer he stepped back into locker number 10B. "Let's go."

"Can't we walk back on the road?"

"Suit yourself. This way is quicker."

I wasn't going to let him go alone, so I followed, closing the door in the floor of the locker behind me.

We made our way through the cave mouth and under the restaurant in no time. Why did journeys always seem shorter on the way back? Gus felt for the trapdoor in the restaurant floor, grunting as he swung it open.

"Wait! Gus, look over there." I pointed toward an object beside one of the pilings. The sun was finally up and cast a shadowy light through the opening between the restaurant floor and the pilings.

"What is it?" Gus came and stood beside me, looking down at the object.

"It's the dead man's backpack. It's been missing since the night of the murder." Gus bent to retrieve it. "Don't touch it!" I scolded. "We need to call the police. Now."

"Not again," Gus moaned.

Chapter 22

I stood with Lieutenant Binder in Gus's parking lot. Sergeant Flynn was under the building, along with two crime scene techs.

"What were you and Gus doing under there?" Binder asked me.

I explained about the photocopy going missing, the unlocked kitchen door, and my discovery of the original photo taken from the yacht club.

"Who did you talk to about this photo?"

I took him back through the whole day. Fee Snugg recalling seeing Caroline Caswell's face on the yacht club wall. Me borrowing the key from Bud, and so on. When I told him I'd shown Caroline Caswell the photo and she'd identified the people in it, he looked uncomfortable. When I said I'd been out to Rabble Point and talked to Deborah Bennett, the skin over his nose pinched into a glower.

"Now I understand. Last night, that's why you thought I was going to say Phil Bennett complained about you. You'd spoken to Mrs. Bennett again."

"She spoke to me. I didn't seek her out. After her, I spoke to Sheila Smith, which you've already heard about, and then Fran Walker."

"It didn't occur to you to come straight to us and tell us about the photo when you discovered it?"

"It *did* occur to me. You and Sergeant Flynn were still out of town. I stopped at the station and left messages for both you and Officer Dawes. None of you called me back. And I tried to tell you last night, but you said you were off duty. I didn't know both the copy and the original photo would get stolen. Anyway, when I told you about the gift certificates, you didn't seem interested in my theory that all the diners in the restaurant the night of the murder were connected." I tried not to sound defensive.

"Julia, there were no fingerprints on the door of Gus's refrigerator except yours, Chris's, and Gus's. There were no fingerprints *inside* the walk-in except the three of yours and the victim's." Binder's voice, slow and steady, underlined the importance of what he was telling me. "Our killer wore gloves. He arrived at the murder scene with a syringe and a fatal dose of insulin. That means our murderer is a dangerous person. Do you understand me? Not someone who lost his temper in a specific situation, but an intentional killer. You cannot go poking around in this. You need to be careful. I mean it."

He blew out a breath, slowing his speech and softening his tone. "We'll follow up on everything you've given us, I promise. But you have to let me do it my way. With any luck, there's an ID for our victim in his backpack and we're halfway home. Give us some time. We'll get this."

There was a shout from under the restaurant. "On my way." Binder headed toward the building.

Moments later, Jamie strolled into the parking lot, a wide grin on his face. "Not even eight in the morning and we've had big breaks in both cases. You and Gus found the backpack," he said, unlike Binder giving credit where credit was due. "And we discovered the identity of our car crash victim."

"Wow. How did you manage that?"

"I sent a general description of the victim to the Hoopers in Costa Rica. They finally remembered that ten years ago, when the husband had a knee replacement, he had several visits from a private nurse during his recuperation. They gave her a key so he didn't have to get up to let her in. Somehow, they dredged the name out of their memories."

"So, spill. Who is she?"

Jamie hesitated. I could tell he was debating whether to tell me. Finally, friendship won out. "A woman named Enid Sparks. We've confirmed she hasn't been seen in her apartment complex since the accident."

I got so excited, I nearly levitated. "Enid Sparks is the name of one of the women in the photo from the yacht club! She was the sister of Madeleine Lowe, the woman who died." I gave him the fastest summary I could of finding the photo, talking to the women in it, and then having it stolen.

Jamie was as excited as I was. "That's it. She got the missing gift certificate and was rushing to meet the others at your restaurant. She got into the accident, became disoriented, and fell off the town pier."

"Maybe. But none of the other gift certificate holders knew it was a reunion, and Enid lived far out of state. Receiving a gift certificate in the mail wouldn't be a reason to take a car without permission and drive all this way."

His shoulders slumped. "You're right. It'll come, Julia. Give us time."

Give us time. Exactly what Binder said.

Enid Sparks. The only living—or rather, recently living—woman from the photograph who was not at Gus's Too the night of the murder. There had to be a connection.

Enid Sparks had "borrowed" a car in Connecticut. Everything in the case kept pointing back to that state. The Bennetts had moved to Busman's Harbor from Connecticut. The diploma on Henry Caswell's wall said Yale School of Medicine. Fran Walker said she and Michael broke up because she "stayed in Maine. He was in Connecticut."

At one point, almost all the members of the Rabble Point set had lived in Connecticut. One of them still did. Or at least she had until very recently. Enid Sparks.

I shook myself, bringing my mind back to the present. Binder, Flynn, the crime scene techs, and now Jamie were under Gus's building. Why was it taking them so long to bring out the backpack?

I went upstairs to my apartment and started my laptop.

It didn't take long to find Enid Sparks's address in North Guilford, Connecticut. The street view on Google Maps showed a well-kept townhouse apartment complex.

I gave my credit card number to a genealogy site and found death certificates for the Lowes. Both had died on January 1, 1974, in Guilford, Connecticut. There was no further information available, so I searched the web, hoping for obituaries or an article about their accident, but I found nothing in the major papers. Apparently the local papers in their area hadn't digitized their back issues yet. The accident was too long ago.

I checked the distance from Busman's Harbor to Guilford. Two hundred ninety miles, five hours of driving. Binder might have a problem with me tramping around Busman's Harbor asking people questions, but he couldn't object to my going to Connecticut. He'd warned me the perpetrator in the case was likely dangerous, but everyone related to the case in Connecticut was dead. That couldn't be dangerous.

I called Chris. "I have to go to Connecticut." I said it right out. Might as well rip the Band-Aid off.

"Whoa." Chris was silent. Maybe I should have built up to it. So I backtracked, filling him in on the events of the morning. Chris asked the obvious question. "Why not let the cops do this?"

"They're so excited about the backpack and the possibility there's an ID for the stranger in it. They'll follow up on what I've told them eventually, but in the meantime I'm sick of being afraid in my own home. I've been more right than they've been all along. The diners are connected to one another, just as I've been saying. And now Enid Sparks connects them to the car accident. I have to keep going."

More silence from the other end. Then Chris said, "Okay. I'll ask Livvie to help with setup and Sam to help me serve and tend the bar."

Sam. He was the perfect solution. As part owner of Crowley's, he'd done every job you could do in a restaurant. And with Crowley's closed during the week, he was available. I hated asking Livvie to do extra work during her pregnancy, but I knew she would come through for us, with a smile on her face. My sister was reliable like that.

"You shouldn't drive that heap of yours all that way," Chris said. "I'm at my cabin. Stop here on your way and switch the Caprice for my cab. It could use the exercise." The long trips to the Portland Jetport were over for the season.

"Thank you." How I loved that man.

Chapter 23

I stopped at the Kennebunk rest stop on 95 to stretch my legs, use the facilities, and get coffee. I made another stop for the same purposes at a Dunkin Donuts off Route 290 in Worcester, Massachusetts, and then made my way into Connecticut, following I-395 to I-95 along the shoreline. Chris had a GPS in the cab. Although they were often wildly misleading in parts of Maine, I trusted it to get me to up-market Connecticut.

Despite the GPS, I somehow missed the exit for Guilford off 95 and had to drive to the next one while she scolded me with a huffy "Recalculating."

On the way into town on Route One, I passed Bishop's Orchards Farm Market, which had a giant apple on its sign. I remembered last summer when I'd driven past Wild Blueberry Land in Down East Maine while searching for a fugitive. I wondered fleetingly if all my quests would be marked by giant fruit.

I came into the center of Guilford and drove around the spacious town green, which was surrounded on three sides by churches of different denominations, along with the town hall, colonial houses, and the Guilford Savings Bank. The green was so pretty and peaceful, I had to remind myself I'd come to town to solve a murder. I'd had the whole ride to think about what I planned to do. I had the address for Enid Sparks's apartment, but I didn't go there right away. After all, I knew she wasn't home.

I had the date Madeleine and Howell died, but I wanted to know more about their accident. I drove to the public library. It was a handsome brick Federalist revival building just off the green, with a new wing that looked bigger than the old building. The town of Guilford obviously cared about its library. Inside, a helpful reference librarian confirmed that issues of the local paper weren't online, but they had microfiche. She set me up at a workstation.

I sat down at the machine, nervously scrolling back through issues, looking for an article about Madeleine and Howell's deaths. According to the genealogy site, they'd died on New Year's Day, so I tried the next issue of the weekly *Shoreline Times* dated Thursday, January 3.

I didn't have to look hard.

The Lowes' deaths were front-page news, accompanied by a huge black-and-white photo of a devastated home. Their house had caught fire in the predawn hours of New Year's Day, after an evening spent entertaining friends. A neighbor spotted the flames from his bathroom window. The house had been fully involved by the time the fire department arrived.

I leaned back in the hard library chair, taking this in. I'd assumed by "accident," Caroline meant automobile. I hadn't been prepared for this. I knew something about house fires, having survived one at our place on Morrow Island in the spring. They were terrifying.

The cause of the Lowes' fire was not immediately determined. The paper mentioned that the guests from the previous night were being interviewed as a part of the investigation. There were photos and bios of Madeleine and Howell. He had commuted to Wall Street, where he worked for a well-known brokerage. She had been active in town life, volunteering at the thrift shop at the Unitarian church and a local senior center.

But there was one thing in the article that I kept reading over and over. The Lowes' son, Austin, had been rescued from his bedroom in a separate wing of the house. The five-year-old had been badly burned, but he had survived.

When Caroline Caswell had said the Lowes "died young" and didn't get to raise a family, I'd eliminated the possibility of children. But "young" for someone Caroline's age had a different meaning than it did for me. The Lowes had a son.

I sat at the terminal for a few moments, thinking about the man at the bar, the scar that snaked up his neck and his prosthetic ear. It had to be. Who else could it have been? I should have been elated at finally making the connection, but the tragedy sat heavily in my chest. A young couple dead. A little boy orphaned and scarred for life.

I scrolled through several more issues of the weekly paper, looking for a follow-up story. Perhaps the news that Austin had been discharged from the hospital, or that the fire investigation had been concluded. But as big as the news about the Lowes had been when the fire occurred, the accounts disappeared immediately afterward.

I was tempted to call Lieutenant Binder right away, or at least call Jamie, who now had an undoubtedly related case, but my instincts told me not yet. The more I knew, the more compelling my information would be.

I wondered if files from fire investigations were housed in the police archives and if I could get someone to give me a look.

Before I left the library, I used one of their computers to look up an address for Austin Lowe in Guilford and for the Hoopers, whose car Enid had stolen. Then the nice librarian directed me to the police records office about a mile away.

"Fill out the form, pay your fee," said the middle-aged woman behind the window at the records office.

"Before I do, I want to ask if you'd even have the record I'm looking for."

"When was the accident?"

I got it then. This was the place to get accident reports that were needed to file car insurance claims after a collision. My hopes dimmed. "1974. An investigation into a fatal fire."

Her officiousness melted away. "Ah, honey, that wouldn't be here. Best case, it would be in the state archives in Middletown. But I wouldn't bet on it. That's a long time ago, and all the files were paper back then."

What had I expected?

I must have looked so dispirited that she tried to help. "Do you have the name of the insurance carrier or agent?"

"No. Sorry."

She leaned across the counter. "I don't know if this will help, but there's a retired insurance agent in town, Tom Dudley. He's kind of a pack rat, and back in the time period you're talking about, he insured almost everyone in town. He's kept every file. It's a long shot, but some other people I've sent his way have had good luck."

I punched Tom Dudley's address into the GPS in the cab. As I drove slowly through the historic district near the green, listening to the dulcet tones of the GPS, I noticed many houses had plaques proudly proclaiming they were built in the 1600s, 1700s, or 1800s.

Tom Dudley lived in a Victorian house on a generous lot. I parked on the curbless street and walked up the drive. A screened-in porch ran along the entire side of the house. My heart sank when I saw its jumble of broken furniture and cardboard boxes. The records clerk had described Tom Dudley as a pack rat. If he had the insurance report about the fire, would he be able to find it? As I got closer, I could smell the mildew coming off the boxes. Even if he could find the report, would it be in any condition for me to read it?

When he answered the door, Mr. Dudley was a surprisingly tidy man somewhere in his late seventies or eighties with wisps of white hair and an impressive mustache.

"Can I help you?"

"Hi. I'm Julia Snowden. I'm sorry to turn up like this. The clerk at the police records office sent me over. I'm looking for any information you have on a fatal fire here in Guilford. She said you might be able to help."

"You better come in, then."

We stepped into his front hall. From there, I could see into the living room, dining room, and den. I needn't have worried. The house was as neat as a pin, though every room was lined with old metal filing cabinets.

"Do you have the date of the fire?"

"January 1, 1974."

"Howell and Madeleine Lowe. I've got that right here."

"You remember."

"I do." He looked at the carpet. "A great tragedy. Early that morning, my late wife and I heard the siren go off, calling the volunteers to the fire station.

We wondered what was going on. I'll remember that call from the fire chief to my dying day." He went to a file cabinet in what should have been the living room and opened a drawer. He pulled out a sheaf of white paper held together by a brad. "You're welcome to sit while you read it." He gestured to a leather chair. "Can I get you something to drink?"

"No, thanks, but I will sit."

The insurance report was four tightly spaced pages, obviously typed on a typewriter. The first part was a form with all the pertinent information, address, owner names (Howell and Madeleine Lowe), age of dwelling (1700s), type of construction (wood frame). No wonder the place had gone up like a tinderbox. The report stated that two victims had succumbed to smoke inhalation and were deceased when the fire department found them. One juvenile was rescued and had been transported to Yale New Haven Hospital and later transferred to the newly opened Connecticut Burn Center at Bridgeport Hospital.

The rest of the report was a straightforward recitation in prose. The fire had begun in a couch, almost certainly from an improperly disposed cigarette. There were no signs of accelerant, though once the couch was burning, the fire had spread rapidly due to the presence of a dried Christmas tree standing in a nearby corner.

There had been a New Year's Eve celebration at the house that night. The report listed the participants. Attending, in addition to the victims, were Enid Sparks,

the female decedent's sister; Deborah and Phillip
Bennett; Henry and Caroline Caswell; Michael Smith;
Sheila Bennett; Barry Walker; and Fran Chapman.
The evening had involved much celebrating and
many cocktails. Everyone except Enid Sparks was a
smoker. All of those present had sat on the couch at
one time or another. Toward the end of the evening,
the couch had been mostly occupied by the women.

I sat back in Tom Dudley's leather chair. The
weight of the tragedy astonished me. The Lowes
were dead, their son grievously injured, and all of
the childhood friends had been in the house that
evening. Had they all spent the last forty-plus years
wondering who left the cigarette? Did they know, or
suspect, who had done it? No wonder they didn't
want to see each other again. They hadn't drifted
apart, separated by geography, as so many of them
had assured me. The Rabble Point set had exploded
on that cold January morning.

The rest of the report consisted of interviews
with all the surviving party guests. No one remembered losing a lit cigarette. Barry Walker confessed
that not only did he not remember losing a cigarette, he didn't remember much of the evening at
all. It was hard for me to imagine that all these ine-
briated people got into their cars and drove home,
though apparently they had. But then, it was hard
for me to imagine a party at which almost everyone
was smoking, and smoking inside the house. A lot
had changed in forty years.

The last interview listed was with Fran—a telephone interview because she had returned to Maine.

Unlike the others, she said she'd had one glass of wine and was able to give a sober account of the evening. She reported everyone's movements in detail. The party had begun with cocktails in the living room. Five-year-old Austin had been there to greet them and then had been put to bed. The adults moved to the dining room for dinner. The celebrants returned to the living room to ring in the New Year. Fran reinforced what everyone else had reported. At one time or another, each one of them had sat on that couch, including Madeleine and Howell. At the end of the evening, the people on the couch had been Caroline Caswell, Sheila Bennett, and Fran herself. I had to admire Fran's straightforwardness with the investigator.

There had been no sign of anything amiss when the guests departed, the report concluded. Howell and Madeleine had evidently gone straight to bed without doing much cleanup. The idea of them leaving the party dishes for the morning, a morning that never came, brought a tightness to my chest and tears to my eyes.

I cleared my throat. "Can I take this to the library and make a copy?" I asked.

"I never let these documents out of my sight," Mr. Dudley responded, as if it were a perfectly reasonable thing to safeguard decades-old insurance reports. "But I can make a copy for you right here."

I handed the report to him, and he disappeared through a swinging door. I heard a copier rev up and then *chunk-chunk-chunk* through the pages.

Tom Dudley was back in a jiff with a neatly stapled copy, which he inserted in a new manila envelope.

"Are you working with the other man?" he asked.

"What other man?" Had the cops already been there?

"A man came here about six months ago asking for the same report. I gave him a copy."

"Was he in his forties, long dark hair, scar on his lower face?"

"That was him. I assumed he was the son. He said he wanted to find out who had left the cigarette. I told him he'd never be able to do it. Couldn't do it back then. Can't do it now. Besides, what good would it do?"

So Austin Lowe had been looking for information about his parents' deaths. That had to figure into his murder somehow. I offered to pay for my copy, but Mr. Dudley waved me away. "This house contains thousands of stories, thousands of people's lives, often the saddest, most difficult parts. I can't bring myself to get rid of these files. I'm always glad when someone can use them."

Chapter 24

Enid Lowe's townhouse was ten miles in the opposite direction, so I decided to visit the other addresses first. According to my phone, the Lowes' burned property was the one nearest Tom Dudley's house. I put the address in the GPS and rode by. The house, near Mill Pond, had been torn down and replaced by a large, bland colonial. Staring at the newer house from inside the cab, comparing it to my memory of the photo in the paper, I couldn't even figure out exactly how the Lowes' antique home had fit on the lot. The scene of the fire told me nothing.

Not far from the address where the Lowes' home had stood was the Hoopers' house, where Enid Sparks had stolen the car. That was one of the craziest parts of this crazy story. Enid was a woman in her sixties, a registered nurse, a respectable person by all accounts. She had worked at the Hoopers' house so many years before, they hadn't remembered she had a key until Jamie had sent them her description. Why would she go to a relative stranger's house, steal their car, and drive nearly five hours to Busman's Harbor? Surely not to redeem a gift certificate.

The Hoopers' house was big and solid. Based on lot size alone, I would have called it an estate. Three bays of an attached garage faced a hard-topped driveway that wound to the street. The yard was carefully laid out. Someone, not the Hoopers I was sure, had put burlap hoods over the smaller bushes to protect them from the rapidly approaching winter. The house was obviously empty, its occupants gone. I drove on.

The next house by distance was Austin Lowe's. I assumed it was a house, because when I'd looked up the address at the library, it contained no identifying information beyond the street number—no apartment number or letter, no "R" to indicate it was a guesthouse or garage. My brief check on the web at the library held no indication of a wife or kids, but bachelors did live alone in houses in the suburbs. It wasn't impossible.

My route took me to a neighborhood on Long Island Sound called Sachem's Head. My plan was to drive by and get a sense of Austin Lowe's life, and if I got lucky, to find an answer the question of whether he was missing. Mail piling up in the box, that sort of thing.

But when I turned the corner, five police vehicles—two Connecticut state police cars, a Connecticut state evidence van, a Maine state police car I recognized instantly, and a Busman's Harbor cruiser—were parked on the lane, which dead-ended at the water just beyond.

As I stared at the house, the front door opened and Jamie stepped out onto the porch. When he spotted me in the cab, his mouth fell open. Mine did the same. What were they doing here? Even more baffling, how did they get here so quickly? I'd talked to Jamie in Gus's parking lot less than half an hour before I left Busman's Harbor.

He shouted something back into the house. As I started up the long path from the street, Binder and Flynn stepped through the open door.

"How did you end up here?" I asked when I reached the porch.

"You first," Flynn commanded.

"I realized all the couples in the restaurant the night of the murder had a connection to Connecticut," I explained. "I came to find out how the Lowes died. I had no idea they had a son until I read the local paper's report on the fire. I decided to check Austin Lowe out to see if he could be the body in the walk-in." I didn't want to say that Jamie had told me Enid Sparks's name. Perhaps he wasn't supposed to. "Your turn," I said to Binder.

"So you know about the fire." Binder paused, then apparently decided to go ahead and tell me what I pretty much already knew. "We found out the drowning victim was a woman named Enid Sparks. She had a nephew, and when Officer Dawes asked the local cops to do the death notification, they came over and found the mailbox overflowing. They reported to us, and we put two and two together."

"See," I said. "I've been right all along. Enid Sparks was the sister of Madeleine Lowe. The diners in the restaurant that night are all connected. And one of them was the killer."

Binder waited for me to take a breath, his mouth slightly upturned, a look of amusement in his eyes. That amusement annoyed me before he even spoke. "You're right. They are all connected, but none of them is our perpetrator."

By that point, I'd had it. "How many times do I have to be right before you give me a little credit? I've been more right about this case than you guys from day one."

Binder stared at Flynn, who looked away in disgust. Then Binder stepped aside so I could enter. "I think you better come inside."

"Don't touch anything," Flynn ordered.

We walked through a well-appointed living room and past a gleaming modern kitchen. "What did this guy do for a living?" I asked.

"Nothing," Flynn answered. "That's one of the reasons no one reported him missing. We figure he inherited a ton of money. Won't be certain until we can follow the paperwork trail on Monday."

That made sense. Deborah had said Howell Lowe's father was so rich he didn't need to work. We went down a long hall toward what I could only guess was a home office or den. The three of them stepped aside so I could be first into the room.

"Oh, my God." An entire wall of the room was

covered with photos and documents. I stepped closer. At the center of the wall was a copy of the photo I'd found at the yacht club. "This is it! This is the photo I've been telling you about. See, everyone who was at the restaurant was there!" In my excitement, I jabbed a finger at the photocopy.

"Don't touch," Flynn hissed.

Next to the photo was the picture of the burned-out home that had been on the front page of the *Shoreline Times*. Radiating out from it were photos of each member of the Rabble Point set as they looked today. I recognized that Barry's was clipped from his store website and Phil's from his company's annual report. Deborah's was from the story in our local paper about the house and garden tour last summer. Sheila's was her official portrait as a judge, and so on. On the far right of the wall was a map with each couple's former home marked on it, as well as their addresses in Busman's Harbor and the year they moved. Below the map was my missing gift certificate and a copy of the insurance report like the one I'd collected from Tom Dudley. Linking all of the photos, documents, and maps were handwritten arrows drawn directly on the wall along with a a scrawl of handwriting every bit as illegible as Austin Lowe's signature in the Snuggles Inn guest book.

"This proves it!" I said. "One of the people in the restaurant that night is the killer. The person who left the lit cigarette in the Lowes' couch is afraid of

being exposed. They're covering up their guilt.
Why don't you see that?"

Binder snorted in exasperation, losing patience
with me. "We found something else. Not here, but at
Enid Sparks's home." Binder gave me a letter, handwritten on lined paper, already in an evidence bag.
Through the plastic, I read:

To Whom It May Concern

*I let myself into my nephew's home after
receiving a cryptic and alarming phone message
from him about his intentions.*

*Austin was gravely injured in a fire that killed
his parents. As a young boy, he spent many
painful months in the hospital, followed by years of
therapies and surgeries designed to prevent scar
tissue from hampering his flexibility as he grew.*

*Perhaps all that has happened is my fault.
I never told Austin that one of the guests at his
parents' New Year's Eve party had probably started
the fire. I never saw what good it would do to
assign blame. But a year ago, somebody in town,
innocently I'm sure, repeated the story that has
always gone around. One of us that night left a lit
cigarette smoldering in the couch cushions.*

*I've never known if the story was true, and even
if it were true, how would we ever know who did
it? It was supposed to be one of the happiest nights
of my life. Barry Walker and I announced our
engagement. There were many toasts and
congratulations. After Dan's death and Phil and*

*Sheila's divorce, we were all joyous to have
something to celebrate.*

*But after the fire, we could never look at each
other again. The loss of Madeleine and Howell
was the final death knell for our childhood
friendship. I devoted myself completely to Austin's
care. I had to grow up quickly. I went to nursing
school in part so I'd have the money to raise him
until his trust fund became available when he was
twenty-one, and in part because I thought it would
help me care for such a profoundly injured child.
Barry saw I had no time for him, no thought for
him, no love left over to give him. Eventually he
moved away, and I settled in to raise Austin.*

*After Austin found out how the fire started,
he became obsessed with figuring out who had left
the cigarette. I thought his interest was unhealthy,
but not dangerous. Then six months or so ago,
he started saying things like, "Wait 'til I get my
hands on the person who . . ." I fault myself. I was
in denial. I couldn't believe the dear, sweet boy I
had raised had turned into a vengeful monster.*

*But then I went into his study and saw what he
had up on the wall. I believe he thinks he knows
who left the cigarette. He has gathered them all at
a restaurant not far from our sunniest days at
Rabble Point.*

*I am going to stop him. I don't have a car, but
I'm going to borrow one, drive to that restaurant,
and prevent him from killing one of my childhood
friends, whatever it takes. I cannot bear to think of*

*my dear, sweet boy spending his life in prison. I
cannot bear to think of him taking a life. I'll do
whatever I have to do to stop him.*

*If you're reading this, it is because my plan has
gone terribly wrong. You're in my home because I
have not returned. All I can say is, I am sorry,
and I pray no one else has been hurt.*

Enid Sparks

"There you have it," Binder said when I'd finished.

"It's so terribly sad." I was still processing what I'd read.

"That it is. We have to get the handwriting verified and prove she had the insulin. She was a nurse, so it's more than likely. We'll do the work, but we've solved both our murder and Officer Dawes's Jane Doe case."

"She killed him and then, out of remorse, jumped off the town pier," Flynn added, in case I wasn't keeping up.

My thoughts were slowly coming into focus. "But even if she killed him with the insulin, who gave him the Valium? That had to have been in his soup or his drink, and I never saw her come into the restaurant."

"It was a busy night. You're the chief waiter, barmaid, and bottle washer there. Perhaps she lingered outside and slipped in when he was in the restroom. She wouldn't have wanted to arouse his suspicion," Binder answered.

"She didn't come in," I insisted. It hadn't been a busy night. "I would have seen her. Or Chris would have. Also, you can't see into the restaurant from the street, so how could she 'linger'? It doesn't make sense." Another thought occurred to me. "If she's been dead since the night of the murder, who's been breaking into my apartment and stealing evidence? Who stole the photograph from the yacht club?"

Binder lowered his head, and then raised it, looking me directly the eye. "I don't discount that maybe something else is going on, but we've found our killer. Rest assured, we'll work with Officer Dawes to clear up the rest of these incidents when we get back to Busman's Harbor. Now it's time for you to go home."

Chapter 25

I was dismissed. I handed Binder the evidence bag with the letter in it and turned to go. I lingered, briefly, on Austin Lowe's porch, looking off across his rolling lawn.

"I believe you."

"What?"

Jamie had come up behind me. "I believe someone has been in your apartment. You're not a careless person, Julia. You don't mislay things. You certainly didn't lose the original photo from the yacht club. I'm going to be stuck here another day, but as soon as I get home, I'll get right to work on your break-ins."

I clasped his forearm through his uniform jacket and gave a quick squeeze. Of all the cops he knew me best, and he believed me.

"Can you tell from the collage on the wall who left the cigarette?" I asked.

He shook his head.

"Can you at least tell who Austin Lowe thought it was?"

"It looks like gibberish to us."

I walked down the winding front path, got into the driver's seat, and sat for a few moments, collecting myself. Then I turned the key in the ignition and put the old cab in drive. As I pulled away, Jamie still stood in the doorway.

I made good time in Connecticut. The GPS took me back a different way than it had brought me, I-91 to I-84, and I was too tired, sad, and worn down to argue with her. The route would keep me well west of Boston, but I was bound to run into somebody's rush hour somewhere. Before I left Connecticut, I stopped at Rein's Deli on 84. There was no way I was going to make to back Gus's Too in time for dinner service. I called Chris as soon as I pulled into the parking lot.

"Did you solve it?" he asked.

"Well, somebody solved it," I said.

"You don't sound too sure."

"Long story. I'll fill you in when I get there. Are you okay for tonight?"

"Fine, fine. Livvie came in to help me set up, and Sam will be here with me tonight. Take your time. Be sure to take breaks. You've put in a long day and you've got a lot of driving left to do."

"Aye, aye."

It was late afternoon and already dark, distinctly off hours even for Rein's, so I managed to avoid its long lines. I ordered a Reuben, and the first delicious bite transported me back to my New York City life. You can't find a Reuben in Maine. You might find something on a menu called a Reuben, but it will not be the same.

I went to the washroom, then got in the cab and pointed it north and east toward home. If you'd asked me a year ago if I would ever call Busman's Harbor home again, I would have said no, emphatically. But at that moment, I couldn't think of a single other place I wanted to be.

I got off the highway in Worcester and made my way back to the Dunkin Donuts where I'd stopped on the way down. I noticed several people waving at me frantically and wondered what could be up, until I remembered I was driving a cab.

I obsessed about the case as I drove. The murderer and the accident victim, all tied up with a bow. The solution was too neat, and at the same time it left too many loose ends. I was sure, from his supportive words on Austin Lowe's porch, Jamie agreed with me. But he was a local cop, and a junior one at that. I had no assurance they'd listen to him. I didn't even know if he'd speak up.

Enid Sparks had written that she'd do "whatever it took" to stop her nephew, but she hadn't said outright she planned to kill him. And yes, as a nurse, she probably had access to insulin, but so did several of the others. Henry Caswell was a doctor. Fran Walker worked at a convalescent home. Phil Bennett was a former pharmaceutical executive, though that

seemed farther fetched. It's not like they'd have free
samples sitting out in the employee lounge.

Which one had the strongest motive? If they had
been working, Phil Bennett the executive, Henry
the doctor, Michael the attorney and Sheila the federal judge would have had the most to lose. But
now that they were retired, the revelation that one
of them negligently caused two deaths forty years
earlier would be hurtful and humiliating but
wouldn't have the same consequences as it would
have had they public reputations to protect.

I was certain, though, that the living members of
the Rabble Point set were involved and one of them
was a murderer. I had been right from the beginning. The state cops had ignored me again and
again, but I was still right.

The green sign on the Piscataqua Bridge that
said STATE LINE-MAINE-VACATIONLAND was the symbol
for every traveling Mainer that they were home. I
was edgy and due for a break, but I pressed on to
the Kennebunk rest stop.

I got back to the restaurant when dinner service
was all but over. A few couples finished their dessert
as Chris cleaned the grill and Sam shut down
the bar. There was a mound of dishes by the dishwasher. No way had they been able to keep up.

I gave Chris a quick hug and ran upstairs. I washed
my hands and face, then went down and started on
the dishes. Later, after Sam went home, Chris and I
lingered over beers at one of the restaurant tables
and I outlined the events of the day. He was shocked

by the story of the fire, Austin Lowe's plot, and Enid
Sparks's desperate act.

He walked the garbage out to the Dumpster
and locked the kitchen door when he returned.
"Considering this case is all wound up, you don't
seem very happy," he said.

"I'm not. If Enid's been dead since the night it
happened, who's been breaking in here? And
her note didn't exactly say she planned to kill her
nephew, just that she would do whatever it took to
stop him."

Chris gave me a hug. "You'll figure it out."

He had more confidence in me than I did.

It had been a long, tiring day, filled with discoveries,
emotion, and a nearly six-hundred-mile round-trip
drive. I should have fallen asleep instantly, but I
didn't. My mind moved relentlessly, turning every
piece of the investigation over and over.

In the past six weeks, I'd gotten used to the
nighttime sounds of the old warehouse—beams
contracting as the weather grew colder, the rattle of
ill-fitting windows, the whir of the ancient apartment refrigerator as it turned on. But that night, I
startled at every sound, heart racing, blood pounding in my ears.

Chris had no such problems. I heard his rhythmic
breathing beside me. He, too, had had a challenging day, in no small measure due to my absence.

Le Roi, sensing a restless soul, jumped onto the

bed and settled at my side, distracting me from the old warehouse's sounds with his purring. I fell into a deep, dreamless sleep.

I awoke instantly, not normal for me, without knowing why. My brain registered that it was pitch dark. Then I heard it. The creak of the door at the bottom of the stairs, followed by one quiet footfall on the first tread. The thief was back! My mind cataloged the available tools to defend myself. I wished for a brief second that, like my father, I slept with a baseball bat under my bed. He had never used it all the years I knew him, but it was there.

The best weapon I could think of was the fire extinguisher in the apartment kitchen, which was all the way across the studio from the bed. Getting there would take me behind the stairwell, which was important. I had no desire to pass in front of the stairs and run smack into the intruder. I slid out of bed and crept across the room. The footsteps kept coming.

I grabbed the fire extinguisher, ran to the top of the stairs, and lifted it over my head, determined to do some damage.

"Julia!" The room lit up and Chris stood at the top of the stairs, hand on the light switch. "It's me."

I was panting from the fear and the adrenaline. "I thought it was the murderer."

"No kidding." Chris dropped his hand to his side. "Did it maybe occur to you to check the bed next to you? To see if I was there, or to wake me up so I could help you, or maybe even defend myself?"

I stared, shame-faced, at my bare feet. "I am so sorry. I'm a little on edge."

He took the fire extinguisher from me and walked it back to the kitchen. "Gus and I boarded up the trapdoor this afternoon. We're not idiots, you know."

"Why were you downstairs anyway?" I wasn't taking the blame for almost clobbering him all by myself.

"I woke up and couldn't get back to sleep. I figured rather than wake you, I'd go down to the restaurant, eat a sandwich, watch a little TV."

I had slept through all of this. "Why couldn't you sleep?"

"Same reason you almost killed me. It doesn't make sense that this Enid woman drowned and then kept breaking into our home. Unless she's haunting us."

"So you agree with me."

"Of course I agree with you." He kissed the top of my head. "I always agree with you."

"Liar."

He laughed.

"I'm glad you boarded up the trapdoor."

"Me too. But I'm not sure it matters. You haven't been all over town today asking people about gift certificates or showing them copies of an old photo. Why would the intruder break in tonight? No bait."

No bait. But I did have bait—the insurance report. Since Binder, Flynn, and Jamie weren't back in

Busman's Harbor, no one in town knew about the discovery of Austin Lowe's study wall and Enid Sparks's letter. I could use that to my advantage.

Chris turned out the light, and we climbed into bed. I fell asleep as soon as my head hit the pillow.

Chapter 26

"We never saw each other again after that night," Caroline Caswell said. I was seated again at the round glass table, watching the birds at the feeder on the deck. "We knew one of us had left that cigarette smoldering in the couch. We didn't know who had done it. Every one of us, except Enid, smoked back then. We all feared we'd been the one. We could never look each other in the eye again."

She put her elbows on the table and leaned toward me. Henry, seated next to her, silently put an arm around her petite shoulders. "The New Year's Eve party was meant as a reunion of sorts. Right after we posed for that photo at the yacht club dance, we began to grow apart. The world felt like it was spinning faster on its axis, pulling us in different directions.

"Henry dropped out of college and joined the navy. Days after their college graduations, Phil and Sheila married. Phil went to business school and joined the family drug company. Three years later, he left Sheila for Deborah. That was the first explosion.

"Michael went to law school to please his parents, but you could tell his heart wasn't in it. His politics became more radical. He went on and on about the rights of the oppressed. Barry attended art school as an undergrad. After college, he drifted. His hair grew down to his waist and his beard was enormous."

I imagined the Barry Walker I knew, with the Bozo-inspired coif, with a beard and hair down to his waist. It was easy to picture.

"Madeleine arranged the New Year's Eve party," Caroline continued. "She thought enough time had gone by for Sheila to be over the divorce, and persuaded her to come. It was meant to be a peace-making, a healing moment for all of us. Barry and Enid announced their engagement at dinner. We toasted them and cheered. Madeleine was the perfect hostess. She smiled and laughed all evening. It made her so happy we were all together. I was happy too." Caroline's voice thickened. "My beautiful friend.

"That night must have been so difficult for Sheila. She and Phil had been together as a summer couple, well, always. We were all friends, but I can't remember a time, even when we were quite young, when it wasn't understood that Phil and Sheila's relationship was special." She paused, considering how to go on. "I think once Phil became a rising star in business, he needed a more glamorous wife. Deborah was always the most beautiful of us. Dan had been dead for three years by then, and she was in Manhattan. Sheila had no idea, but Phil found Deborah and wooed her. He left Sheila and married Deborah the day his divorce was final."

"And then Sheila married Michael?"

"Yes, stole him right out from under Fran. Sheila started working on Michael at the New Year's Eve party. She got stumbling drunk, elbowed Fran out of the way, and kissed him, open-mouthed, on the lips on the stroke of midnight." Caroline stopped talking and looked at me, as if she was still shocked by Sheila's behavior. "I knew Sheila and Michael had married," she continued. "She sent me a wedding invitation, but Henry was deployed, and I didn't have the heart, or the nerve, to go alone. I wasn't ready to see any of those people again. Later, she wrote me that none of us had come."

"You told me the first time I came that you stopped sending Christmas cards to Sheila because her life was so sad, but it sounds to me more like Sheila got what she wanted and Fran was left out."

"You might think so," Henry answered for Caroline. "But Michael wasn't his father. He was never going to work in his dad's Wall Street law firm. Michael became a public defender. According to Sheila's letters, they lived in a roach-infested cold-water flat in the East Village."

"But mostly," Caroline took up the tale, "Sheila was brokenhearted because she couldn't have children. Henry and I had three daughters in six years. I couldn't stand to rub her face in our happiness any longer. I stopped the correspondence, and our last tie to the Rabble Point set was gone."

"As for Fran," Henry finished, "we never saw her after that New Year's Eve. Sheila reported she was living at a commune on a farm outside Belfast, Maine. I couldn't have been more surprised when she walked through the door of your restaurant with Barry Walker."

"I went out to Rabble Point," I told them.

"Sad, isn't it? After Mr. Lowe bulldozed the cottages, any hope that we would ever get over the trauma of Howell and Madeleine's deaths and be friends again disappeared along with Rabble Point," Caroline said. "It was like being cast out of Eden. I always believed that if those of us who were left had kept going to Rabble Point in the summer, if our children had grown up together, we would still be friends today." She sighed, lost in the what-ifs. "I have no idea who owns the land now."

"I know," I said. "The Bennetts own it. They live in the Lowes' old house. They've renovated it extensively. Even moved the front door so it faces Eastclaw Point Road, instead of Rabble Point, but it's the same house."

"Isn't that something?" Caroline's eyes were wide. "I've longed for Rabble Point ever since my last summer day there. Henry left the navy to finish college and go to medical school. He thought that was what he wanted, and I pictured myself as a physician's wife, settled in some suburban town. But he missed the navy terribly, and after med school he reenlisted and stayed in for twenty years until he went to Johns Hopkins Hospital." She took a deep breath, fighting off tears. Henry patted her shoulder and she continued.

"During the navy years, I got quite good at setting up our house and making new friends. But I never got over longing for Rabble Point, and for the friends who knew me when I was young and unformed, and anything was possible." Tears cascaded down her cheeks, tracing rivulets through powder. "I miss my old home. I miss my friends. I have never again felt as surrounded by people who cared about me. I have never felt as *known*."

Henry gave her his handkerchief. His pain at seeing her pain was obvious in his eyes.

"Your friends are here," I said. "You can call them. Visit them." I thought of Sheila Smith, so obviously in need of friends, and Deborah Bennett, living her isolated life out on the point.

Caroline shook her head. "I can't. Ever since that New Year's Eve . . . I just can't." She dabbed at her eyes with Henry's white hanky.

I wanted to go. I felt terrible that I stirred up so many deeply unhappy memories for Caroline, but I had to bait the hook. "While I was in Guilford, I met with the Lowes' insurance agent," I said. "He gave me the insurance company's report on the fire."

"Does it come to any conclusion?" Henry asked. He didn't seem rattled or fearful.

"I don't know," I lied. "I haven't looked. The agent gave me his original in a sealed manila envelope. I don't want to disturb it. It's evidence. I'm handing it over to Lieutenant Binder tomorrow when he's expected back in town."

Caroline looked at me. "I want to know what it says, but I'm afraid to know."

"The police will know what's in it soon enough," I said.

I said my good-byes, and Henry saw me out. "What does the report say?" he asked as we stood on the front stoop.

"Honestly, I don't know." People always say "honestly" when they are being anything but, and I was no exception.

Henry's bright blue eyes held mine. "Caroline thinks of Rabble Point as home. That's why I brought her back here. Through all the years of moving and deployments, all I ever thought about was her. Wherever she and the girls were, that was home. I was an angry, sullen young man. Caroline, with her common sense and her generous heart, turned me into a better human being. Everything I have in my life, I have because of her. I would do anything in my power to make her happy. Anything."

I wondered as I walked toward the Caprice: *Anything?*

I saw Fran's car parked at the curbside when I pulled up at Walker's Art Supplies and Frame Shop. I hoped that meant both Fran and Barry were in the store.

The little bell tinkled as I walked in. Barry was at work on a painting in the far corner of the store.

Fran was behind the cash register. She looked up as soon as I entered, while Barry continued to work. I cleared my throat loudly. When he didn't turn around, I shouted, "Barry!" just a little too loud.

"What? What? Julia, you scared me."

"I'd like to speak with you both."

Fran stepped quickly from behind the counter. "Certainly, dear. What's the matter?"

I walked to the high framing table and waited for Barry to join us. He reluctantly scraped the knife he was using to apply the thick paint on his palate, then put it down.

"I went to Guilford, Connecticut, yesterday," I said. Better to get straight to it. Both of them looked at me expectantly, like they knew that couldn't be all my news. "I know about the fire."

Barry stepped closer to Fran, though he didn't touch her. "That was such a tragic part of our lives," he said. "We try not to dwell on it."

Fran shook her head in agreement. "Not a happy time."

"No," I said. "I'm sure it was very stressful. Even more stressful for you, Fran, because you were pregnant when it happened. Quinn is Michael Smith's daughter."

Fran sat heavily on a stool. "How did you guess?"

"It took a long time," I admitted. "Something bugged me about that yacht club photo. It wasn't until I saw Quinn here in the store on Wednesday that I saw the resemblance and the pieces fell into place."

"If you'd known Michael when he was younger, you'd see it even more clearly," Barry said.

"Does Michael know about Quinn?" I asked.

Fran shook her head. "I was living in Maine. Michael was in Connecticut. We'd been drifting apart for a while, but our bond had been so strong, and our relationship gone on for so long, neither of us had the strength to break it. Or so I thought." She paused, gathering herself. "I planned to tell him I was pregnant that New Year's weekend. Instead, I watched him spend the evening flirting with a drunken Sheila. As we drove back from Madeleine and Howell's house to his apartment in New Haven, Michael told me it was over. I was so upset, I made him take me straight to the train station. I was on the first train to Boston at four that morning. I didn't hear about the fire until Michael called me the next day."

"Yet you still didn't tell him about the pregnancy."

"No. His parents had never accepted me, the cleaner's daughter, in all the years we'd been to-gether. I'd always feared he'd cave in to their pres-sure and settle with someone more appropriate. Sheila was back in his life and available. I could imagine what his parents were going to say when they found out I was expecting. Poor girl traps rich guy by getting knocked up. Why would I put myself in that situation?

"I couldn't stay here in town, either. My mother had been expecting disaster the whole time I was with Michael. She predicted—well, exactly what hap-pened is what she predicted. That he would marry a college-educated girl who knew what fork to use at a dinner party and I would end up alone and pregnant. So I did what any other self-respecting person did at the time. I joined a commune."

Fran smiled, and the mood in the room lightened. "What idiots we were. We were going back to the land—in a place with more rocks than soil in the ground and the shortest growing season ever. Still, it was a good place for Quinnie to spend her early years. Lots of fresh air and a house full of caring adults and children to play with. It took the sting out of being the only child of a single mother."

"But, how did Barry . . . ?"

"Barry showed up three years later. He'd called my mother to find out where I was. He was a natural for the commune. He moved in on his first visit. When the commune finally went belly-up, we were among the last to leave."

"Enid and I had announced our engagement at the New Year's Eve party," Barry said, unaware I already knew. "But after everything that happened, it was clear she was going to devote her life to that little boy. On top of everything else, she was broke. Austin's grandfather had left everything in trust until he turned twenty-one. Old Mr. Lowe never anticipated the kid's parents would die so young, and then he died himself before he changed his will. I tried to stick with Enid, to support her, but I didn't have two nickels to rub together, and fewer prospects. She finally told me she needed to focus only on Austin. I was heartbroken, but I understood.

"After we broke up, eventually, I wondered why I

was hanging around in Connecticut. My heart was in Maine. When I arrived in town, I called Fran's mother. I expected to hear that Fran and Michael were married. Instead I got an earful about boys From Away who use local girls then shirk their responsibilities. But she did relent and tell me how to find Fran. From ten minutes after I walked into that drafty, rickety commune farmhouse, I wondered why I hadn't been with Fran all along. And Quinn . . .''

Fran put her hand over mine. "Those days after the fire were the darkest of my life. I was alone, traumatized, broke, pregnant, and cut off from my friends. But now, when I look back on it, everything turned out the way it should have. Michael was an immature man, dominated by his parents and rebelling in unproductive ways. I couldn't see it then, but I see it clearly now. He used to complain to me about how hard his life was. His life! With his prep school and his Ivy League education. The crazy part is, I fell for it. I was head over heels for him." She released my hand and turned both of hers hands palm up, as if willing me to believe. "Barry is ten times the man Michael Smith could ever be. Ten times the father. Ten times the husband to me."

"Aw, luv." Barry kissed the top of her head, pulling more strands of hair out of her bun. I doubted he heard sentiments like that very often from his acerbic, Mainer-to-the-bone wife.

"Does Quinn know?" I asked.

"She knows Barry isn't her biological father. She

could handle it if we told her. But Michael . . ." Fran
shivered. "I don't fear Michael. I fear the wrath of
Sheila."

"Which is what makes it so scary that someone
else knows. Right, Barry?" I asked.

Barry studied a crack in the table, tracing it with
his finger.

"Tell her," Fran said. "She's already guessed."

"When Phil came into the store that first time,
Quinn was here. He recognized her resemblance to
Michael instantly. He's a portraitist, after all." Barry
sighed at the inevitability of this collision. "The
second time, when Phil and I went to lunch together,
he asked me flat out if Michael knew. I said neither
Fran nor I had heard from Michael in decades."

"I had heard some people named Smith bought
the Fogged Inn," Fran added. "But it's such a common
name. I didn't think anything of it."

"Phil felt strongly that Michael should know,"
Barry continued. "That's when he told me that
Michael had married Sheila and they were here in
the harbor. They'd been unable to have children.
Phil swore he hadn't seen Michael in years, but he
seemed to know an awful lot about how Michael
and Sheila's lives had gone. It struck me as curious
at the time. As if he'd been keeping tabs on them
all these years."

"Since that day, that lunch, Barry and I have
been worried that Phil would go to Michael. I've
lost so many nights' sleep, I can't tell you," Fran
said. "But if Phil did tell him, Michael's given no

indication. Sheila doesn't know. I'm certain of that. She never could have hidden it that night in your restaurant. I almost died when she and Michael walked in right behind us. But after that man was murdered, my worries seemed petty."

"Do either of you have any idea who started the fire at the Lowes'?" I asked.

Fran looked at the floor. "No one knows," she said. "But all these years, I've feared it was me."

"Why you?"

"I sat on that sofa most of the evening. They weren't nearly so strict about smoking during pregnancy then. I'd cut way back on the drinking. I think I only had a glass of wine at dinner and sipped a little champagne for the toast. But I was so livid at Michael and Sheila, I was smoking furiously all evening, especially as it got later and their shenanigans escalated."

Barry got up from his stool and put his arm around Fran. "Oh, girl, I've told you so many times, you can't worry about that. No one knows who it was."

"So everyone fears," Fran said. "And everyone feels guilty. I've thought of that poor, injured little boy so often."

It was my turn to look down at the tabletop. I couldn't bear to tell them that Austin Lowe's body had gone from the walk-in at Gus's to a refrigerated box at the medical examiner's office. Unless, one of them, or both of them, already knew that. I put out the bait. "When I was in Connecticut yesterday, I met with the Lowes' insurance agent. He gave me his copy of the insurance examiner's report. He told me it does draw a conclusion about who left the cigarette smoldering in the couch."

Fran looked up sharply. "Who was it?"

"I don't know. I brought it back in a sealed envelope. I'll turn it over to Lieutenant Binder when he's back in town tomorrow. I don't want there to be any question about the integrity of the evidence."

We said our good-byes, though they were both obviously preoccupied with what I'd said. The bell over the door jingled as I let myself out. I still had two stops to make.

Chapter 27

I left the Caprice parked in front of the frame shop and walked the few blocks to the Fogged Inn. I climbed onto the porch and glanced again at the list of "no's." Greeting guests with a long list of prohibited acts made more sense now that I knew Sheila hated being an innkeeper. I pressed the bell.

Footsteps clattered down the staircase, and then Michael Smith opened the front door. "Ms. Snowden. Lieutenant Binder was supposed to speak to you about bothering us at home."

"He did. In fact, he spoke to me in my restaurant right after he met you outside. Why were you hanging around anyway?"

Michael glanced to either side of the porch, as if to make sure no one had observed us. "I think you had better come in."

"Where's Sheila?" I asked.

"Garden Club meeting."

Our local garden club put on a fund-raiser at the Coast Guard station every year where they decorated fifty or so Christmas trees and auctioned them off for charity. As the calendar rolled over into advent, the preparations would be intense. I guessed that just like me, Sheila was trying to find a way to fit into her new community.

Michael didn't ask me to sit or take off my coat, and I didn't really expect him to. We stood face-to-face in the front hall.

"I'm only going to say this once, because I want you out of here before Sheila gets home. Leave us alone. Don't come around here with that photo. Don't ask upsetting questions about friends we left behind more than forty years ago. Just stop."

"I can't come around with the photo because someone stole it from me and stole the one at the yacht club. Any idea why *someone* would do that?"

"If you're accusing me, you're barking up the wrong tree. But in the interests of getting you to leave, I can think of several reasons. The photo is old and upsetting. Three of the people in it are no longer alive. Others were at the dance that night with partners they didn't ultimately end up with. I imagine most of us want to forget that time. I certainly do."

"You're Quinn Walker's father." The effect on Michael was stunning. He recoiled as if the words were a physical slap. "That's why you didn't want me showing that photo around. She's a dead ringer for you when you were younger. Phil Bennett told you about her, didn't he?"

Michael's bluster deflated. He motioned for me to follow him into the kitchen. He gestured me toward a seat at the table. I unzipped my jacket but didn't take it off. I might have to leave quickly.

"Is it so obvious?" he asked.

I considered. "I made the connection because I saw the photo of you when you were twenty-one. I knew Quinn when she was that age."

"So I was right to be worried about you showing that photo to everybody."

"Is that why you stole it?"

He leaned forward on the table, bringing his face closer to mine. "I didn't steal it. But I'm not sorry it's gone."

"Have you told Sheila about Quinn?"

"No, and I don't intend to. Our childlessness has been an enduring wound for her. I don't want to reopen it now. But I have no doubt Fran's daughter is mine. One day I stood outside the window of the art supplies shop and watched her work. You may think she looks like me, but she's really the spitting image of my mother. It makes me sad they never got to meet." He fooled with a saltshaker, turning it over in his hands, scattering white grains on the maple tabletop. "I didn't know Fran was pregnant when we split."

"When you left her for Sheila, you mean."

"Yes. My parents objected to Fran. Vehemently. They always had, but as my law school graduation got closer, they really put the pressure on. When I saw Sheila again the night of Howell and Madeleine's party, she was available and interested. She and I were both in Connecticut. Fran was here in Maine. The long-distance thing was killing us. Once Sheila was back in the picture, my parents found ways to throw us together. Sheila and I took the path of least resistance. She wanted to show Phil she was desirable to someone, even if she no longer was to him. And she wanted to be married. The path for a single woman wasn't nearly so clear in those days. I was tired of fighting my parents. I caved. I didn't fight nearly hard enough for Fran. Or for myself."

"But then something changed."

"The world changed. It felt like overnight. My generation came to the foreground, and my parents and their stifling rules and restrictions faded to the back. I woke up married to a woman I didn't love. I vowed never to let my parents push me into anything again. I never joined my father's law firm. I became a public defender. I was radically transformed by the lives of the people I defended. I'd always known, of course, in the abstract, that many people lacked my advantages. But confronting it head on was an eye-opener. I grew my hair. I made some questionable friends. But more than anything, I believed. I believed in the rightness of what I was doing.

"My parents assumed I'd grow out of it. Sheila did too. Truth be told, she'd gotten nothing of what she signed up for when she married me. She wanted to be the county club wife of a rising associate at a prestigious law firm. Instead we ate soup from a can and macaroni and cheese from a box. She hated it."

"But you stayed together."

"My job wasn't the worst of it. Then came the real

blow. Sheila was diagnosed with type 1 diabetes, late onset. At the time, the popular advice was against having children. So now she had a serious disease that had to be managed and no prospect of children. In the beginning, we stayed together because she was sick. She was afraid, and I didn't want to be the jackhole who left his seriously ill wife."

Type 1 diabetes. So Sheila and Michael Smith presumably had access to insulin. Did Binder and Flynn know this? Probably not. Proof they were closing the investigation too soon. "Then what happened?" I asked Michael.

"Then things changed. I give all of the credit to Sheila. She was the first of the two of us to grow up. She accepted her situation. She had a chronic illness, she was advised not to have children, and she was married to a guy who was never going to make much money. She went to law school, made law review, and joined my father's firm. It wasn't easy for her in that boys' club, but she was ten times the lawyer I would ever be. She became the son my father never had. Seventeen years ago, she was appointed to the federal bench.

"Our marriage started as a disaster. One person on the rebound and the other knuckling under to his domineering parents. But we found a path to happiness."

"Why did you come back to Busman's Harbor?"

"I left the public defender's office when I was in my forties and joined a small law firm. I did criminal defense work for the few people who could pay, and some family law. When my billings could no longer cover the rent for my office, my partners forced me out.

"I'd always dreamed of running a B&B, so when I retired I looked around for one. I found the Fogged Inn and talked Sheila into it. As to why this town—because we'd always loved it. We felt like it was destiny." He paused. "When Phil told me about Fran's daughter, I nearly fell apart. I can't bear to think of what it might do to Sheila." He used a finger to trace a path through the salt on the table-top. "I think we'll leave town soon anyway. Sheila hates the inn."

So he knows that too.

We heard the sound of a car going up the drive. A door slammed, and footsteps came across the deck. The back door opened, and Sheila came into the kitchen, shedding her coat as she did.

"Well, hullo," she said when she saw me.

"Julia dropped by for coffee." Michael told one of the least convincing lies I've ever heard.

"Then maybe you should offer her some?" Sheila seemed more amused than suspicious. "Would you like coffee?" she asked me.

"No. I have to get going. I had a long day yesterday. Drove all the way down to Guilford, Connecticut."

She turned from fussing with the coffeemaker to face me.

"I know how the Lowes died," I said.

Sheila sat down heavily in a kitchen chair. "I can still barely think about it."

"Hon—" Michael started.

She began to cry. "It was me. I left the lit cigarette in the couch. I was so drunk that night. I thought I was prepared to see Phil with Deborah, but I was wrong. Everyone else there was coupled up. Barry and Enid announced their engagement. It was crushing. I made a pass at Michael in front of Fran."

Michael leaned across the table and laced his fingers through hers. "It all turned out okay. We're happy. Fran's happy. She is, isn't she?" he asked me.

Before I could answer, Sheila said, "It didn't turn out okay for Madeleine and Howell, or for their little boy." She took a napkin from the holder and wiped her tears. Then she gestured around the dreary old kitchen. "You call this happy?" She sobbed into the napkin.

Michael looked so discouraged, I almost couldn't go through with it, but I had to. "While I was in Connecticut, I talked to the Lowes' insurance agent and picked up the insurance report on the fire."

"Does it say who left the cigarette?" Sheila's voice quavered.

"I haven't opened it. I'm saving it to give to Lieutenant Binder tomorrow. It's still in the manila envelope, in the tote bag, in my apartment."

They didn't respond to that, so I rose and said my good-byes. Neither of them walked me out. When the kitchen door swung shut behind me, I heard the murmur of their voices as I walked down the hall.

One more visit to make.

* * *

The Bennetts' luxury SUV was parked in front of their massive garage addition. Deborah answered the door.

"Julia. How lovely to see you."

"Is Phil around?"

"In his studio. Do you need to talk to him? You look very serious."

I consciously unfurrowed my brow. "Yes, but I'd like to speak to you first." I needed Deborah's take on some things, and I wasn't sure how many questions Phil would let me ask her.

She stole a glance up the stairs toward the studio. Had Phil heard the Caprice in the driveway, I wondered. Would he come down?

"Phil usually paints with headphones on," Deborah told me. "He listens to classical music. I think we have some time before he realizes someone is here." She led me to the kitchen, and we sat at the island.

"I know Phil was married to Sheila before he married you," I said.

Deborah looked me straight in the eyes. Now that I knew her, I was able to return her gaze without being distracted by her face. "I know what they say about me, said about me back then," she responded. "Phil was on a fast track in his family's business and needed a more glamorous wife, but none of that was true. None of us is all one thing. Phil may have been a genius at corporate life, but he was also an artist in his soul. During the summers at Rabble Point, he used to go off painting with Barry and his father. Barry's dad thought Phil had something really special.

"That side of Phil held no attraction for Sheila. It's ironic that I was viewed as the corporate wife when I had no interest in entertaining or making appearances at functions to support his career. It was Sheila who loved those things. Phil got satisfaction from his job, as one does when one is good at something, but it was so stressful. He needed a home life that nurtured his other side, the artist. That was the part of him I loved. Had always loved, all those summers, though I kept it to myself."

Sheila had gone on to success in her own career. Perhaps her ambitions for Phil masked thwarted desires of her own. "For what it's worth," I said, "Sheila and Michael seem happy. Sheila was a federal judge until she retired last year. She's had a good life, though I think she's feeling isolated and lonely since they moved here, trying to adjust to retirement and find friends in a new town." I paused. "Perhaps you understand some of what she feels."

Deborah's face didn't move, but I thought I saw recognition in her eyes. "I made peace with our situation years ago, but Phil has always felt terrible guilt about what we did to Sheila. He knows they had no chance for happiness. He never should have married her. He knew it was wrong from the start."

"Phil may know how Sheila's doing," I said. "He's seen Michael Smith since they've been in town."

"I've what?" Phil stood in the kitchen doorway,

shirtsleeves rolled to his elbows, paint flecks on his skinny forearms.

"I was telling Deborah that you've visited Michael Smith since you've been in town."

"Phil, why didn't you tell me?" Deborah asked. "I thought we'd agreed to let the past stay in the past."

Phil rolled his shoulders and looked pointedly at me. I wasn't going to say anything about Quinn. Let her parents, real and biological, figure it out. I wondered if Phil would tell Deborah after I left. Now that I had them both in the room, I did what I'd come to do. "I was in Connecticut yesterday. I know about the fire that killed the Lowes."

Deborah's mouth opened in surprise. Phil, the former executive, was better at hiding his reaction.

"When Caroline Caswell told me the Lowes died in an accident, I assumed she meant car accident," I continued. "I wondered for a while, Deborah, if your automobile accident was connected to their deaths."

"It was," she answered. "Though not in the way you're thinking. For years I pretended that terrible night had never happened. I blocked it completely, avoided any place or person that would remind me. But when my boys were little, I don't know. With the stress of the responsibilities of motherhood, being alone with them. Phil was traveling all the time. I started to drink. Heavily."

"You don't have to tell her this," Phil said from across the room. But he didn't go to her.

"My two little boys were in the backseat when I was thrown through the windshield. Child car seats were not as good then as they are now, but they were good enough. Neither boy was seriously hurt." She wiped tears away with the back of her hand. "Julia, I had been drinking. Alone, at home, before I went off to the nursery school to pick them up."

She let that sink in. It wasn't my story, yet I could barely breathe.

"After I got out of the hospital, I went straight to rehab, with my face still a horror. I had to get better, for my boys. And I did, though my younger son had nightmares for years after the accident. Thank God we've all left it behind us." She turned to face me head-on. "So I'm glad for my ruined face. I'm alive. My boys are alive. My new face reminds me every day of the person I had to become. Not looking like I did then has helped me move past all that happened. Excuse me."

Deborah went off in search of a tissue while Phil stared daggers at me. I felt terrible. The events that had rippled out from that single New Year's Eve were staggering. So many lives profoundly changed.

"Now look what you've done," Phil snarled. "I asked you to leave her alone."

Deborah returned from the powder room holding a box of tissues. "It's okay," she said to Phil. "I wanted to tell Julia what happened. Why did you go to Connecticut?" she asked me.

"Because that was where the woman from the accident at Main and Main was from. I've believed for a while that the accident and the body in our walk-in are related."

"And are they? What do they have to do with us?" Deborah asked.

By plan, I'd told none of the other couples what the police had discovered in Connecticut, but none had asked as directly as Deborah Bennett. I hated to inflict more pain, but she had been honest with me at great personal cost. I decided I owed an answer. "The accident victim was Enid Sparks. The murder victim was her nephew, Austin Lowe."

The words were no sooner out of my mouth than Deborah grasped her chest, took a deep breath but didn't exhale, and crumpled onto the hard kitchen floor.

Phil beat me around to the other side of the island. "Dammit, Julia! I begged you not to upset her!" He cradled Deborah's head in his arms as she gasped for breath. "Get her medication from the shelf in the pantry!" He turned his attention back to his wife. "Slow, deep breaths, Deborah. Help is on the way." I returned to Phil with her medication, a Valium prescription, and a glass of water. Since I'd had panic attacks myself, I felt awful for Deborah, and guilty about what I'd done to her. Unless she was an Oscar-worthy actress, she'd had no idea of either Enid or Austin's identity. And, clearly, she hadn't put the past as much in the past as she thought she had.

Phil helped Deborah to her feet, then looked at me. "Go," he ordered.

But I had to fulfill my mission. "Okay," I said, loud enough for both of them to hear, though I doubted I had either's attention. "I have to go anyway. While I was in Connecticut, I visited the Lowes' old insurance agent. He gave me the report from the fire. It's in a manila envelope on the coffee table in a tote bag in my apartment. When Lieutenant Binder gets back into town tomorrow, I'll give it to him."

Phil muttered, "Go away, Julia," but his attention was clearly on his distressed wife. I let myself out the front door.

Chapter 28

I put the Caprice in my mother's garage and fast-walked back to the restaurant. Gus would be winding down for the day. I had just enough time to grab a late lunch and help Chris get set for the evening.

I sat at the end of the counter, the only customer in the place. Gus served me one of his famous grilled cheese sandwiches and I chowed down. I savored the sharp tang of the cheese, the perfect crunch of the bread. It was the taste of my childhood and my current existence. My life had come full circle, the past united with the present.

That couldn't happen for the surviving members of the Rabble Point set. Caroline had been the one to use the words "cast out of Eden," but they all had lived for years in a state of exile. Their lives had been varied and rich. Some had successful professional lives, some loving families, some both. All had been in long-standing marriages that were, to all appearances, loving and supportive. But when they'd had the opportunity, they'd returned to the place where they'd felt they belonged. As Caroline had articulated it, where they'd felt *known*.

One of those people, I was convinced, was willing to kill to keep the past in the past and prevent it from destroying the now. And maybe, I was beginning to believe, not to cover up their own culpability but that of a beloved spouse.

But which one? I'd spread a lot of misery today. I'd forced people to tell me things they didn't want to talk about, remember times they'd tried to forget. I'd made grown-up humans cry. It didn't feel good. I hoped the guilty party would take the bait I had so carefully laid out at a high cost to everyone else.

Chris arrived as I took my last bite of sandwich. Gus finished cleaning and turned the place over. Because the restaurant had been so busy the night before, I set every table in the dining room, cut up extra fruit for behind the bar, washed more lettuce for the salad station. Livvie came by at four and dropped off the evening's desserts—blueberry cheesecake and chocolate mousse. "We're coming for dinner tonight," she said. "And bringing Mom."

I ran up to my apartment and changed. While I was there, I fed Le Roi, who tried to feign indifference but at the last minute couldn't hold out and ran for his bowl. Then I headed back downstairs.

The restaurant was busy again that night. In addition to the couples and foursomes, there were families. For the first time, I seriously considered a children's menu.

Mom, Sonny, Livvie, and Page arrived around seven. Forewarned, I'd kept a big booth in the dining room open for them. Page greeted Chris with her usual enthusiasm, calling from across the counter.

"Hey, squirt," he responded, but didn't have time for much more because we were slammed.

Kendra Carter was there with her husband and their two kids. "I hope we'll see you Tuesday night at the Sit'n'Knit," she said.

"I don't know. I'm such a terrible knitter."

Kendra leaned in close. "It's not about the knitting," she whispered.

Exactly what Livvie had said. Maybe they had a point.

By seven thirty the place was full, and a couple of tables had even turned over. I finally found my way back to the bar, where I attempted to tidy up before I had to rush off again. The restaurant was noisy from the people and their chatter. In the center of it all were the members of my own family. Mom's face was animated, the tiredness of the long shifts at Linens and Pantries washed away. She, Livvie, and Page laughed at some story Sonny told.

I walked across the room to where Chris stood, momentarily caught up with the cooking. I put my arm through his and turned him toward the room full of people enjoying the food and celebrating the weekend. "We did this," I whispered to him. "We did all of this."

"Thanks to Gus," he said.

"Yes, thanks to Gus. And to us. We've worked hard. We need to enjoy it."

"Yes, we do." His lips grazed my cheek.

I spotted a table that needed to be cleared, a dessert order to be taken. Another group signaled for their check. I was off and running again.

The crowd around the bar lingered, and it was after midnight when the last couple left. I cleaned up and checked on the state of the restrooms. Chris finished battening down the kitchen. I heard the walk-in door open and rumble shut, though the food had been put away hours before. I knew Chris was making a final check of the premises, just as I was.

"Going upstairs!" he called to me. "You coming?"

"One minute." I made one last circuit of the restaurant to make sure it was shipshape for Gus in the morning, dousing the lights as I moved around. I shot the shiny, new deadbolt across apartment door at the bottom of the stairs.

"Everything okay?" Chris glanced at me as I came up the stairs. He was on his way into the shower after a sweaty night of cooking.

"Fine."

"Because you seem a little distracted."

"Do I? Sorry. Long day."

While Chris was in the shower, I tried a variety of activities—book, TV, computer, but none held my interest. I changed into the old Snowden Family Clambake T-shirt I slept in, pulled the covers up, and put my head down on the pillow. Not long after, Chris climbed into bed and gave me a kiss on the cheek.

As soon as I was sure he was asleep, I slipped out of bed.

I pulled on my jeans and sweater, stuffed my feet into my sneakers, grabbed my phone, and crept quietly down the stairs, undoing the deadbolt at the bottom. In the restaurant, I took Gus's hammer and the big flashlight out of his toolkit under the lunch counter and then pried off both two-by-fours that Chris had nailed over the trapdoor behind the bar. The boards screeched as I pulled them up. Between that and the grunting and the swearing, I worried Chris would appear. I waited a few moments, heart pounding, but he didn't. I positioned a chair opposite the bar, by the wall under the light switch. And waited.

And waited. Waiting in the dark for something that might not happen turned out to be stupendously boring. I shifted on the wooden restaurant chair, stiff and cold.

And waited.

The harbor was quiet in the dead of the night. Quiet in a way my apartment in New York never was or could have been. The streetlight on the other side of the parking lot threw a tiny sliver of light into the room, but not enough to see much of anything.

In spite of my best intentions, I dozed.

"Julia?"

"Aieee!" My eyes sprang open, but I couldn't see

a thing. I flailed at the intruder, who grabbed both my wrists and held on.

"It's me, Chris! I woke up and you weren't in bed, so I came to find you. Good grief, Julia. What is going on?"

I sagged against him. "Shhh. Quiet. I'm hunting wabbits."

Chris found a chair and pulled it next to mine. "Seriously, what in the world are you doing?"

"I told everyone who was in the restaurant the night Austin Lowe was murdered that I had the only copy of an insurance report that named the person who left the cigarette that started the fire at the Lowes' house. I figure that'll cause whoever's been breaking into the apartment to show up one last time."

Beside me in the dark, I heard Chris open his mouth several times, but he produced only sputtery noises. Finally, he spoke. "Why didn't you tell me?"

"I worried you'd think I was insane."

"Well then, mission accomplished."

We sat for a moment, then he said, "Julia, we have to talk about this. I'm serious. This is the second time you've tried to brain me. And the second time you've put yourself in danger without telling me. I think, after all this time, after all we've been through, I'm owed a heads-up on your intentions." His voice had an edge to it I'd rarely heard. He was angry.

I felt my face flush. "You're right. You are. You are owed that, and so much more."

"We'll talk in the morning," he said. "When we've had some sleep."

"Maybe we should go to bed. It looks like my plan hasn't worked. I've been sitting here for hours."

"It's still dark."

"Then we should quiet down. Just in case."

Chris took my hand and we sat in silence. In a few minutes, his chin dropped slowly to his chest.

I was about to drop off again myself when I heard a creaking noise from behind the bar. I shook Chris and then elbowed him. He jerked awake with a "Wha?"

"Shhh!"

The trapdoor banged as it fell open. I put my hand on the light switch. Soft footsteps made their way around the bar. Whoever it was wore a head-lamp like bicyclists wear but didn't shine it in our direction. Instead, the person made straight for the apartment stairs.

When I judged the intruder was in the middle of the room, I flipped on the lights.

"You!" I shouted, pointing at Phil Bennett, who stood in the center of the room.

"You!" he yelled simultaneously, pointing at Chris and me. Then he turned and, with surprising agility, fled back the way he'd come.

I thrust my phone into Chris's hands. "Call nine-one-one," I shouted, and ran after Phil. He jumped down through the trapdoor, grunting as he hit the rock not far below. I jumped after him, hit the rock, and aimed the flashlight just in time to see him slip through the opening to the cave.

I followed, pointing the flashlight ahead of me. Bennett ran on, apparently sure of the way. I'd been in the tunnel only once before and moved more cautiously than he did, worried about running headlong into a wall of packed dirt despite my flashlight. I pushed myself to go faster. If he made it to the ladder and pulled it up behind him, I'd have to turn around and go back, and he could easily get away.

Behind me, I heard the slap of bare feet on the tunnel floor. I assumed it was Chris. I had to believe it was Chris. If someone else was pursuing me, it was too scary to think about.

Ahead of me, I saw the ladder in the light of Phil's headlamp and heard the creak as he stepped on the bottom rung. I aimed my flashlight and caught Phil's back as he vanished upward. I leapt toward the ladder, grabbing the sides as he thundered to the top and began to pull it up. "Oh, no, you don't!" I stepped down forcibly on the bottom rung.

I thought for a moment I might bring him tumbling down on top of me. But he released the ladder. As I clambered up, I heard him slam the door of locker 10B. I was afraid he might have locked it, and I threw myself against it as hard as I could when I reached the top. It sprang open, my own momentum propelling me to the floor. I scrambled to my feet. I could hear Bennett running toward the front door. I jumped for him, bringing him down. I landed on his back, my knees on either side of his ribs. I heard a distinct crack that might have been bone breaking.

"Oof."

There was a thump and a bump and the sound of someone patting a wall. The overhead lights blazed on. Chris stood by the switch, barefoot and blinking. Jamie and Officer Howland broke down the front door seconds later.

"What's going on here?" Howland demanded.

"Phil Bennett broke into my apartment to steal evidence three times, trying to cover up that he murdered Austin Lowe and Enid Sparks!"

"Mrgh, mrgh, mrgh, mrgh!" Bennett protested from beneath me.

Jamie shook his head. "No, Julia. He didn't kill anyone." Then he added, "Get off him. You're hurting him."

So I did.

Chapter 29

"Every once in a while, you should trust us to do our job." Lieutenant Binder's mouth was a thin, straight line as he sat across the folding table from me in the multipurpose room. Flynn was so angry, he couldn't keep still. He paced the room, not looking at me, as we spoke.

I'd spent a couple of long hours sitting in the Busman's Harbor police station, waiting while Binder and Flynn made their separate journeys to town. I suspected Binder had been called at his home in Augusta, while Flynn was roused in Portland from Genevieve Pelletier's warm bed. Both had been summoned in the early hours of Sunday morning to deal with a case they were sure they had closed. No wonder they weren't happy with me.

"Enid Sparks killed Austin Lowe and then jumped or fell into the harbor and drowned," Binder said. "It's true her note didn't explicitly say she planned to kill him, but she procured the insulin and syringe before she left Guilford. She was prepared for what she thought she had to do."

"Lowe's backpack was filled with cans of Coleman fuel," Flynn spat. "The kind used in camp stoves. He spent the time between when he left the Snuggles and entered the restaurant gathering kindling along the road and pushing it through the opening under your building. He never did figure out who left the burning cigarette that killed his parents and maimed him. His plan was to burn all of them—and you and Chris—alive." Flynn's eyes blazed with fury at my foolishness.

I shuddered to think of it. If Austin Lowe hadn't turned up in the walk-in, I would have described that evening as a normal, after-holiday weekday evening at the restaurant. I had no idea what was going on beneath my feet.

Binder took up the story. "Enid Sparks must have lurked by the kitchen door, waiting for Lowe to leave. When he came through the parking lot to get the gas cans, she led him into the restaurant and into the walk-in, so no one would hear them arguing. She wore winter gloves, which is why she left no fingerprints.

"Despite his plan, Lowe was feeling mellow from the effects of the diazepam and the Wild Turkey. He went along willingly. When she saw there was no other way to stop him, Enid did what she thought she had to do."

"That poor woman." It broke my heart to think of her, killing the person she had raised.

"That kind of desperation, seeing no other way out, is what drives normal people to murder." Binder paused, then continued. "When she saw that wall her in nephew's study and understood what he planned to do, she was so shocked, she lost all capacity for rational thought. Then add in the trauma of her car accident . . ." He shrugged. "There's no doubt about it, Julia. That's what happened."

My face flushed with embarrassment. I had been so sure Enid couldn't have been the killer. "But how did she give him the Valium?"

Binder looked at Flynn who glowered back, but nodded.

"You weren't completely wrong," Binder said. "Of all the diners, only Phil Bennett recognized Austin Lowe." *The portraitist. Just as he'd recognized Michael Smith's features in Quinn's face.* "When Bennett realized that all but one of the living guests from the fatal New Year's Eve party were there in your restaurant, he figured there was something wrong. He put the Valium in Lowe's drink. He's confessed to this. He's also confessed to breaking into your building three times and to stealing the gift certificates, as well as your copy of the yacht club photo, along with the one from the yacht club. Apparently tonight he was after the copy of the insurance report you picked up in Guilford, though why he thought getting rid of a copy would make a difference, I don't know." Binder squinted. "You wouldn't know anything about that, would you?"

I sat, still and silent. I was already in enough trouble.

When Binder understood I wasn't going to speak, he said, "There's no one left to prosecute for Austin Lowe's murder. I'll talk to the DA's office about bringing charges against Bennett on the Valium, but I doubt they'll want to pursue it." He moved some papers around on his desk, obviously buying time for whatever was coming next. "In the meantime, it's a local matter, but I'd recommend you drop the trespassing and burglary charges against Bennett in exchange for his dropping the assault charges against you."

"Assault charges!"

"You broke at least two of his ribs, Julia."

"I was defending my home."

"Were you in your home when you assaulted him? You chased the guy for a hundred feet underground and up a ladder. And what was the monetary value of the items he took?"

Flynn looked at me for the first time in the interview. His face was triumphant.

I was crushed, and mortified. On three previous cases, I had been a real help to these detectives. Now I'd shredded whatever standing I had with them in a single day.

Binder took my silence as indecision. "Perhaps

it would help if you and Mr. Bennett spoke," he suggested.

We sat side by side in folding chairs. Binder and Flynn had left the room to give us privacy. Bennett was obviously in pain. His next stop was the hospital.

"You broke into my place three times." I wasn't cutting him any slack. "You stole from me. You scared the crap out of me. And Chris."

"I'm sorry. I really am." Phil shifted in his seat. "That whole evening at your restaurant was like a bad dream I couldn't wake up from. To walk in and see Henry and Caroline sitting there. And then the Walkers and the Smiths. Deborah had her back to the room, but I was staring out at all those people. And that man had come in and sat at the bar.

"Even though I hadn't seen him in forty years, those eyes of his were something I'll never forget. I thought they would drill right through me. When I got up and went to the men's room, I came back by way of the bar. As soon as I spotted the scar on his neck, I knew absolutely the man was Austin Lowe.

"I wasn't sure what was planned, but we were all there, including Austin, so it felt ominous. I went back to our booth, hurried Deborah through her meal without telling her why, and got ready to leave. Just as we finished, Officer Dawes arrived to say the road was blocked. We were stuck. My anxiety climbed by the minute.

"When we moved into the bar, I observed Austin

more closely. He was jumpy, no doubt about it. I became convinced he planned some sort of public accusation."

A public accusation. If only that had been all Austin Lowe had planned.

"I carry Deborah's anxiety medication in my jacket pocket whenever we go out," Phil continued. "I went into the restroom, crushed ten tablets with a spoon, and on my way back, I stopped at the bar and slipped them into his drink. I didn't want to hurt him. God knows we'd hurt that boy enough. I wanted him to be sleepy or mellow and forget about whatever he'd planned to do.

"I thought I'd succeeded. There was no public scene. No one was more astonished than I was to wake up the next morning and learn he'd been murdered. And I never, ever would have hurt you or Chris. I only wanted to get rid of the evidence of our connection to one another and to the fire. You have to believe me."

"You took a lot of risks," I said.

"I didn't do it for myself."

I realized he was telling the truth. As I'd guessed, Phil Bennett had crept out in the night, broken into my apartment, and stolen evidence all for love. "You did it for Deborah, because you're afraid she was the one who left the cigarette."

"Deborah?" Phil sat back in his chair. "I never thought Deborah burned down that house. I thought it was Sheila." He looked down at his lap. "I did it for her."

"Sheila?" *The last piece of the puzzle and I couldn't*

even get that right. I was never interfering in police business again.

"I was the reason Sheila was drunk and out of control that New Year's Eve," Phil said. "I had hurt her, and then she killed Howell and Madeleine. She never intended what happened. So much time has gone by. To prevent the truth from coming out was the least I owed her."

I hadn't liked Phil much when I first met him, but my heart went out to him. This tortured man deserved the truth. "The insurance report was inconclusive. Austin Lowe never figured out who was to blame. His plan was to kill you all by setting fire to the restaurant. Enid Sparks murdered him to stop him."

"Oh, my God." Bennett gave into his emotions and his physical pain. Like a landslide, his defenses came down. He took off his glasses, put his head in his hands, and wept. "We were all so young and careless. Look at what we've done."

I trudged back along the road toward the restaurant. The sun had come up while I was at the police station. Gus would be busy with his early morning crowd. I had to have one more conversation I dreaded this morning.

What I had done to Chris might be unforgiveable. Why hadn't I trusted him enough to tell him my plan? Was there a problem in our relationship?

No. There was a problem with me. Somewhere

deep in my brain I had known the plan was stupid and I hadn't wanted anyone to tell me so. Especially not the person whose opinion I most valued. The person who would tell me the truth.

I thought about the couples in the Rabble Point set. Each of them had been together for decades. And though they'd lived lives haunted by the fire that killed the Lowes, within their marriages they had supported one another. Sheila and Michael had become grown-ups together. Caroline had supported Henry's career, despite the disruption the frequent moves caused in her own life. He, in turn, valued her sacrifice and had brought her back to Busman's Harbor as she wanted. Fran and Barry were good parents to Quinn and good grandparents. They still loved each other, despite the challenges, financial and otherwise, in their lives. Phil and Deborah had overcome her alcoholism and injuries and the demands of his career and stayed together throughout. There was a lot of resilience there. I thought if I could achieve a relationship like that in my lifetime, I would have a good life.

And yet, love wasn't quite enough. Caroline, Deborah, and Sheila, all strangers in a new town, longed for friends. Despite the trauma caused by the Lowes' deaths and awkwardness of the changing partnerships, Phil had sought out both Barry and Michael, and neither had turned him away. Even people in good relationships needed friends.

At Gus's, I entered through the kitchen door and snuck up the stairs to the apartment. It had been a

morning full of painful conversations, and I had
to have one more before I could sleep. Part of me
hoped Chris had gone back to bed after our crazy
night, but he was sitting on the couch, waiting.

"I thought we weren't going to have any more
secrets." The hurt in his deep voice stabbed me in
the heart. I'd been so focused on proving I was right
about the murder, I'd done the one thing we'd
promised each other we'd never do. Kept secrets.
I was ashamed of myself.

"Forgive me," I pleaded. "I've been such an idiot."

He rose from the couch and turned toward me.
"Do you know how you keeping things from me
made me feel?"

I shook my head. The long, sleepless night; the
embarrassment; and now the regret at how I'd
treated Chris took their toll. A tear slid down my
cheek.

"It made me feel shut out and not trusted. I was
hurt that you were keeping a part of yourself from
me. I was scared, after all we've been through, that
we weren't going to make it." He took a breath.
"In other words, it made me feel exactly what you
felt last summer when I was the one keeping the
secrets. Secrets about things that put me in danger.
Secrets about stupid, wrongheaded, bullheaded
stuff I did." His voice was ragged. "I can't believe
you stayed. Or that you forgave me. Or that you
still love me."

"Of course I do." I could barely breathe. "Now
you need to forgive me."

In three long strides, he took me in his arms.

"You are the smartest, bravest person I know. There is nothing to forgive. But we have to promise, whenever one of us is going to do something stupid, we have to tell the other. Full disclosure."

"I promise." We kissed, a deep and satisfying kiss. My heart pounded and my knees went weak.

No end of that in sight.

Chapter 30

They stood in a circle on Rabble Point Road. The mid-December wind cut through the vacant land, sucking out our breath. Everyone was bundled in heavy winter coats, scarves, and gloves. Deborah's face was hidden behind enormous dark glasses, even though so near the winter solstice, the sun barely crept over the horizon.

Jamie and I stood outside the circle, a few yards back. We wanted to show respect and acknowledge their loss, but we didn't want to intrude. He was off-duty and we'd ridden out to Rabble Point together in his pickup. As the miles had rolled along on deserted Eastclaw Point Road, I thought about my friend. I couldn't get the image of him, alone in his patrol car on Thanksgiving Day, out of my head. I hadn't valued our friendship enough. I hadn't even called him when I first got back to town. And then this summer . . .

"I miss you," I said. "I want us to be friends again."

"Oh, Julia. Me too." He kept his eyes on the road. "I can't stop thinking about what happened this summer. If I hadn't kissed you, we'd still at least have what we had."

"That's gentlemanly of you, but we kissed each other. It was a mistake. We were drunk. Can we put it in the past and move on? I don't think I can stand to live in Busman's Harbor without us being friends."

"Deal," he said, taking his right hand off the steering wheel for a fist bump. "Friends."

They scattered Austin's ashes first. It was painful to think of this man, whose life had devastated by fire, consumed by flames at the end. But his and Enid's wills had been specific. Both had requested cremation, and Enid had asked for her ashes to be scattered at Rabble Point. The police were never successful in notifying a next of kin for either of them. Austin and Enid had just had each other. Austin left all his money to the Connecticut Burn Unit.

The group was largely silent as the wind carried Austin Lowe away. They hadn't known him, though each of them had probably thought of him every day for the last forty years. For these people, he'd remained the wide-eyed boy who'd haunted their imaginations. But they were the only ones left to mourn him.

Henry produced the urn that contained Enid's remains. Barry took it and scattered the first handful. "I loved Enid," he said. "She was my first love, and that never leaves you." He stepped back next to Fran. "I found happiness after we parted. I hope she did too."

Fran stepped forward next. "Enid gave me my greatest gift. My husband. I will be grateful forever."

Caroline was next. She stepped to the center of the circle, took a handful of the ashes, and opened her hand, letting the wind carry them off. "Enid was my friend. She and Madeleine were sisters by blood, but during those long childhood summers, I was their sister too. I'm ashamed of myself that I let my own guilt and horror of what happened to Madeleine and Howell separate us for all these years. I want Enid back." Her voice broke, and she picked her head up, pivoting to look at each person in the group in turn. "I want you all back in my life, before we lose the chance again." She stepped back into the circle and finished. "You cannot make any new old friends."

Henry put a hand under Caroline's elbow, and Deborah stepped forward to hug her. Slowly, the rest of them circled in, until they all embraced.

I stepped closer to Jamie, and he put his arm across my shoulders. I'd teared up as Caroline spoke, and now the tears came freely. "I love you," I said to Jamie. "You are my oldest friend."

"I love you too." He hugged me tighter. "I'm so glad you've come home."

In front of us, at the edge of the group of old friends and lovers, Caroline held aloft the vessel with the last of Enid's remains, and she blew off into the wind.

Recipes

Split Pea Soup with Ham

From the time Fogged Inn *was conceived, it was inevitable the book would have a recipe for pea soup. This one was contributed by my friend Pat Kennedy, and it is delicious.*

From Pat: I am of the opinion that split pea soup is infinitely better with the addition of ham, so this is not a vegetarian option. It is, however, hearty and delicious, and makes a perfectly satisfying main course. I like to add some diced carrots at the end because it adds a little crunch and a lot of cheerful color. This recipe makes quite a bit of soup, so plan on eating some for dinner and freezing the rest in serving-size portions for a quick dinner on a night when you're too tired to cook.

Ingredients

1 meaty ham bone
12 cups water
1 small onion, chopped roughly
2 carrots, chopped roughly
2 stalks celery, chopped roughly
1 clove garlic, minced
Salt
Pepper
2 packages (14 ounces each) split peas (I prefer green, but you can use yellow)
Optional: 2 additional carrots, diced

Instructions

Remove as much visible fat and tough skin from the ham bone as possible. Carve off and dice larger pieces of meat clinging to the bone. Set aside.

Place ham bone into large stockpot with the water.

Add the chopped onion, two chopped carrots, celery, garlic, and a liberal sprinkling of salt and ground pepper.

Add split peas to the pot.

Bring water to a boil and then turn down to a simmer. Cook gently for 1–1½ hours until the peas are thoroughly softened. Stir frequently. Continue cooking for another hour.

Remove pot from heat source and let the soup cool.

Remove the ham bone and the chunks of celery, carrot, and onion (if possible). If there is any meat left on the bone, remove and dice it. (Optional: At this point, you could take the soup from the pot and put it through the food processor for a smoother, creamier texture.)

With the pea soup in the pot, add the chopped ham and the two (fresh) diced carrots (optional).

Heat to serving temperature.

Season to taste with salt and pepper.

Serves: Lots. Plan to freeze some.

Gus's Too Date Night Stuffed Chicken Breast with Lemon-Tarragon Sauce

Chris and Julia worked hard to develop a menu for Gus's Too that meets a lot of differing needs. Chris wants to cook good, fresh food that is fun and engaging. Julia wants the restaurant to offer couples stuck on the peninsula for the winter the possibility of a "date night." They both know the restaurant needs to be affordable. Gus is adamant that they not serve anything on his menu. Although their menu changes daily, Date Night Stuffed Chicken Breast is one of Chris's go-to offerings.

Ingredients

Chicken

4–6 ounces pancetta, cut into ¼-inch cubes
8 chicken cutlets pounded ¼-inch thick,
⅛-inch thick at the edges
1–2 cups baby spinach leaves
4–6 ounces Fontina cheese, cut into ⅛-inch
cubes
2 cups panko bread crumbs
1 cup grated Parmesan cheese
1 cup flour
3 eggs

Sauce

3 Tablespoons unsalted butter
3 Tablespoons flour
2 cups chicken broth, warmed
2 Tablespoons lemon juice
1 Tablespoon tarragon, chopped

Instructions

Fry the pancetta over medium heat until browned.

Lay each cutlet flat on a board. Put a small handful of spinach leaves and 1 Tablespoon each of pancetta and Fontina cubes in the center. Roll the cutlet into a packet, folding the sides into the center and pinching to seal.

Put cutlets in the refrigerator for at least 1 hour to complete sealing process.

Preheat oven to 350 degrees.

Mix bread crumbs and Parmesan in a bowl and put half on a plate. Put flour on another plate, and lightly beat eggs with a fork in a separate bowl.

Remove chicken from the refrigerator. Roll each packet first in flour, being sure to shake off excess, then in egg, and finally in bread crumbs. Place on a wire rack set on a sheet pan.

Cook chicken for 40–45 minutes or until an instant read thermometer inserted in the center reads 165 degrees.

In the last twenty minutes or so of cooking time, melt butter in a saucepan over medium heat. After it stops foaming, add flour and whisk together constantly for about 3 minutes.

Begin adding broth slowly, whisking together, and continue to slowly add broth, whisking all the while.

Cook on medium-low heat until sauce thickens, 3 to 5 minutes.

Add lemon juice and chopped tarragon and cook for 1 minute more.

Season with salt and pepper to taste.

Serves: 4

Roasted Hake Loin
with Warmed Pineapple-Avocado Salsa

*Chris uses hake because it's a budget-friendly white fish,
even in December. People tend to shy away from it because it's less familiar than cod or haddock, but Chris
knows once it's cooked, it will be tasty and visually
appealing.*

Ingredients

Salsa
   1 avocado, diced
   6 grape tomatoes, halved and then quartered
   1 shallot, chopped
   ½ jalapeño pepper, seeded and diced small
   ½ red pepper, diced
   1 cup pineapple, diced
   1 Tablespoon cilantro, chopped
   2 Tablespoons lime juice
   Salt and pepper to taste

Fish
   1 hake loin
   ½ teaspoon sugar
   1 Tablespoon olive oil

To finish
   ¼ cup white wine
   Chopped cilantro for garnish
   Lime wedges

Instructions

Preheat oven to 425 degrees.

Prepare salsa by stirring together first eight ingredients. Salt and pepper to taste.

Pat hake dry with paper towels and sprinkle one side with sugar.

Heat olive oil in nonstick skillet until nearly smoking. Add hake, sugar side down, and cook for 2 minutes.

Turn fish over and pop into the oven. Roast 7–10 minutes or until internal temperature reaches 135 degrees.

Remove fish to warmed platter.

On stovetop, pour white wine in the skillet the fish was cooked in and deglaze over medium-high heat.

Let bubble for 1 minute, then add salsa. Cook until warmed through, about 2 minutes. Adjust seasonings.

Spoon salsa over fish and garnish with cilantro.

Serve with lime wedges.

Serves: 2

Slow-Cooker Sweet-Braised Short Ribs

Chris is alone in the Gus's Too kitchen, so it's critical that he have some dishes he can prepare ahead. These delicious ribs fit the bill nicely. He often makes them the night before they are served, after things quiet down in the kitchen.

Ingredients

3 Tablespoons dark brown sugar
2 Tablespoons kosher salt
1 Tablespoon ground black pepper
1 Tablespoon smoked paprika
1 Tablespoon ground mustard
6 short ribs, English cut, 3-4 pounds
2 onions, chopped
2 green bell peppers, chopped
1 jalapeño pepper, seeded and chopped
1 cup dried apricots, halved
1 cup pitted prunes
1 bottle red wine
2 cups apricot jelly
1 can (15 ounces) diced tomatoes
buttered noodles for serving

Instructions

Stir the first 5 ingredients above together. Put 3 tablespoons of the resulting dry mix aside for later. Rub spices into the short ribs.

Lay the chopped vegetables in the bottom of a slow-cooker. Nestle the short ribs in with the vegetables. (Brown the short ribs if you prefer, but it is not necessary.)

Scatter prunes and apricots over the top.

In a large bowl or pitcher mix jelly, diced tomatoes, wine, and the three tablespoons of reserved dry mix and stir to combine. Pour over everything.

Cook on low in slow-cooker for 8-10 hours.

Remove short ribs to heated platter. Skim the fat and strain the liquid to remove solids. Discard the solids. Boil down the liquid until reduced by half.

Serve meat with buttered noodles. Serve the sauce over the meat or noodles.

Serves: 4-6

Baked Hake Filet with Leek & Fennel Tomato Sauce & Scallop Buttons

Another hake dish, but with the filet instead of the loin. Chris uses scallops, expensive in December, as a garnish, which is another way he keeps the price of meals affordable.

Ingredients

Sauce

2 Tablespoons olive oil
1 shallot
1 clove garlic
1 Tablespoon tomato paste
¼ cup white wine
1 medium leek, white part only, split, washed, and sliced
½ large fennel bulb, sliced thinly
1 can diced tomatoes, drained
Salt
Pepper

Fish

1 pound hake filet
Olive oil
Salt
Pepper
Smoked paprika
Parsley
Lemon wedges for serving
2 scallops

Instructions

Preheat oven to 350 degrees.

Heat olive oil in a pan and sauté shallot for 2 minutes.

Add garlic and cook 1 minute.

Stir in tomato paste and white wine and let bubble for 1 minute.

Add leek, fennel, and tomatoes, and cook together until vegetables are tender but retain a little crunch.

Season with salt and pepper to taste.

Put sauce in a baking dish.

Rub hake all over with olive oil.

Sprinkle with salt, pepper, and smoked paprika.

Tuck hake into sauce and bake for 15 minutes or until fish is cooked through and flaky.

While hake is cooking, pan sear two large sea scallops in olive oil on both sides.

Remove from pan and slice in half.

Garnish hake with parsley, top with scallop buttons seared side up, and serve with lemon wedges.

Serves: 4

Lobster & Corn Chowder

This hearty soup is derived from one of my treasured family recipes. It was originally Corn and Turkey Chowder, a Depression-era meal popular in our house after Thanksgiving. Bill Carito adapted it for lobster and brought it into the current millennium.

Ingredients

4 Tablespoons unsalted butter
2 onions, chopped
3 Tablespoons flour
6 cups lobster stock or fish stock, warmed
1 can creamed corn
1 pound frozen corn
½ pint heavy cream
½ pound lobster meat, chopped
Salt
Pepper
Corn nuts for garnish
Chopped chives for garnish

Instructions

Melt butter over medium-high heat.

Add onions and sauté for 5 minutes.

Add flour and stir constantly for 2–3 minutes.

Add warm stock, a ladleful at a time, stirring constantly. Bring to a boil, then simmer gently for 5 minutes.

Add creamed corn and frozen corn and continue simmering for 5 minutes.

Stir in heavy cream and lobster meat and continue simmering for 5 minutes.

Season with salt and pepper to taste.

Ladle into bowls, and garnish with corn nuts and chopped chives.

Serves: 6–8

Deborah's Fish Tacos

Deborah Bennett makes this meal in Fogged Inn. *Her recently retired husband expects a "proper lunch." In reality this recipe was contributed by my soon-to-be son-in-law, Luke Donius, who began playing around with these ingredients when he was in graduate school and has continued to perfect the recipe.*

Ingredients

Sauce
  ½ cup mayonnaise
  1 cup sour cream
  ⅓ small shallot, finely chopped
  1 medium jalapeño, diced
  Juice of one medium lime
  Salt and pepper to taste
  2 cilantro sprigs

Tacos and Toppings
  8 corn tortillas, warmed
  2 jalapeños, chopped
  ⅓ (remaining portion) shallot
  2 tomatoes, chopped
  Chopped cilantro sprigs
  1 lime cut into wedges for squeezing
  1 small radicchio, chopped

Fish
  1 pound any seasonal white fish
  2 Tablespoons butter

Seasoning

⅛ teaspoon cayenne powder
¼ teaspoon paprika
⅛ teaspoon pepper
⅛ teaspoon garlic powder
⅛ teaspoon salt

Instructions

To make the sauce

Combine the sauce ingredients in a bowl and mix. Prepare at least 1 hour in advance and let sit in the refrigerator. (If you have leftover sauce, it makes for a great chip dip!)

To make the fish

Cook fish in butter and ½ teaspoon of the seasoning. Cook the fish until it is opaque. Squeeze lime juice from one wedge on the fish, then break up the fillet.

To serve

Serve fish on warmed corn tortillas with toppings and sauce.

Serves: 4

Acknowledgments

I first heard the expression "You cannot make any new old friends" at the commencement address given by actor and writer Mike O'Malley at my daughter's graduation from the University of New Hampshire in 2006. I admit I went into the event rolling my eyes. Former presidents Bill Clinton and George H. W. Bush had already been announced as the joint speakers for 2007, and it didn't help when my daughter explained who O'Malley was by referencing his show on Nickelodeon. (Of course, now that I know who he is, he's *everywhere*.)

It turned out, as it so often does, that my low expectations were dramatically wrongheaded. O'Malley's speech was heartfelt and wise, and resonated all the more because he had sat where those graduates were sitting. The relevant portion of the speech is this: "Try as often as you can to give tribute to your friends, to stay in contact, to be at their momentous occasions. Drive across the country and go into debt to go to their weddings, fly across the country and be with them when their parents pass away. You cannot make any new old friends." (The whole address is worth a read at http://en.wikipedia.org/wiki/User:IanManka/Mike_O%27Malley)

That speech is what got me thinking about a group of old friends and the reason they might not drift apart, but be blown apart. The reason it happens in *Fogged Inn* is from a story my mother once told me. I have no idea if it was true, but I have remembered the story for more than thirty years.

I thought this book would take much less research than the previous three. All the suspects are baby boomers, and I'm one, too. But the group in *Fogged Inn* is about seven years older than me, and as anyone who was there will tell you, the sixties and early seventies were a fast-moving time. College deferments from the draft changed to a lottery system that included all eligible men, and then to a time when no one was called up. By the mid-1970s, female students entered law schools and medical schools in numbers truly unthinkable just a few years before, reflecting a larger, dramatic change in young women's expectations for their lives. The leading edge of the baby boom had a very different coming of age than the middle, who had a very different coming-of-age than the trailing edge. I found myself constantly checking reference points and looking at photos as I pondered the lives of this group of recent retirees. So thank you, World Wide Web.

For this book I'd like to thank my agent John Talbot, my editor John Scognamiglio, and the team at Kensington Books for giving me the opportunity to tell more of the Snowden family's stories.

Thank you to Sherry Harris and Bill Carito, who read drafts of the material and provided critical feedback. You always help me get out of my own way. Sherry was also on a deadline for her Kensington series, the Sarah Winston Garage Sale Mysteries, so I particularly appreciated her support for this book.

I'd especially like to thank fellow writer A.J. Pompano for reviewing and making such wonderful suggestions about the scenes that take place in Guilford, Connecticut.

Pat Kennedy, Luke Donius, and Bill Carito contributed recipes to *Fogged Inn*. The delicious pea soup is Pat's. The scrumptious fish tacos are Luke's. Bill provided all the others, as well as ideas about how Chris would go about developing tasty and innovative, but affordable, menus for Gus's Too.

As always, I'd like to thank my blog sisters at Wicked Cozy Authors—Jessie Crockett, Sherry Harris, Julie Hennrikus, Edith Maxwell, Liz Mugavero, Sheila Connolly, Kim Gray, and Sadie Hartwell, and the whole gang at the Maine Crime Writers blog. Also to my writer's group—Mark Ammons, Katherine Fast, Cheryl Marceau, and Leslie Wheeler.

Because *Fogged Inn* takes place the first week in December, we don't make it to the Snowden Family Clambake in the book. However, I still want to take the opportunity to say that if you want to go to a real Maine Clambake on a private island in Maine, check out the Cabbage Island Clambakes at http://www.cabbageislandclambakes.com/.

Thank you to my family for their unflagging support—Bill Carito, Rob, Sunny and Viola Carito, and Kate Carito. I truly don't know what I would do without you.

Finally, I would like to acknowledge my old friends. We don't make nearly enough time to see each other, but you are the people I can go years without seeing and then pick up the conversation as if it were yesterday. Thank you for being in my life, friends of my youth—Hilary Hinds Kitasei, Amy and Thom Fritz, Vida Antolin-Jenkins, Jon Anton, Pat McGrath, and Paul and Paula Dowd. Love you all.